"You continue to amaze me, Gregory Bowman."

"I can say the same of you. You haven't let your condition take control of your life." She warmed at his words.

"I don't intend to let it." She wiped her mouth on her napkin. "I was almost a prisoner of my home, but that's when I decided to see a therapist. I knew I needed help, but I was embarrassed."

He shook his head. "You have nothing to be ashamed of, Renee. It's courageous to ask for help when it's necessary."

"Enough about me. You're the brave one. Are you sure you're ready to leave the military?"

"I'm getting older... I'd like to have a family while I'm healthy and young enough to enjoy them."

"So, you're really sure about this?"

"I am."

Renee wanted to believe him, and she did for the most part, but there was a tiny part of her that wasn't convinced he was being entirely truthful.

Dear Reader,

Don't you just love a man in uniform? I do. Especially a man in the military. But they were the men I avoided dating for reasons very similar to my character Renee Rothchild. In fact, this is the inspiration for *Her Marine Hero*. Renee Rothchild and Greg Bowman have feelings for one another, but both must give up something to find their happily-ever-after.

I truly enjoyed writing this story, which is the third book in the Polk Island series. It has been a joy for me to watch Renee's growth throughout the series, as well as her success as a fashion designer. I also enjoyed getting to know Greg, a man who knows exactly what he wants out of life, despite what others think. Both characters are unapologetically organic.

I hope you will enjoy getting to know Greg and Renee as they navigate their feelings for one another and face off challenges that threaten to derail their relationship. Thank you for your never-ending support of the Polk Island series.

Jacquelin Thomas

HEARTWARMING

Her Marine Hero

—

Jacquelin Thomas

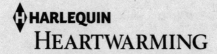

HARLEQUIN
HEARTWARMING

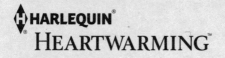

ISBN-13: 978-1-335-58465-6

Her Marine Hero

Copyright © 2022 by Jacquelin Thomas

Harlequin Enterprises ULC
22 Adelaide St. West, 41st Floor
Toronto, Ontario M5H 4E3, Canada
www.Harlequin.com

Printed in U.S.A.

Jacquelin Thomas is an award-winning, bestselling author with more than fifty-five books in print. When not writing, she is busy catching up on her reading, attending sporting events and spoiling her grandchildren. Jacquelin and her family live in North Carolina.

Books by Jacquelin Thomas

Harlequin Heartwarming

A Family for the Firefighter
Her Hometown Hero

Harlequin Kimani Romance

Five Star Attraction
Five Star Temptation
Legal Attraction
Five Star Romance
Five Star Seduction
Styles of Seduction
Wrangling Wes
Five Star Desire
Forever My Baby
Only for You
Return to Me
Another Chance with You

Visit the Author Profile page
at Harlequin.com for more titles.

CHAPTER ONE

GREG BOWMAN OPENED the door and stepped out of the car. He sniffed the salty ocean air, a smile tugging at his lips. His heart kicked up a happy beat upon his return to beautiful Polk Island.

Locals claimed there was something magical about the island located off the coast of Charleston, South Carolina. Greg believed it in every atom of his being. Tall, majestic oaks; magnolia trees; colorful flowers; sandy beaches and small-town charm welcomed tourists year after year.

He glanced up toward the heavens. The twentieth of April had ushered in a dazzling sunny morning, with no signs of dark clouds in its bright blue sky. Humming to himself, Greg opened the left passenger-side door and retrieved a black leather weekender bag.

By the time he stepped onto the porch, the front door had swung open, and his best friend walked out, a cane in his left hand to aid in walking with his prosthetics and help balance his gait.

"Trey Rothchild…!" Greg exclaimed. "It's good to see you, brother."

"It's a good day to be seen and not viewed," his friend responded with sunny cheerfulness as he stepped aside to let Greg enter the house. *"Rah."*

They sat down in the living room. Trey asked, "How was the drive?"

He'd left in the middle of the night, driving down from Camp Lejeune without having to deal with a lot of traffic. "It was smooth the entire way here. I had good music to keep me company." Greg stifled a yawn. Now that he wasn't behind the wheel of his car, he was struggling to stay awake. "How's Renee?" He made it sound casual, but he couldn't help but ask after her.

"She's good. Making a name for herself across the country with her clothing line." Trey smiled, leaning back in his seat. "I remember when Renee made her first skirt. It had this thick elastic waist because she didn't know how to sew in a zipper. Now she has famous folks from all over contacting her. We're all real proud of her."

"She has a gift," Greg said.

A flash of humor crossed Trey's face. "Are you still crushing on my cousin?"

Grinning, Greg responded, "She clearly doesn't know a good thing when she sees him, but Renee is a really sweet person." Greg had crushed on her hard when he'd met her a few years ago. She didn't seem interested, despite his trying to convince her to go on a date with him, and in the intervening years, his expectations had cooled a bit. He was happy to consider her a friend.

Trey's gaze flickered with amusement. "Renee's got the Rothchild stubborn streak."

Greg lifted his chin. "You're right about that. She shot me down from the very beginning, but I'm not one to give up on something I really want. Remember when I wanted to join MARSOC? I didn't quit until I got in."

His mouth quirked with humor. "True, but that's nothing compared to my cousin's determination."

Greg chuckled—it felt good to talk to his friend again. Which brought him to the reason for his visit. "One of the reasons I wanted to come down is because I need to talk to you about something."

"What is it?" Trey asked.

"I'm thinking about getting out," he announced. "I've already started my paperwork."

Trey stared, complete surprise on his face. *"Really?* After everything you did to make MARSOC. *Are you sure about this?* Are you really ready to just walk away from all your hard work?"

"That's why I came to talk it out with you," Greg responded. "These last two years have been great, but the truth is that I'm not getting any younger, Trey. I love being in the military, but I was never planning on being a lifer."

"From the moment we met in boot camp— following your father's path as a Marine Raider is all you talked about."

"I also said I didn't want the same ending. I meant what I said about family. I'm thirty-one years old. I'm ready to settle down, and I can't do that with a high-risk job." He eyed his friend. "I hope you were serious about me working with you at the museum."

"Yeah…of course," Trey stated. "Just wasn't sure you'd take me up on it. A museum job is kinda boring compared to high-intensity reconnaissance and attack missions."

"You know how much I love history," Greg responded. He'd soon have his master's and was even considering a PhD in historic preservation.

Trey weighed him with a critical eye. "I can tell that you're seriously considering this."

He sighed. "I'm really ready to settle down, but then there's the adrenaline junkie part of me who isn't ready to give up the action."

"So why now? Have you met someone?"

"I'm not dating anyone," he responded. "But hopefully one day…"

An image of Renee floated to the forefront of Greg's mind. Her warm, friendly smile had the ability to brighten a person's day, even someone in poor spirits. Her dark eyes and thick eyelashes matched those of the other members of the Rothchild family, flattering her unblemished cocoa-colored skin. Renee possessed a commanding presence whenever she entered a room, but Greg knew of her struggles hidden beneath the surface of calm she wore daily. He found her courageous in fighting this private battle—it was a quality he greatly admired. As soon as the image came though, he forced it from his mind. It wouldn't do to dwell on hopes of him and Renee like he'd done two years ago.

"Then why don't you just wait? What's the

rush?" Trey asked. "You're single… Enjoy being a Raider while you can."

Greg didn't respond.

"Wait a minute… Does this have anything to do with Renee? Tell me you're not getting out in the hopes of the two of you getting together. 'Cause that's just crazy."

Of course he wasn't. "Your cousin and I are just friends." He was getting out for himself. He'd meant it when he said he wasn't a lifer. He'd served his time and was proud of it, but he was ready for a different life.

Thoughts of that must've relaxed him because Greg yawned a second time and then a third.

"Why don't you go upstairs and get some rest," Trey suggested. "You can barely keep your eyes open. I know you're tired after driving half the night."

"I don't want to be rude, but I think I'll do just that. Man, I didn't expect it to hit me like this."

"Go on upstairs," Trey encouraged. "We'll catch up later today. We're not done with this conversation."

"Thanks, brother." Greg picked up his bag and carried it upstairs with him.

The guest room was a welcome sight as he

opened the door. He undressed, showered and then climbed into the inviting comfort of the queen-size bed awaiting him.

INSIDE THE FIRST-FLOOR master suite, Trey gently pressed a cool, wet washcloth to Gia's forehead as she kneeled on the floor with her head over the toilet, emptying the contents of her stomach.

She moaned softly. "I h-hate this…"

"Hopefully, it'll end soon," he said. "The book I'm reading says that women usually have it only in the first trimester."

Gia glanced up at Trey. "Morning sickness sucks. I hope I can avoid being nauseous around Greg." They'd decided to hold off telling anyone about the pregnancy until she was in her second trimester. Gia was at ten weeks now, so she and Trey planned to share their announcement soon.

"He's in the guest room, catching up on some sleep. Greg was so tired when he got here, he didn't even want anything to eat."

Moaning, Gia pressed a hand to her stomach. "That's good because I'm certainly not in the mood to cook."

"Come November, we'll have a beautiful little baby, and you'll forget all about the throwing up."

"I doubt that." Feeling a bit unsteady, Gia rose to her feet with Trey's assistance. "Right now, I need to brush my teeth."

"Why don't you lay down for a bit?" Trey suggested. "I'll make you some toast. That seems to help settle your stomach."

She gave him a grateful smile. "Thanks, babe."

Gia eyed her reflection and was stunned by how pale she looked. She worried that she was also losing weight due to her inability to keep food down most days. She made a mental note to ask her doctor about it at her prenatal appointment later in the day.

She joined Trey in the kitchen fifteen minutes later. Gia paused in the doorway for a moment, admiring her handsome husband. He was doing well with his prosthesis; his PTSD episodes and nightmares were happening less frequently. Gia had never seen Trey as happy as he was the day they found out they were expecting a baby. Life for them was great and perfectly normal.

While Trey ate a full meal of bacon, scrambled eggs and grits, she sat across from him, nibbling on a piece of dry toast.

"Feeling any better?" he asked.

"Somewhat," Gia answered. "Give me another half hour and I'll feel like normal. I just need to stay away from the coffee at work. The smell of it makes me nauseous. It's been a challenge keeping this pregnancy a secret from everyone. I'll be glad when we announce it."

"We can do that anytime you're ready, sweetheart."

"I know… But let's just keep it between us for another week or so."

"I'm ready to shout it from the rooftops." Trey finished off his juice. "I can't wait to tell the family."

Gia grinned. "I know it's been hard for you to keep something like this from your family. Actually, I'm surprised you haven't told Aunt Eleanor or Leon." He'd always been close with his older brother—and the aunt who'd raised them.

He gave her a mock offended look. "What are you trying to say? You think I can't keep a secret?"

"I'm not saying that… I just know how excited you are about this baby. To be honest, I almost told Misty, but I didn't. I held out."

Trey laughed. "Are you sure you didn't tell her?"

"I didn't, but if we don't say something soon—I might cave. She and Shelley have already noticed that I'm not drinking any wine." Not drinking during ladies' nights with her sister-in-law and her friend had been a tricky part of keeping her secret.

"Let's plan a family dinner and announce it then."

"We should do it after Talei's birthday celebration," Gia said. "Her special day should be all about her." Gia loved Trey's niece—now *her* niece. She knew the little girl would be a wonderful older cousin to her baby.

"Sounds good to me," Trey responded.

She dabbed at her mouth with her napkin. "Greg must really be tired. I haven't heard any movement upstairs."

"He looked exhausted when he got here."

Gia finished off her toast.

"You're looking much better," Trey observed. "Not so pale."

"I'm starting to feel more like myself." She pushed away from the table and stood up. "Thank goodness, because I need to get going. My first client is at nine o'clock."

"Do you have some time in your schedule to have lunch with your loving and devoted husband?" Trey asked.

"I don't have any appointments between noon and two. I'll swing by and pick you up. What about Greg? I figured you'd be hanging out with him."

"I'm just going to let him rest. Maybe he'll be up by the time we get back."

"Well, he's welcome to join us if he wakes up beforehand," Gia said. "Love you."

"Love you, too."

After straightening her purple scrubs, she kissed Trey, grabbed her tote off the counter and headed out the door.

An hour and a half later, after she'd finished with her first client of the day, Gia made a quick stop at the boutique owned by Trey's cousin, Renee.

Gia knew Renee was attracted to Greg, and she secretly hoped the woman would let her guard down and give him a chance. He was a good person, and it was obvious that he cared for Renee. The two had kept in touch since meeting during a visit Greg had made to the island one summer. Gia smiled fondly, recalling the memory. It was the summer she'd fallen for her husband, and now that she was pregnant, she couldn't be happier with how things had turned out.

She'd promised Trey that she wouldn't play

matchmaker, but Gia saw no harm in giving Renee a tiny nudge in Greg's direction.

"GREG'S HERE," GIA announced when she walked up to Renee as she was arranging a display of new scarves. "He got in early this morning. He was sleeping when I left home."

Renee's stomach churned a little upon hearing his name. "That's wonderful," she said as casually as she could manage, ignoring the huge grin on Gia's face. "I'm sure Trey's happy to see his best friend." She hoped her body language wouldn't betray her true feelings—her elation and anticipation of seeing Greg again. Renee had missed him beyond reason—as a friend, of course. The last time she'd seen Greg was at Trey and Gia's wedding two years ago.

Gia pressed on. "What about *you*? Are you looking forward to seeing him again after all this time?"

Renee moved to a nearby rack and focused on adjusting one of the dresses on a hanger. Careful to keep her expression neutral, Renee murmured, "Of course I am. He's my friend. I'm looking forward to seeing Greg during this visit."

Feeling the heat of Gia's intense scrutiny,

she fluffed up the curls of her pixie haircut with her fingers.

Despite her reluctance to date Greg when he'd first asked, they'd been able to maintain a friendship through phone calls and emails whenever he wasn't on one of his secret deployments. She hated the stress those brought on. Renee had been battling panic disorder for years. She avoided anything that might set off an attack—and dating a military man would certainly leave her open to triggers. Having a friend deploy was bad enough.

Whenever Greg was sent away to whereabouts unknown, Renee had to force herself not to become consumed with worry over his safety, which proved that not getting involved with him romantically was the right decision. It was best that they'd spent the past couple of years building a platonic friendship. Whenever he was home, they talked and texted frequently. They'd watch the same movie on Netflix while on the phone; they had become close enough to confide in one another.

She couldn't avoid being drawn to Greg more than she'd like, despite fighting her attraction to him. But they could only ever be friends—his military service was a solid black mark against him. She'd rather have him as a friend than completely out of her life.

"We're hosting a dinner for him tonight, you know," Gia said.

Renee gave her a slight smile. "I know. I heard y'all discussing it with Misty last Sunday."

"So you're planning on coming, then."

It was more of a statement than a question, but Renee responded, "Yes, I'll be there." She held up a multicolored sundress. "This is what I plan on wearing to the dinner."

"Wow. That's beautiful." Gia lifted a brow. "Girl, I can't believe you're gonna do this to Greg. Come to his party dressed like a goddess. You know he's crazy about you."

"I keep telling you that we're just friends," Renee said with a short laugh.

Gia didn't seem convinced. "He wants more than that and so do you."

Renee dropped her eyes from her friend's. There was an undeniable allure building between them, but she fought to keep that awareness of Greg under control. As long as he was enlisted, nothing could ever happen between them.

"You never know… One day he may decide to leave the military."

"Maybe if he hadn't joined MARSOC," Renee said. "Gia, you know that was a dream come true for him. He's not about to give that up." And even if he was, Renee wasn't sure she was ready to date again. Not after what had happened with Kevin.

Gia gave her an assessing look. "Can you really just be Greg's friend?" she asked. "Caring for him the way you do?"

Renee gave a slight shrug. "I don't have any other choice. He's doing something he loves—I'm really happy for Greg. We're both living our dreams."

A knot of sorrow twisted inside her. Her dream *was* coming true. She had a successful clothing boutique, and her goal of having her own design house was just within her grasp... but she had no one to share it with.

Almost six years ago, she'd been planning her wedding to the man she thought she'd spend the rest of her life with; but Kevin had abruptly called it off, saying he didn't want to marry a woman with "issues." At the time, he'd been running for office. As far as he was concerned, she was damaged goods. Renee dropped her lashes quickly to hide the hurt that still lingered. She gave herself a mental shake; she wasn't going down that particular alleyway of memory lane ever again. She'd moved on. She was proud of all she'd accomplished since—she'd gotten there by relying on the one person she could trust. Herself.

I can do this. I'll see Greg tonight and we'll have a great time together...as friends.

Gia placed a red-and-white-striped dress on the counter. "I've been trying to make up my mind about this one. I've decided to buy it."

"It's going to look great on you," Renee assured her. "But you should get a smaller size. This will be a little big on you."

"I tried it on the other day, and I like the way it fits."

Renee walked behind the counter and rang up the sale.

Gia paid with cash, accepted the shopping bag and said, "I'll see you at the café later."

"I'm looking forward to it." She smiled as Gia left. Deep down, Renee couldn't deny she was a tiny bit disappointed that Greg hadn't come by the boutique to say hello. But Gia had mentioned he was getting some rest.

Besides, he doesn't owe me that. I'll just have to be satisfied with seeing him tonight.

Renee was about to leave the sales floor when she heard someone enter the shop. She glanced over her shoulder. For a moment, shock stole her capacity to think. "Greg… I didn't expect to see you until dinner. I figured you'd spend the day relaxing after the drive down."

He greeted Renee with a friendly hug. "I couldn't wait another minute to see this beautiful smile of yours."

Without looking away from his face, she backed out of his grasp. "I can't tell you how relieved I am that you made it back stateside. It was difficult not knowing if I'd ever see you again." Renee gave him a playful punch. "You know, I thought we were friends… I had to hear from Trey that you were back at Camp Lejeune."

"As soon as I got back, my focus was putting in for my leave for a visit," Greg said. "I couldn't wait to get back here to the island."

She awarded him a smile, shoving aside the fluttering in her stomach at his words. "Well, I'm glad you're here, because I need my card partner to redeem me. Gia and Trey have been whipping me. Rusty is a sweetheart, but he's not very good at Spades." Rusty, who'd married her aunt Eleanor a few years back, had immediately become a big part of their family.

"I got you," Greg said with a laugh.

Renee walked around him, studying him.

"It's hard to believe that I haven't seen you in two years. You've added more muscle... toned up quite a bit." It was true. Tall, muscular. Subtle hazel eyes and skin the color of caramel. His close-cropped black hair lay in neat waves—he was very handsome. "You look good."

Now, why had she let that slip out? She risked a glance at him, and when she glimpsed the heartrending tenderness of his gaze, she had to fight her overwhelming need to step closer to him in that very moment.

We're just friends. FRIENDS.

"I have to meet up with Trey," Greg announced, stepping back. "But I'll see you tonight, won't I?"

"Yeah, you will," Renee responded.

He embraced her again. "So good to see you again, friend."

She laughed. "Bye."

"I told you I don't like goodbyes. It sounds final."

"See you later," Renee murmured.

He smiled. "Much better."

CHAPTER TWO

THE POLK ISLAND BAKERY & CAFÉ had closed early for the private party Trey was hosting for Greg.

He glanced around the newly renovated dining room. A red, white and blue welcome banner with his name on it hung in the center of the ceiling along with balloons in the same colors.

"Trey, you didn't have to go through all this trouble for me, but I appreciate it." He picked up one of the finger sandwiches and popped it in his mouth after pulling the flag toothpick out.

"We wanted to properly welcome you to the island, especially if you're seriously planning to relocate here."

"Shhh… I haven't said anything to anyone yet," Greg whispered. "I don't want to say anything until it's a done deal. Don't even tell your brother or Gia." He glanced around, realizing he was looking for Renee. He thought she'd be here by now.

Trey gave him a knowing look. "Don't worry. She'll be here. She wanted to go home first and freshen up before the dinner."

Outside, the sun was setting among the tree-tops. His gaze shifted toward the entrance just as Renee strolled in, looking like a super-model. He often told her that, but Renee had no interest in a modeling career—she loved designing clothes.

He got up and crossed the floor, stopping her in her tracks. "Hello. Glad you made it…"

She gave him a smile. "Greg…"

Her sultry voice caused a brief shiver to ripple through him. It had become so familiar to him over the years as they'd kept in touch over the phone. "We didn't really get to talk earlier, but I want you to know that I didn't intend to stay away this long. It couldn't be helped."

"I understand," Renee murmured. "You have a job to do and no say as to when or where it takes you. At least we have you with us for now."

"I'll be here for ten days." Happiness filtered through Greg like an overflowing river at the thought of it. He hoped they could catch up properly. "You look absolutely stunning. Is this one of your designs?"

Renee smiled once more. "It is."

He couldn't look away, his gaze held captive by her beauty. Realizing he looked like a complete fool, he rushed to fill the silence. "The seat beside me is empty. It's yours." He'd waited so long to see her, he didn't want to tear his attention away from her.

"Thank you." She followed him to the table.

Her smile was so warm, vibrant and alive. He enjoyed her closeness as his long stride matched hers.

They joined Trey, Gia, Misty, Leon, and Trey's aunt Eleanor, who were already seated.

"You look great," Misty said. "I *love* that dress."

"Thank you," Renee responded as she sat down beside Greg.

His eyes traveled around the room, and he relished being with friends again. "It's so good to be back here with y'all. It feels good to be able to sleep as late as I want, do nothing but hang out at the beach or anything else I want to do."

"Hmm… A vacation," Renee said wistfully. "I used to take those, once upon a time."

"Me, too," Leon's wife, Misty, stated. "Before I became a business owner."

Renee nodded. "I'm finally able to hire another full-time employee so I can take some time off. I've been working really hard on the designs for Fashion Week."

"We know," Trey said. "We've hardly seen you."

"How are you able to have a show in New York?" Eleanor asked. "You made it to the big time now, but something like that has to cost a lot of money."

"It's definitely not cheap, but I was able to get sponsors, which helped with a lot of the costs of my show," Renee responded. "The biggest expense is the venue. My dad's company paid for that. And the DuGrandpre Law Firm donated money for the decorations, lighting and sound system." Greg knew the DuGrandpres were cousins of the Rothchild family— Greg had always loved how close they were and how they helped each other. "Everyone in this family has been so supportive, and I truly appreciate it."

"Were you able to get any additional sponsors?" Gia asked.

"Yes. The Alexander-DePaul Hotel chain is

one of my sponsors. That's where I'll be hosting the party after the fashion show."

Greg noticed the way her eyes lit up as she
talked about her upcoming debut during Fashion Week. Renee had talked about this for a
while and now it was really happening. He was
thrilled for her.

"The other sponsor is a national beverage
company. I was able to hire two very popular
models, a hairstylist and a makeup artist. The
rest of the models are lesser known, but they're
coming from a top modeling agency in Manhattan. My only out-of-pocket cost is the PR
agency I'm using to create a buzz to reach the
masses, the invitations, swag items and mis-
cellaneous stuff."

"Sounds like you have everything under
control," Gia responded.

"I'm blessed to have a super-organized assistant designer," Renee practically gushed.
"Kayla has amazing administrative skills.
She's wonderful and keeps me on task. She
pretty much runs the boutique for now, until I
hire a store manager so that I can focus on the
couture collection."

Greg met her gaze. "I know you're busy getting ready for your fashion show in September,

but I hope I'll get to spend a day or two with you while I'm here."

Renee grinned. "You don't have to worry about that because I've already penciled you in."

He touched a hand to his heart playfully. "Thank you."

"I pulled some long hours over the past couple of weeks just so I could take some time off for your visit."

"She sure did," Gia confirmed. "We didn't see much of her. Trey and Leon both threatened to send out the police if she didn't return texts or phone calls."

Greg was looking forward to their time together. He silently debated whether to share his news with her.

It could change everything between them, or it might not. Maybe they were just destined to remain friends.

HE SMELLS SO GOOD, like warm skin, amber and spices. Sitting beside Greg, she reveled in his closeness—so male, so bracing. His broad shoulders heaved as he breathed.

Everyone at the table joined in conversation as they nibbled on appetizers. Her favorite was the hot sausage dip with homemade tortilla chips.

Renee's heart beat with the pulse of the music. She began swaying in her chair as she finished off a couple of meatballs.

"Let's dance," Greg said.

Eager to get on the dance floor, Renee pushed away from the table and stood up. He swept her into his arms as if she were weightless.

Renee broke into a grin as they moved to the rhythm of the song playing. She burst into laughter when Greg suddenly went old-school with his version of the robot.

"You don't know anything about that," he said.

"I remember watching my parents do something similar," she said smugly. "I was never a fan."

"You sound a little jealous to me."

Joy bubbled inside her, and she let it out with laughter. "Next you're probably going to break out with the moonwalk." Renee loved Greg's sense of humor and outgoing personality. She always had a great time with him, even just on the phone.

Misty and Leon joined them on the dance

floor. They danced through a couple of songs, then went back to the table.

It was a little past nine o' clock when everyone left the café.

"Renee, are you coming by the house?" Trey asked as he and Gia walked to their car.

"Actually, I'm going home. I have a long day tomorrow."

"Do you mind if I come by?" Greg asked. She hesitated for a moment before agreeing. She didn't want the night to end just yet. "I promise I won't stay long."

"Well, I guess we've been abandoned, sweetheart." Trey glanced at his wife, then handed a key to his friend. "Just let yourself into the house."

Greg followed Renee to the beachfront condo she rented from Misty. After Trey and Gia had gotten married, Renee felt they needed time alone, so she'd moved out of the house she once shared with Trey and into her own space, right by the water.

Renee and Greg settled down in her living room after she'd locked the door. "That was fun… I really missed you," he said.

"I missed you, too," she responded. Before his visit, their contact had been cut off by his latest deployment. "It was hard not knowing if you were safe."

"This last mission wasn't bad."

"I know you can't talk about it," Renee interjected. "But I have to tell you that I'm proud of what you're doing to keep this country safe."

"I appreciate it, ma'am."

She gave him a sidelong glance. "No, you didn't just *ma'am* me."

His brow furrowed. "It's not an insult, Renee."

She chuckled. "I know. I'm just teasing you."

Their gazes locked.

"So…" he began, "it sounds like you have everything set up for Fashion Week?"

Renee nodded, latching on to the safe subject. She couldn't remember a time when she didn't love designing clothes. As a child, she would design outfits for her paper dolls, and after learning the basics of sewing in her home economics class, she began making clothes for her teddy bears. She earned money for college by designing prom dresses and outfits for her friends. She loved the way her designs made other people feel when they wore them. "The best I can say right now is that we have a plan. I'm still trying to come up with a theme and the music. We have to find the right set designer. There's still a lot of stuff to do. The clothing line is pretty much complete—I keep making changes here and there." She glanced over at him. "I'd like for you to come if you're not deployed somewhere."

He nodded. "I'll put in a request for leave when I get back to LeJeune."

"Great. You can help keep me calm. I get nervous just thinking about it sometimes," she admitted. "This is such a great opportunity. If all goes well in New York—I'm going for Fashion Week in Milan next."

He grinned at her. "I can see that happening, so you might as well get ready."

She exhaled a long sigh of gratitude. "You've been such a good friend to me, Greg. Leon and Trey are wonderful, but they have to be supportive because they're my family. It's nice to be able to talk to someone who isn't related to me who also thinks I can do this."

His hazel eyes darkened with emotion. "I'll always be here for you."

For a heartbeat, they simply stared at each other.

"Renee..." he said, so softly it was barely more than a whisper. She tingled as Greg said her name. "I really want to get to know you better."

He leaned forward and pressed his lips to hers. Warmth flooded through her.

The world stood still.

Her heart stuttered in her chest, and Renee forgot to breathe.

It was too much. Too real and too confronting. She broke the kiss.

She couldn't look him in the face, could barely force herself to lift her gaze, because she was afraid of what he'd see in her eyes. "I thought we agreed to keep this within the friendship zone."

"I couldn't help myself. My apologies if I crossed the line. I don't want to make you uncomfortable."

"The kiss was nice." She grappled with what to say next. "I just don't want things to get out of hand or awkward between us. Let's just chalk it up to a kiss between friends who haven't seen each other in two years."

Who am I fooling?

Greg rose to his full height, and she couldn't decipher the expression on his face. "It's getting late, and I remember you said you have a busy day tomorrow. I told you I wouldn't stay long, so I'm keeping my word."

"The reason my day is a busy one is because I'm taking a few days off to hang out with you."

When he looked as if he were about to kiss her again, Renee stood up and walked toward the front door. She gripped the knob. It twisted beneath her hand as she unlocked it.

He followed her.

"Renee—"

"See you tomorrow, friend."

Greg smiled gently and left.

Renee entered her bedroom and sank down on the upholstered bench at the end of her king-size bed. Her mind was plagued with thoughts of what it would be like to kiss Greg again—for real this time. Thoughts of what her life could be if she and Greg were a couple.

A smile formed on her lips, then disappeared. There was no point in thinking about what could never be. Greg was so handsome and a good man. The type of man she could see herself spending her life with—but because of his occupation, there couldn't be a future with him. Her own fear kept them apart. She hated living with chronic panic disorder— how it meant avoiding situations that would trigger her. It was a burden she wouldn't wish on anyone. But on this matter, there could be no compromise.

"Hey, Dr. Wiley," Renee greeted as she took her seat on the plush sofa. Without looking around, she knew every painting on the wall, every degree. She knew every inch of her therapist's brightly lit office in Charleston. She'd been coming here since moving to the island; their biweekly therapy sessions had helped her cope with her chronic panic disorder.

"How have things been going?" Dr. Wiley asked.

"Better," Renee responded, picking up a plump throw pillow and cradling it. "The friend I'd been so worried about arrived yesterday. He'll be in town for ten days."

As usual, Dr. Wiley kept her face blank as she asked, "How do you feel about this?"

She gave a slight shrug in nonchalance. "I'm relieved that he's back safe."

Her therapist nodded. "Do you have any concerns?"

"It's nice seeing Greg again. He's a lot of fun," Renee answered. "I just have to maintain control over my feelings." *Easier said than done.*

"It sounds like you really care about this friend. What strategies do you have in place to keep your emotions in check?"

"I do care for him," Renee admitted. "But we'll never have any type of future together."

"Because he's military?" Her therapist knew her well.

"Yes," she responded. "You know how hard it was for me whenever he was on a mission. I can only imagine it would be much worse if we were together." It reminded her of how much she worried whenever Trey was deployed. She would never forget the day they received the call that Trey was injured. It was her worst fear coming true.

"You have no control over what happens."

"I know that." Renee shifted her position on the sofa. "But my brain automatically takes me to the worst-case scenario. I've tried shutting down the thoughts, refocusing… Sometimes it works, and other times it doesn't."

"What frightens you about pursuing a relationship with this man?"

"I'm a bit of a mess," Renee responded. "The whole deal with my panic attacks… I told you how it ruined my last relationship. It's also his being in the military."

"Greg is a different man. He's not Kevin."

She nodded in agreement. "I know you're right. When I first told Greg about the panic disorder, he was concerned and very understanding. He even took time to research it." She smiled at the memory. "But I'm not sure he can handle something like this in a relationship. He's never seen me have one of my attacks."

Dr. Wiley studied her. "Focus on one day at a time and on controlling what you can, Renee. The rest of it will fall into place."

She took a steadying breath. "I'm trying."

Renee continued to talk through her week with Dr. Wiley, and after her session, she left the office. She was soon back on the island, driving straight to her shop.

"Did we have many customers come through?" she asked Jade, one of her employees, noting there were only a couple of shoppers in the store.

"You should've been here about fifteen minutes ago. It was crazy busy. We've already sold out of most of the swimwear." Jade grinned. "People are getting ready for the summer."

"That's great," Renee said. "We have more coming in this week."

"Good. I had to sell the one I wanted."

Renee laughed. "Wait until you see the new inventory of swimwear," she said. "You're going to love them."

Her assistant designer, Kayla, entered through the double doors of the boutique.

When she met Renee's gaze, she said, "I just had the most amazing lunch at the café."

Kayla had interned at the design house where Renee worked in New York a few years back. Renee had reached out to her when she was financially prepared to hire an assistant fashion designer. She was thrilled when Kayla had accepted her offer of employment and moved to the island. She had a keen eye for market trends.

Renee grinned. "I told you the food is delicious…"

"Yes, you did. I wasn't quite sure about it, but you've made a believer of me. And Misty is so nice. Actually, everyone working there was friendly." Holding up a paper bag, Kayla said, "Misty sent over some chocolate-raspberry brownies for everyone."

"They're a staff favorite," Renee responded. She looked around the store. "Looks like y'all have everything under control. I'm going to take a couple days off."

"I'm really glad to hear that," Kayla said. "You've been working some long hours. You need a break."

"That I do," Renee agreed. "And Greg's here for ten days, so I plan to spend some time with him."

"That's great," Jade responded. "He seems like a really nice guy, and you two look good together."

Kayla eyed her. "You've never mentioned this man to me."

"That's because he's just a friend," Renee said, hopefully not too forcefully. She changed the subject. "A young lady called earlier about a wedding dress. She doesn't want the traditional white. She wants a sapphire-blue gown. And silver for her bridesmaids. I made an appointment for her to come in to discuss in more detail tomorrow afternoon. I told her she'd be meeting with you, Kayla."

"Sounds great," she responded. "Oh, I checked on that warehouse space in Charleston we looked at last week, and it's still available. It's perfect for the design house."

A rush of excitement filled Renee. "Did you set up a meeting with the owner?" In September, she would debut the Renee Rothchild couture collection, and from there, she planned to open her own fashion house. Having a space just across the bridge would be perfect. Despite her parents' reservations, she'd moved to Polk Island six years ago with the dream of owning her own boutique filled with her ready-to-wear collection. She was soon designing custom pieces, including wedding gowns for VIP customers. Through word of mouth, her name had spread, and she could hardly believe where she was today.

"Yes," Kayla answered. "He's leaving town tonight but will be back on Sunday. We meet with him on Monday at noon."

Renee grinned. "This is really happening, Kayla."

"I know…"

She went through her phone, reviewing her notes. "I don't think I've forgotten anything."

"We're fine," Kayla told her. "Go. Enjoy your time off."

Picking up her tote, Renee said, "Thanks for all you do. I'll see you in a couple of days."

CHAPTER THREE

LAUGHTER DRIFTED FROM Greg as he watched Renee, Gia and Misty cavorting in the ocean with the children. Talei and her little brother, Leo, were having a good time splashing around. He sat with Trey and Leon on the beach while the others swam around in the water.

As mesmerizing as the ocean surrounding them was, Greg couldn't take his eyes off Renee. He took in her big brown eyes and the way her hair lay in tiny curls when wet. She was an extremely beautiful woman. Not skinny—she had more of an athletic build, with curves in all the right places. But it was more than her physical beauty that attracted Greg. He liked her gentle nature, her sense of humor, even her competitive spirit. In truth, he liked everything about Renee.

"What are you thinking about so hard?" Trey asked, cutting into his thoughts.

Greg snapped out of his reverie. "I was

thinking about your cousin. She's beautiful, intelligent and creative… She's special."

"Yeah…she is very special," Leon responded. "Renee's been through a lot, but you wouldn't know it to look at her."

He agreed.

Renee waved and gestured for him to join her in the water.

Greg rose to his feet. "I'll talk to y'all later. I'm being summoned."

He walked across the warm sand and into the ocean. There was a bit of a chill in the air, but it didn't faze him.

He began to swim toward Renee. "You just couldn't stay away from me any longer. Just admit it."

"You don't quit, do you?" Laughing, Renee playfully splashed water at him. "Friendship zone. I'm serious."

Greg shook his head. "Let's not get serious about anything. Not today."

Grinning, Renee responded, "I can get with that."

She had the prettiest smile. Floating in the water, Greg drifted closer to her. He'd been looking forward to this—strolling the beach with Renee, swimming. He intended to make the most of their time together. It would be over far too soon, and then he'd be back on base, having to settle for phone calls with her.

Greg lost count of how long they stayed in the ocean.

When they returned to the beach tent where the others had gathered, Gia announced, "I'm in desperate need of a nap, so Trey and I are leaving."

"I think I need one, too," Renee said.

"Are we still on for Saturday?" Greg asked her as they packed up their belongings.

She smiled at him. "Yeah, we are."

"I'll drop you off," he offered.

"No need," Renee responded. "My condo is right over there. I can walk. Besides, I didn't get to run this morning. I can use the exercise."

Greg wanted to plant a kiss on her cheek but settled for a quick wave. "See you later." It was a struggle to stay within the boundaries of friendship for him, but not having Renee in his life at all wasn't an option. He held on to hope that one day, what they shared would turn into something more. But before that could happen, Greg had to make peace with his decision to not reenlist.

Renee's laughter pulled him out of his thoughts again as he followed Gia and Trey to the SUV parked a few yards from Renee's condo.

When they returned to Trey's house, Greg went upstairs to take a shower.

His phone rang as he ascended the stairs, and he answered once he entered the guest bedroom. "Hello?"

"Staff Sgt. Bowman, my name is Edward Morris." The voice on the other end wasn't familiar to him. "I know that you're currently on leave, but I'd like to meet with you when you return regarding a job opportunity."

Intrigued, he asked, "What's the job? And where is the job location?" Greg closed the bedroom door behind him.

"Washington, DC."

He sat down on the edge of the bed. That was farther than he'd like to go. "Look, I've already made plans to relocate to South Carolina when I get out."

"Working from that location may not be a problem. I hope you'll at least hear me out. You possess the knowledge, experience and particular skill set in the candidate we're looking for."

It was nice knowing that there were companies interested in hiring him post-military. There was a time when he questioned what he'd do if he ever decided not to reenlist. During his previous visit to the island, Trey talked about his plans to open a museum highlighting his family's history and contributions to Polk Island. Greg's help with the project at the time led to Trey offering him a job.

His mind was already made up, but Greg didn't see any harm in hearing what Edward Morris had to say. "Mr. Morris, you're a recruiter for what company?" he asked. He knew that his special-operative skill set was a natural fit for intelligence-analyst positions within law enforcement or other three-letter agencies.

"I'm not at liberty to disclose that information, but I'll explain everything when we meet."

"Now you have my attention…"

TODAY HAD BEEN PERFECT, as far as Renee was concerned.

Releasing a soft sigh of contentment, she sprinkled drops of raspberry vinaigrette over leafy greens before mixing the ingredients around the bowl with metal salad tongs. She tossed bacon bits and garlic croutons on top, then carried her dinner to the sofa to eat in front of the television.

The cool, calming colors in her spacious living room helped erase the tension from her body. As she ate, Renee took in her surroundings, decorated in a minimalist style. She preferred her living space airy, without a lot of furniture.

She absolutely loved her condo, with its marble fireplace and patio facing the ocean. It was very different from the small studio apartment she'd had in New York, and the more Renee thought about it, the more she recognized this place was exactly her style.

She stabbed her fork into a leaf of spinach and stuffed it into her mouth, chewing slowly. She reached over, grabbed the remote from the coffee table and flipped through several channels before settling on a show.

When Renee had finished eating, she shifted her position on the sofa, lay back and closed her eyes. She wasn't sleepy—she knew that was because she couldn't stop thinking about Greg. It was hard to avoid thinking so much about him. He was unforgettable.

He's your friend, and he's leaving soon. She needed this constant reminder to keep her emotions in check.

An hour passed; it was almost midnight. Since she was still very much awake, Renee went through her calendar.

She had a wedding to attend on Saturday at noon. She considered not going, but the bride was one of her top clients. Renee decided she'd attend the ceremony but skip the reception. While she found the bride sweet and friendly, she didn't care much for the woman's mother or her sister.

Renee had had her fill when it came to dealing with them, and she didn't want to be rude—it wouldn't be a good look for her business. She'd rather spend her time in the peaceful surroundings of her home than around mothers and daughters who enjoyed making snide comments about other women. Renee had zero tolerance for cattiness. She preferred instead to empower women; it took too much energy to do otherwise. It was why she'd hired Kayla as assistant designer, and why she loved designing clothes—to help women feel beautiful and confident.

She stared at the painting of Iao Valley in Maui, Hawaii, above the fireplace, trying to lose herself in it. It was a gift from her brother, Howard Jr., and a favorite of hers. Their parents had taken them there on vacation when she was sixteen. They'd chosen paradise to inform her and her brother that they were separating. A year later, her parents divorced.

Although her parents chose to end their marriage, they were able to remain friendly toward one another. Their breakup hadn't destroyed Renee's hopes of one day finding her Mr. Right. Although, her broken engagement had left her shaken. Still, Kevin hadn't been her Mr. Right, and he was better off in her past than as her husband—the man was manipulative and had never understood her. She didn't regret that things had ended between them, but it had certainly left her more cautious about dating ever since.

She shook the thought away, again finding calm in the picture on the wall. Strangely, the news of her parents' breakup had done nothing to mar her happy memories of spending most days on the beach and swimming in the beautiful North Pacific Ocean. The trip had reminded her a little of summers spent with Aunt Eleanor here on Polk Island. She'd never regretted giving up her fast-paced life in New York to move here permanently.

This was her happy place.

"THE WEDDING RING is an outward and visible sign of an inward and spiritual bond, which unites two hearts in endless love. It is a seal of the vows..." the pastor was saying to the bride and groom.

Renee smiled through unexpected tears. She glanced over at Kayla and handed her a tissue.

The bride's sister relieved her of the enormous wedding bouquet she had insisted on carrying down the aisle. Both Renee and Kayla had tried to convince her to go with something simple to avoid it competing with the beading and sequins on her gown—but what Halle Bryant wanted, she got.

"It is a seal of the vows Tom and Halle have made to one another..."

Renee witnessed the exchange of rings between her client and her new husband, silently wishing them love and happiness for the rest of their lives.

When her own engagement had ended, Renee wouldn't take any bridal clients—it was too much for her. She'd thought she would be the one walking down the aisle when that dream came to a crashing halt. The gown she'd designed for her wedding was buried in the back of her closet. However, she loved bridal design and couldn't continue to ignore that call.

The pastor's words drew her attention back to the ceremony.

"You may now kiss your bride."

Three hundred guests erupted in applause as Mr. and Mrs. Thomas Ryan were introduced. The music began, prompting the newlyweds to lead the recessional from the sanctuary.

Outside in the foyer, Renee and Halle embraced.

"Congratulations," Renee whispered. "I'm so happy for you."

"Thank you for everything, Renee. You and Kayla were great to work with."

"It was a pleasure working with you, as usual," she replied, hiding her true feelings from her client to stay professional.

Renee moved toward the exit doors as the wedding guests filed out of the sanctuary, each one pausing to congratulate the bride and groom.

"I'm not going to the reception," Renee told Kayla as they walked to their cars.

"I'm not staying too long. My boyfriend's flying into Charleston. I have to pick him up from the airport." Kayla paused in her tracks. "I have a confession—I'm so glad this wedding is done. That woman and her mother…"

Renee chuckled. "I know what you mean." She had designed some cocktail dresses for this family in the past, but she would be happy to have a break between her next commission with them. They were demanding clients.

After a final goodbye to Kayla, Renee left the chapel and drove straight to the condo. She had enough time to change out of her semiformal dress and into a pair of shorts and a tank top before Greg showed up at her door. They were planning to do some shopping at a mall in Charleston.

If Renee had to describe their friendship, she'd consider Greg her best friend and confidant. They'd spent quite a few late nights on the phone over the past two years, sharing their goals, their woes, triumphs…she could tell him anything without fear of judgment. Although it was clear he wanted more, he respected her wishes. Deep down, Renee had to often caution herself against blurring the lines of that relationship.

The struggle was real.

CHAPTER FOUR

"How was the wedding?" asked Greg.

"It was beautiful, but Kayla and I are both glad that it finally happened. My client has always been a sweetheart until she got engaged. Then she turned into a bridezilla. She looked like a little girl's dream when she came down the aisle in that gown, though. My assistant did a fantastic job."

"You sound like a proud mama."

"That's because I am." They kept walking, pausing every now and then to look at the rows of dolls on the shelves.

Greg picked up one and asked, "What do you think about this one?"

Renee bit back a smile as she noted the intensity with which Greg searched for the perfect birthday present for Talei. "I think she'll like it. Talei seems to prefer the ones she can feed, change and cuddle."

"I read up on what is considered age-appropriate toys for eight-year-olds," he admitted.

She stopped in her tracks. "You actually re-searched this?"

"Yep. I wanted to make sure I bought a gift that wasn't too young for her or too old."

He was so serious about this. Renee resisted the urge to hug him since they were inside a busy store, but he deserved one for putting so much thought behind a gift.

Greg even purchased a backup present just in case Talei didn't like the doll, prompting Renee to do the same. She was not about to be outdone by *Uncle Greg*.

Not that it was a competition or anything.

Renee and Greg left the toy store in Charleston laden with presents. They put them in the trunk, got in the car and headed to the cele-bration dinner.

"Is Talei still a fan of hot dogs and French fries?" he asked during the drive to Leon and Misty's house.

Renee chuckled. "She seems to be over the hot dogs for now. Her new favorite is pepper-oni flatbread. She also loves cheese fries with bacon and ranch dressing."

"I have a feeling you introduced her to that little treat."

"I did because they're the best."

Greg smiled. "And addictive. Only I add jalapeños to mine for that extra kick."

Renee grinned. "That sounds delicious. I'm going to have to try it."

They arrived at Leon's house, minutes after Gia and Trey. Greg parked his rental right behind their SUV.

He got out, walked around to the passenger side and opened the door for Renee.

Smiling, she got out.

They retrieved the gift bags from the back seat.

Talei greeted them at the door. "It's my birthday!"

Renee chuckled. "I know, little cousin. Did you think I'd forget?"

The little girl beamed. "I wasn't gonna let you forget."

Greg laughed. "We brought presents for the birthday girl."

"Wado."

"You're welcome," Renee responded to the girl's expression of thanks in Cherokee. She handed the gift bags to Talei, who put them with the other gifts. Misty had been teaching her daughter the Cherokee language since she was a toddler. She wanted Talei to grow up proud of both her Native and Black heritage.

Misty embraced her, then Greg. "Welcome to the party."

"Do you need help with anything?" Renee asked.

"My mother's taken control of the kitchen. Let's just leave her be. She's making Indian tacos for the children and salmon for the adults."

Hands up, Renee uttered, "I'm not messing with Miss Oma."

Elroy and Clara Hayes, Talei's paternal grandparents, arrived a few minutes after them. Leon had met Misty the day her ex-husband and his best friend, John, died. The two eventually fell in love and married. However, Misty still wanted her former in-laws to be an active part of her daughter's life.

Renee glimpsed Gia slipping away from the gathering. She got up and followed her outside to the patio. "Hey, are you okay?" Renee asked out of concern. "You look a little pale."

"I'm fine. Just needed some fresh air."

She glanced down at how tightly Gia was gripping the railing and responded, "Naw... something's up. You look like you're about to pass out." Renee gestured toward a nearby lounge chair. "Why don't you sit down for a minute? I'll get you some water."

She went inside, grabbed a water bottle and then returned. "Here you are."

"Thank you," Gia murmured, accepting the water.

"Do you want me to get Trey?" Renee inquired, her concern for her friend growing.

"No, I'll be okay. Really." Gia eyed her, then said, "I'm pregnant. Trey and I weren't going to say anything for another couple weeks. We were waiting until my second trimester before announcing the pregnancy."

Renee released a sigh of relief. "This is wonderful news. I was a bit worried about you because you haven't really been yourself these past few months."

"Don't say anything, please," Gia pleaded softly. "Trying to hide the morning sickness hasn't been easy."

"I won't," she promised. "It's your and Trey's story to tell, but I'm so happy for you both. Congratulations." She tried to keep it low-key, but deep down, she was ecstatic over the news. She knew how badly Trey wanted to become a father. Renee had never really believed in soul mates until Trey and Gia. Watching them fall in love had offered her a firsthand view of what true love looked like. Even during his worst moments after coming home from the

Marines, Trey was gentle and loving in the way he treated Gia.

Misty stuck her head outside. "I wondered where you two were. Everything okay?"

"Yes," Renee responded. "We're just getting caught up with some girl talk. We'll join everyone in a few minutes."

"Okay. We'll be eating soon."

Gia awarded Renee a grateful smile. "Thank you. Certain smells make me nauseous these days. I'm hoping I can make it through dinner without getting sick."

"It happens. Don't worry about it."

They went inside the house to join the others.

Gia walked over to Trey, who looked instantly concerned, but she seemed to quickly reassure him she was fine. A smile tinged with sadness tugged at Renee's lips as she watched the couple. If things had gone well with Kevin, maybe she would have been a mom by now... She shook away the thought. It was a good thing they were no longer together. He could be borderline verbally abusive at times and so could his mother. The day she'd had a full-blown panic attack, Kevin had the nerve to say she'd embarrassed him. She'd needed his love and support but instead received a lecture and was told her panic disorder wasn't a real thing.

Her eyes strayed to Greg. Now, *he'd* make a great father—she was sure of it. He would never treat a woman the way Kevin had. But Renee wasn't ready to take that leap and open her heart again, so there was no use lingering on that thought.

It was time to eat.

"Gia, you don't want any greens?" Aunt Eleanor, the matriarch of their family, asked when they were seated at the table. "You love mixed greens."

"Not tonight," she responded. "I don't have much of an appetite right now, but I'll take some home with me for sure."

"We ate a lot during lunch," Trey interjected. "We didn't save much room for dinner, but we didn't want to miss Talei's birthday." He winked at his niece. "I left room for cake and ice cream, though."

Nice save. No one seemed to suspect a thing. Gia's lack of appetite was soon forgotten as Trey changed the subject.

"Aunt Eleanor, I hear you and Rusty are going on vacation in a couple of weeks," he stated.

Surprised, Aunt Eleanor looked over at her husband. "We're going away?"

Rusty nodded. "We're visiting my brother in Connecticut."

"Oh yeah… I remember now. I need to start getting my packing done. You know I hate waiting until the last moment. I always forget when I do." Aunt Eleanor's battle with Alzheimer's had been tough on the family the past few years, but they tried to support her as best they could.

"Me, too," Renee replied reassuringly. "I have to actually make a list of the things I need to pack."

Aunt Eleanor took a sip of her water. "Maybe I should do that. I'll write it down in my journal."

"That's a good idea, my darlin'," Rusty said.

Trey wiped his mouth on a napkin, turned to Talei and said, "You're a big girl now. I hope you're still going to want to spend time with your uncle."

"I will," the girl responded with a grin. "We're still gonna do our beach dates and… and you're gonna teach me how to play Spades. You promised when I got older you'd teach me. *I'm older now.*"

Trey shrugged. "You're already beating me at Go Fish… I don't know, sweetie."

"You scared, Uncle." Talei giggled.

Talei's younger brother, Leo, began imitating a chicken.

"Sounds like you just got called out, cousin," Renee teased. "You don't want people thinking you're scared of a little girl."

"I'm the reigning king of Spades in this family," Trey said as he stared down Talei. "I'm not ready to relinquish my crown."

Arms folded and staring back at him, Talei uttered, "I'm getting that crown."

Greg burst into laughter. "Did y'all just see that look she gave Trey? This is one determined little girl."

Renee nodded in agreement. "She just let it be known that she's coming for you, Trey."

"That's my daughter," Leon said proudly.

Everyone at the table laughed.

"Talei is definitely competitive," Misty stated. "You should see her on the soccer field."

"I have a game tomorrow morning," Talei announced. "I want all y'all to come. You, too, Uncle Greg."

"I'll be there," he said.

"Me, too," Renee responded.

From across the table, they caught each

other's eye. There was no denying that she and Greg shared an awareness of each other. She forgot how intense it could feel but seeing him in person again reminded her—and Renee wasn't sure it was a good thing. She broke eye contact as everyone started getting up from the table so Talei could have her cake and presents.

THE MORE GREG THOUGHT about not reenlisting, the more uncertainty crept within.

How would he feel tomorrow, and after too many days on the island? Restless? Would he love life as a civilian?

One thing was for sure—Greg couldn't have it both ways. He had to decide and then stick to his decision. The absolute truth was that he was still weighed down with indecision.

"Why so quiet?" Renee asked, intruding on his thoughts.

Her question pulled him out of his reverie. "Just thinking about the future." Greg now realized that deciding to get out over the idea of a family at the beginning of his military career wasn't really all that smart. He'd never counted on loving his job. Back then, it was all about his hopes and dreams of following in his father's footsteps.

She nodded slowly. "Me, too. I've been fantasizing lately about what it'll be like to be a fashion icon like Calvin Klein, Ralph Lauren or Stella McCartney…"

"I believe Renee Rothchild will outshine them all."

"See…that's why you're one of my best friends. If I said I'm going to fly to the moon, you'd cheer me on."

"That's because I believe in you," Greg responded.

"I know you do, and I appreciate it so much." Greg knew she had a lot riding on her show this September at Fashion Week, and that soon, her hard work would pay off.

"I want you to have that kind of faith in me, too." He also knew she had trouble coping with his deployments. He kept thinking about what she'd said the other day, about how it had been hard on her not being in touch with him on his last mission.

Renee looked him in the eyes. "I have a lot of faith in you."

"Then trust that when I'm on a mission, I am doing everything in my power to stay safe. I'm not some reckless person." He grinned "I enjoy being alive, and I intend to stay that way.

Prayers are always welcome, but I don't want you to worry so much."

Not too long after Talei opened her presents, everyone left. Greg dropped Renee off, then headed to Trey's house.

He crept up the stairs as quietly as he could so as not to disturb his friend and Gia. He was beginning to suspect that Gia was pregnant, although no one had said anything. Greg was almost positive an announcement would soon be forthcoming.

He showered and climbed into bed.

Renee was the last thought on his mind before he closed his eyes. If he ever got a chance with her, he didn't want to disappoint her. He wanted to be the type of man she deserved.

Greg shifted his position in bed. He kept trying to convince Trey that Renee wasn't the reason he was thinking of getting out of the military, but it was kind of a half-truth. If he hadn't met her, getting out most likely wouldn't be on his mind right now.

He just wasn't sure she'd ever let down her guard enough to allow him inside her heart.

TALEI'S GAME WAS scheduled at eight o'clock Sunday morning.

Greg got up with Trey and Gia to head over

to Leon's house. They'd volunteered to help prepare snacks and pack up the supplies for the game. Renee arrived at the house as Misty was putting orange wedges into baggies, and then they headed out.

The four of them followed Leon's vehicle to the elementary school three blocks away from the house.

Leon and Misty gathered the soccer team together and led them out on the field while Renee and Greg followed Gia and Trey to the bleachers.

Greg began cheering as soon as the game started. He was already considering volunteering to coach a sport once he began civilian life. He enjoyed working with children, and he loved sports.

"Go Ravens!" Renee cheered.

"Did you play any sports growing up?" Greg asked.

"I didn't," she responded. "I was more into sewing, fashion—that sort of stuff. I had zero interest in being an athlete."

"I'm surprised, because you're so competitive."

Renee gave him a sidelong glance. "Is that your way of saying I don't like to lose?"

He grinned. "You don't."

"True," she murmured. "But that's not why I never wanted to play sports. I simply wasn't interested. I do love to exercise, though. Running helps to clear my mind."

Greg leaned toward her and whispered, "I don't like to lose, either."

Renee gave him a look filled with mischief. "Don't I know…"

"C'mon, Talei," Trey yelled. "Great job, sweetie."

Renee and Greg joined in, cheering the little girls' team to a victory.

After the game, they decided to drive to the café for pizza.

Watching Talei and her teammates had ignited a yearning within Greg. He was looking forward to days like this—coaching his son or daughter's team, cheering for them, celebrating a victory or being supportive after a loss. He wanted to create special memories like these.

That part of him reared its head once more. He loved serving his country. Had he lived, his father would've been proud that Greg had followed in his footsteps.

But you're not here. You died when I was young and never got to see me grow up.

I don't want that for my children.

But am I making a mistake? It was a question he'd avoided asking himself up until now. And now that he had, he found it necessary to answer it.

"Earth to Greg..."

He glanced over at Renee and smiled. "Sorry about that. Just thinking about how much fun I'm having with you and everyone. I love being around your family."

"We *can* be a lot of fun," she said with a chuckle.

Greg had grown up an only child. After his dad had died young, it was just him and his mom. Their family wasn't big, but he loved it all the same, and he'd always dreamed of having a big family of his own someday. He smiled at her. "I'm seeing that more and more."

CHAPTER FIVE

"You still feel like going to the beach?" Greg asked when lunch had ended, and they were in the car.

She broke into a smile. "I'd love to, but I should probably put in a few hours working on my designs. This opportunity to debut my collection during Fashion Week could be a huge break for me. If any of the buyers place orders, I'll need to be able to fulfill them. I've been looking at industrial space in Charleston. I'll also need to hire additional staff...patternmakers, cutters, a textile designer, pressers, production manager and sewing machine operators. Not to mention someone to handle quality control, packaging and customer support—"

"Breathe..." Greg said gently. "You've got this, Renee."

She inhaled deeply and exhaled slowly. "Thank you. Sometimes I get overwhelmed when I think about all the stuff that comes with a design house… I can't believe I'm really doing this. When I first mentioned this to my parents some years ago, they weren't very encouraging. It was my father's idea that I start small with a boutique. I think it was the right move, but now I'm ready for more." Renee wished her parents had had more faith in her when she'd announced her desire to be a fashion designer. Instead, they'd pointed out all the negatives and tried to redirect her career goals. However, her Rothchild stubbornness had kicked in, and she was more determined than ever to make her dreams a reality.

"It's real," he responded. "You're a fashion designer, and your brand's taking off. Just don't put too much pressure on yourself. Now, this is just a suggestion—why don't we go to the beach and give Leon a hand with the kids?"

"That ocean must really be calling your name."

Greg put a hand to his ear. "Can't you hear it, too?" he teased.

They stopped at Renee's condo long enough for her to change into a swimsuit and cover-up.

"Leave your car here and let's walk," she suggested.

Greg relieved Renee of the tote filled with

sunscreen, bottled water and towels. "Sure. It's right at your backyard."

They made their way to the location where Leon had set up his tent. He waved when he saw them walking in his direction.

"Thanks for coming," Leon said with a chuckle. "I could use some adult conversation."

"We weren't going to leave you hanging," Renee responded.

"*I* wasn't going to leave you hanging," Greg corrected.

She gave him a playful shove. "Really? You're just going to throw me under the bus like that?"

"Daddy, I wanna go get into the ocean," Talei said.

Leon smiled down at her. "In a few minutes, baby."

"If you don't mind, I'll take her just far enough for her to get her toes wet," Renee offered.

"I'll go with them," Greg added.

Leon nodded before glancing at his son. "I'll be right behind you. Leo's finishing up his juice."

In the ocean, Renee tried not to let the rivulets of water streaming down Greg's face to his chest distract her from all the beauty around her. He was a very handsome man indeed, she had to admit.

Clearing her throat, Renee turned away, hoping he couldn't tell just how much he affected her.

She was surprised when Misty showed up an hour later and took a seat next to her on the sand. "I didn't expect to see you. Leon said that you had to work."

"Silas was able to come in and help out. I promoted him to head cook so that I can take off time to spend with the children and Leon." Misty gave a slight nod toward Greg. "It looks like you two are really clicking."

"I can't deny that we have a good time together."

"Are you open to something more?" Misty asked.

Renee smiled. "We're just taking it day by day." She picked up a handful of sand, relishing the grainy texture as it slid through her fingers. "I've learned from experience that everything seems perfect when two people meet. Everybody's on their best behavior. It's like a new house—once it starts to settle, you begin to see cracks." Her previous relationship had taught her as much—Kevin was fun in the beginning, but by the end, she couldn't make him understand her. He'd been skeptical of her design career and her panic disorder.

"True," Misty responded. "But a relationship will stand if it's built on a firm foundation."

Greg walked over where they were sitting. "Talei is a good little swimmer."

"Yes, she is," Renee responded, happy for the change in subject. "Misty, you've done a great job with her."

"She took swimming lessons at the YMCA. It was Leon's idea. To be honest, I wasn't completely on board initially, but Talei took to the water like a fish. Now we have Leo in swim class, too."

They watched the children playing in the ocean with Leon.

Greg held up a hand to ward off the sun. "I'd better go out there and rescue your husband. I think Leo and Talei are getting the best of him."

They laughed as he walked away. Renee adjusted the hat on her head. "I feel like he's just too good to be true, Misty. He's such a sweet person. The only thing is—"

Misty reached over, giving Renee's hand a gentle squeeze. "Stop looking for reasons why the two of you shouldn't be together. Instead, focus on the reasons why you *should* be with him. Enjoy this time together and see where it goes."

Renee couldn't deny that Misty had given her some solid advice. She only had to take it.

That was the hard part.

RENEE'S FRAME WAS wrapped in a vivid green swimsuit that highlighted her curves. Greg noted the pink rose tattoo on her shoulder. She'd mentioned she was thinking of getting one right before he went on his last mission, but he didn't realize she'd gone through with it.

"I like your tattoo," he said.

"Thanks." Renee laughed. "This is the first and last one I get. I have zero tolerance for pain."

"When it's done right, it's worth it."

Shaking her head, Renee said, "I don't think I agree with you on that."

Chuckling, Greg pointed to a young woman selling homemade Italian ice out of a cart nearby. "I haven't had one of those in a while."

Renee stood up and shook the sand off her. "Then we need to change that right now."

She ordered raspberry lemonade while Greg chose cherry.

"Mmm… This is delicious," she murmured.

"I used to eat these all the time when I was younger," Greg said.

"I heard you once mention that you grew up in Hinesville, Georgia. What was that like?"

"Small," Greg chuckled. "Not too different from Polk Island, but no beach. I had good friends, extended family—I think it's the only way my mom survived losing my father. Most of her family lives in Texas, but I'm sure she stayed in Georgia because of the solid support system she found in Hinesville. We'd visit Texas from time to time, but my mom worked so much—she only took time off to be at my games."

"It's wonderful your mom had that kind of support," Renee said. "That's not always the case."

"True."

"She still lives in that area?" Renee inquired.

Greg nodded. "Yep. She never considered leaving. She said she never really liked living in Dallas. A small town is more to her liking, but I think it's because my dad is buried there, too."

"That's one of the reasons I moved back here. I wanted to live in a place where I felt safe. Don't get me wrong—I love New York.

But it never really felt like home to me. I need a place of calm, and this island does it for me."

Greg agreed. There was something really soothing about this place—he could see how easy it would be to create a life here. "You belong here, Renee."

She looked up at him and smiled. "I believe it. That's why I decided to open my boutique here. I would've loved having the design house on the island, but the space I need can be found in Charleston."

"That's just across the bridge."

She nodded. "I appreciate how supportive you've been, Greg. Not everyone has always been like you—not even family members."

He knew she meant her parents.

"Leon and Trey have always had my back, but my parents—they wanted me to do something great like become a doctor or a lawyer. My only interest was in fashion."

"I'm no fashion expert, but I know that you have a gift," Greg said. "Some people are afraid to step out on faith, but not you." He admired that about her.

"Only when it comes to design and the shop. Truth is, everything else scares me." Renee chewed on her bottom lip. "I know that I have a lot of unrealistic fears, and at times, they get really out of control. There are times when the episodes just come whether I'm triggered or not." She shook her head. "I *hate* living this way."

"What helps you cope with panic disorder?" he asked. Greg really wanted to learn as much as he could about it. He hadn't seen her experience an attack, but he'd heard about the one she'd had some years back. She and Trey had gone to the movies. Everything was fine until they were on the way home—that's when she had suddenly started to hyperventilate. According to Trey, it just came out of nowhere.

"I try to avoid anything that might potentially trigger me. But if I start to feel anxious, I work on refocusing my thoughts. If that doesn't work, then I'll take my medication."

He couldn't help but think again on what she'd said the other day, about how it was hard for her not knowing if he was safe. Greg stopped in his tracks. "Tell me the truth, Renee. Do I trigger you in any way?"

"No, of course not," she responded quickly. "I feel safe with you."

He smiled. "I want to be a safe haven for you. Always."

RENEE TREASURED GREG'S obvious concern for her. He didn't dismiss her panic attacks as her overreacting or accuse her of being a drama queen. It still bothered her that Kevin and his mother had said those things. She often felt like she was bracing herself for the next person to diminish her panic disorder that way.

She finished off the last of her Italian ice.

Greg took her empty cup and stuck it inside his own. "Renee, you're special. Don't you ever forget it." It was like he knew where her thoughts had gone. "I don't know how or why you have to deal with panic disorder, but I have faith in you. I believe you can overcome anything."

"I've been dealing with them for years," she stated. Eight, in fact. "I don't think it's going to change. The best I hope for is to be able to survive the attacks without feeling like I'm dying or losing my mind." She'd never been able to be so transparent with anyone outside of Trey and Leon. She hadn't even shared the depth of her fears with Misty and Gia. Renee didn't want them to see her as weak.

An hour later, Leon walked over to where she and Misty sat on the beach, stretched and yawned. "I'm tired, so I think I'm going to head home and take a nap." Brushing sand off his swim trunks, he added to his wife, "Babe, you can stay as long as you want. I'll take the kids home with me."

Misty stood up to give her husband a hug. "I won't be too long."

"Enjoy this break."

She kissed him. "Thanks, hon."

Greg was still in the water, swimming around.

He's going to shrivel up like a prune. Renee smiled to herself.

They spent another hour on the beach before walking back to the condo. Before he drove away, Greg made dinner plans with her for later.

"I want to try your cousin's place in Charleston."

She was happy he'd suggested it—she had been talking up Manoir Bleu to him for years. "You'll love the food there. I'm always down for eating there."

He gave her one of his winning smiles. "See you later, then."

Renee entered her house and walked straight to her closet. She had to find the perfect outfit—one that didn't scream *date*. Especially since it was just two friends getting together to enjoy a meal.

She pulled out dress after dress, tossing

them on the bed, unable to decide. Renee eventually chose a jumpsuit in royal blue.

Now that she knew what she was wearing, she padded barefoot to the bathroom and quickly jumped into the shower, humming softly.

Afterward, she dressed quickly, then ran her fingers through her short hair, fluffing up the curls.

By the time Greg rang the doorbell, Renee was ready.

"You look beautiful," he said.

"Thank you." He looked as though he'd jumped off the page of a men's fashion magazine in the dove-gray suit he wore.

Renee picked up her clutch. "Let's go."

As they walked to the car, she said, "You're going to love the food. Everything is delicious."

Forty minutes later, Greg pulled into the parking lot of the restaurant in Charleston.

He was always the perfect gentleman, opening doors for her and escorting her safely into the building.

The smell of freshly sautéed garlic and herbs tantalized her senses, and her mouth watered.

"Aubrie... Hey," Renee said when her cousin

greeted them at the entrance. She had texted Aubrie earlier about tonight.

"Greg, this is my cousin Aubrie DuGrandpre. She's the owner of this fine establishment."

"It's nice to meet you," she said to him. "I have the perfect table for you."

Shortly after they were seated, a server outfitted in a crisp white shirt, a black vest and slacks approached to take their drink orders.

Renee glanced at the woman's name tag, which identified her as Meg.

When she walked away, Greg suddenly turned serious. "I want you to know that I value our friendship. It's really important to me," he said, keeping his tone low to keep their conversation private from the other patrons around them. "Especially if it means taking advantage of your connections to get a table at a place like this." He winked.

Renee laughed. "I feel the same way." Kevin had never made her laugh like Greg did. They also didn't have any shared goals or dreams— which she was once told didn't matter when it came to finding the perfect match. Suddenly, the realization hit Renee that Kevin had never made her feel safe; in fact, she was often on edge whenever they were together. He wanted her to be a vison of perfection.

His words not hers.

Renee raised her eyes heavenward and once again gave thanks that she no longer had that politician wannabe in her life.

Greg, on the other hand, seemed to respect her. And he'd seemed genuine when he'd complimented her after picking her up earlier.

Stop. You're not dating him, so you can't compare the two.

Meg returned with glasses of water, a Cadillac margarita for Greg and a strawberry margarita for Renee. They gave her their entrée orders. She smiled, then disappeared into the sea of servers.

Renee fell back into an uneasy silence, and the sounds of the dining room suddenly seemed amplified: forks against plates, the rushing of servers' feet against the tile floor as they brought out drinks and food.

Meg soon returned with their meals.

Renee had ordered fettucine Alfredo with Cajun shrimp, and Greg had ordered the shrimp étouffée.

"What I'm trying to say is that we have a good time whenever we're together." He flashed his perfect teeth. "Our interests, our goals, our values—they all click. That's what counts, right?"

Renee forced her lips to curve up in agreement. Because Greg was right—they *were* in tune, and they *did* have a great time together. So why was she holding back?

"That's all important," she said, pushing her barely tasted Cajun-shrimp Alfredo aside to reach across the table and take his hand. "Are all those things important to you in a friendship?"

"Definitely… And I believe that friendship is the basis of a strong romantic relationship."

"It certainly would've helped to have been friends with Kevin first. Maybe then, my panic disorder wouldn't have scared him off." She'd told Greg a bit about her broken engagement over the years, but not everything.

Greg twined his fingers with hers. "Well, I'm not bothered by the fact that you have chronic panic disorder."

"You say that now…"

"I mean it, Renee. It doesn't scare me. I'm not that guy." He pulled his hand away. "I have a family member who suffered from panic attacks to the point that it was hard for her to leave home at times."

"Does she still deal with them?"

"From time to time," Greg answered. "Not as much since she's been on medication and has identified her triggers. Her therapist has helped her with coping strategies and changing her thought behaviors."

"You suddenly seem to know a lot about them."

"I called my cousin after our chat today and asked a lot of questions so I could gain a better understanding."

Renee took a deep sip of her strawberry margarita. The fact that he was taking the time to understand what she was going through touched her. "You continue to amaze me, Gregory Bowman."

"I can say the same of you. You're a fighter, and I admire that. You haven't let your condition take control of your life."

"I don't intend to let it," she responded before wiping her mouth on her napkin. "I was almost a prisoner of my home, but that's when I decided to see a therapist. I knew I needed help, but I was embarrassed. Kevin had me thinking I was having a nervous breakdown. His mother even told him that he should have me committed to a psych ward. At that time, I didn't know what was going on with me—I'd never been so scared. Finally, I confided

in my parents, and they took me to see someone. That's when I was diagnosed with panic
disorder."

He gave her a tender look. "You had nothing to be ashamed of, Renee. It's courageous
to ask for help when it's necessary. I'm glad
you didn't listen to your ex."

His words meant a lot to her. "Enough
about me. You're the brave one…protecting
this country. Protecting *us*. I know I've said
it before, but I really mean it. Thank you for
your service."

"You're welcome." He smiled. After a moment, he added, "But I won't be in the military forever…" He seemed to be watching her
closely.

And her surprise probably showed on her
face. She knew that, but she figured Greg had
years of service ahead of him still. "You mean
you're not interested in doing twenty years or
more?" she teased.

"You never know," he responded. "I might
surprise you one day and tell you I'm getting
out."

Renee busied herself by stabbing a shrimp
with her fork. "That would definitely be a surprise."

She wanted to believe him—and she did,

for the most part. The thought of seeing him more often—not once every couple of years—made hope rise in her. But it was quick to dissipate. She felt awful for feeling it, but there was a part of her that wasn't convinced he'd ever leave his unit or the military in general.

CHAPTER SIX

SUNDAY EVENING, GREG and Renee weren't very hungry, so they picked up dinner from the café—caramelized Vidalia onion tarts with goat cheese, lobster-and-chive-risotto fritters and crab cakes.

While they sat at the dining room table, Greg's eyes traveled to Renee, and the thought of having to return to Camp Lejeune put a slight damper on his mood.

"Are you okay?" she inquired.

He gave a slight nod. "Yep. I'm fine."

"Days are flying by, huh?" The time after their dinner at Manoir Bleu had passed so quickly. He wished they had more time.

Greg sliced into his crab cake. "Yep. We still have a bit longer before I'm North Carolina bound, but you're right. They seem to be coming fast. I'm actually trying not to think about it at all."

"Well, maybe I can come visit you," Renee said.

Greg broke into a wide grin. "You'd really do that?"

"Yeah. Camp Lejeune isn't that far away. Besides, I've never seen that part of North Carolina."

Renee's willingness to visit him led Greg to consider that they were getting closer. Maybe she would eventually warm up to the idea of them being more than friends. She was still guarded when it came to her emotions, but her beautiful, expressive eyes often revealed more to Greg than she realized.

He stayed until it was almost midnight, then left. He knew she had a busy day scheduled for tomorrow, especially after taking a few days off to hang out with him.

Trey was still up when Greg entered the house.

"Were you waiting up for me?" he asked.

"Naw... I wanted to see the end of this movie."

Greg sat down beside his friend on the burgundy leather sofa. "What's it about?"

"Some dude looking for the man who left him for dead." Trey turned down the volume on the television, then asked, "How was your date with my cousin?"

"First off, it wasn't a date. Just friends having dinner together. Just so you know, I was a perfect gentleman," Greg said.

Trey chuckled. "I'm not worried about that—Renee is more than capable of taking care of herself."

Greg nodded before rising to his feet. "I think I'm calling it a night. Is Gia feeling any better?"

"Yeah. She just had an upset stomach," Trey responded. "She's been working a lot, trying to get everything in order with the new clinic here on the island."

Greg gave a slight nod. "I'll see you in the morning."

In the guest bedroom, he changed out of his clothes and into a pair of pajamas.

While he waited for sleep to overcome him, Greg thought back to his conversation with Renee at Manoir Bleu. He was glad she'd opened up to him about her panic disorder. Few women could handle being married to a soldier, especially one in MARSOC, and it would be an even bigger struggle for someone coping with that. Renee had told him from the beginning, when he'd first asked her out years ago, that she didn't have the emotional capacity to do so, and Greg appreciated her honesty.

However, in the intervening years, she'd

managed to steal his heart. Renee dominated his thoughts, and he knew what he felt for her was real. Greg couldn't deny that he hadn't considered getting out of the military until after he met Renee. It wasn't an immediate decision, but the more he got to know Renee, the more his feelings for her developed. The past few days, spending time with her in person, had only made him more sure of that.

When it was time for Greg to reenlist, he decided he was going to take a different path for his future.

He propped up his pillows and lay back, staring at the ceiling.

THE WEEKEND HAD come and gone, with Renee spending most of her time with Greg. Now it was time to return to work. She was the first to arrive at the boutique, with Kayla arriving minutes behind her, on Monday morning.

"I didn't expect to see you here today," she told Renee.

"It's going to be a short day for me." Renee let them into the boutique and set her bag on the checkout counter. "I need to finish some designs for a client. I told her I'd have something to show her this afternoon, but after I meet with her, I'm leaving for the day. How did the meeting go last week with our bride?"

"It went well," Kayla responded. "She knows what she wants and brought in some visuals. She also wants us to design her mother's dress for the wedding—a simple sheath with a matching coat."

They were joined by the two morning staff members, Jade and Lucy.

"Good morning," Renee greeted them. "How was the weekend?"

"Busy," Lucy said. "We sold out of the new cover-ups and the last of the swimwear."

"There's a new shipment arriving this morning," Kayla said. "I had the order expedited."

Renee released a soft sigh of relief. "Thank you for doing that."

When the shipment arrived, she helped her staff with unpacking, tagging and hanging clothes out on the sales floor.

"These are gorgeous pieces," Jade said. "I really like this one." She held up a turquoise two-piece. "I love the rose gold trim."

"You should get it," Lucy encouraged.

Renee and Kayla agreed.

"I think I will," Jade murmured. "Wait until my boo sees me in this…"

"He's definitely going to love it." Renee

grabbed her tote. "I'll be in the office if any-one needs me."

She checked the items in the stockroom against what had sold over the weekend, then made a list of clothing to be marked down and placed on clearance.

Her client arrived. After the meeting had ended, Renee packed her tablet into the tote and strolled out of her office. She paused at the counter to tell Kayla, "I'm leaving for the day. Call me if anything comes up."

"We'll be fine."

Shortly after arriving at her condo, Renee made a couple of phone calls regarding Fashion Week from her home office. Her insides jangled with excitement every time she thought about it—her dream come true.

She ended her last call and was about to head to the kitchen to make blackened salmon for lunch when her cell phone rang again. Renee's heartbeat quickened, and a shiver snaked down her spine when she saw the caller was Greg.

What was that shivering about? Why was she reacting this way to his phone call?

She clicked on her phone. "Hello?"

"Hey, how's your day going?"

Renee wished that Greg didn't sound as good as he looked.

"Trey and Gia are hosting a special dinner party tonight. Are you interested in joining us?" he asked.

"Sure, I'd like to come." Renee had a feeling they were going to announce the pregnancy. "I never turn down any opportunity for a free meal."

"Maybe we can take a moonlight stroll on the beach afterward," Greg suggested.

"I'd love that." She knew he loved taking moonlit strolls as much as she did and staring up at the stars adorning the heavens. The thought made her chuckle.

Renee sighed as the memory rushed through her mind. She had to find a way to maintain some sort of control over her emotions. She'd known so much heartache and preferred not to become reacquainted with it.

GREG INSISTED ON picking Renee up and bringing her to the house that evening. Trey hadn't said what this dinner was about, but Greg was happy for the chance to see Renee again.

When they arrived, Leon's family was already there, along with Eleanor, Rusty and

Gia's mother, whom Gia introduced to Greg as Patricia.

"Thank you all for coming," Trey said when everyone was seated at the dining room table. "Tonight's dinner is very special to Gia and me because we have something to share with y'all."

The room seemed to grow silent in anticipation.

Placing his hand on his wife's belly, Trey announced, "We're going to have a baby."

"Oh, my goodness," Eleanor uttered. "Blessings on top of blessings. A new baby…" Tears ran down her cheeks. "I'm so happy."

Patricia burst into what Greg thought were happy tears.

Everyone offered their congratulations and well wishes. He was genuinely thrilled for Trey and Gia. He'd suspected that they were pregnant. He'd noticed moments when Gia would appear nauseous, and she seemed to do a lot of sleeping whenever she was home.

Greg looked forward to fatherhood, but first he had to find the right woman. He stole a peek at Renee. Okay, he was pretty sure he'd found her—he just needed to convince her that he was the right man for her. Would she go out with him if he asked her again?

First, he'd have to clear all the obstacles ahead of him. He couldn't seem to shake the thought for the rest of the dinner.

"Did you know about the pregnancy?" Greg asked when he walked Renee to the car after their beach stroll later that evening.

"Before tonight?"

"Yeah."

"Nope," Renee responded. "You?"

"Naw… I suspected but Trey didn't say anything, so I didn't, either. I figured I'd just wait until he was ready to tell me."

"I'm happy for them," Renee said. "After everything Trey went through, they deserve to live happily ever after."

"I agree," Greg said. "I believe we all deserve a happily-ever-after."

Staring out the window, Renee uttered, "That might be true—but unfortunately, it doesn't always work out that way."

CHAPTER SEVEN

RENEE DIDN'T RELISH lying to Greg, but she hadn't been about to betray Gia's confidence either. Now back home for the night, she thought back to how happy Gia and Trey had looked when they announced the pregnancy. There were times when she'd envied what they shared. She was guarded but still very much capable of loving. She'd learned that she couldn't give her heart to just anyone. The right man would have to prove himself worthy.

She had hope she would find that man, but she also lived with fear. She'd tried to build a cushion to insulate herself from the harsh realities of this world—and she'd faced quite a few. She'd been confronted with death at a very young age when her favorite aunt and uncle died, leaving Trey and Leon orphans. Then a few years later Uncle Walter, Aunt Eleanor's first husband, had passed away.

Renee's parents had left the island after his death, and adjusting to life in New York became complicated when they later divorced. Renee and her brother were shuffled back and forth, from one parent to the other. It hadn't taken long for her mother to remarry. Her step-dad was nice enough, but Renee had always been close to her own father. As for her mother, they seemed to clash over almost everything.

The only thing that had got Renee through the pains of her childhood was learning to sew. She'd realized even back then that she didn't want to face the ugliness of the world—only the beauty. After her first home economics class, the only thing she wanted for her birthday was a sewing machine. After that, she began making her own clothes.

Her parents had tried to persuade her to go to college for anything other than fashion design, but Renee stuck to her calling.

She was grateful for Greg's faith in her. It touched her beyond words that he readily supported her in anything she did. He was the first person she'd called to share the news about debuting her collection during Fashion Week. He was also the first person to donate money to her show, only he didn't want to be listed as a sponsor.

Renee got up off the sofa and made her way

to the bedroom. As she prepared for bed, her cell phone rang.

Greg's picture came up on the caller ID.

She answered it. "I had a feeling you were going to call."

"I'd planned to call you earlier, but I'm just getting off the phone with my mom. She's back from her training in Dallas, and I'm going to drive down to see her tomorrow. Would you like to go with me? It's about a three-hour trip one-way. We'd be gone most of the day, but I'd appreciate the company."

Renee sat straight up in bed. "You want me to meet your mother?" She was thankful that he'd ask, even though nerves started to set in.

"Yep. You're my friend, and she knows all about you."

"You've told her about me?"

"I discuss my friends with my mom from time to time." She could hear him holding back a laugh. "She met Trey shortly after we got out of tech school."

She was overreacting—there was nothing to be nervous about. "Sure, I'll ride down with you."

Greg wasn't making a big deal out of this trip, so neither should she.

They talked until she could barely keep her eyes open.

Renee stifled a yawn.

"I'll see you tomorrow," said Greg.

They ended the call.

Despite trying to stay calm, she was both nervous and excited about meeting the woman who'd raised Greg. Renee hoped she would make a good impression. She recalled her experience with her ex-fiancé's mother. The woman had tried to make her over into a younger version of herself.

When Renee had refused, she and Kevin began having problems in their relationship, and she suddenly wasn't good enough for him. By the time he had ended things, his mother already had Renee's replacement picked out and apparently on standby—a woman Renee had once considered a close friend. Her best friend, actually. This time was different, though. She wasn't meeting Greg's mother as his girlfriend—just as a friend. That thought brought her some relief. After her last experience getting to know the mother of the man she was seeing, she wasn't sure when she'd be ready to do that again.

GREG MADE THE introductions upon their arrival in Hinesville, Georgia. "Mom, this is Renee

Rothchild. She's the friend I've been telling you about."

Renee extended her hand. "It's very nice to meet you, Mrs. Bowman."

Greg's mother shook it. "Why, she's lovely. It's a pleasure to meet you. Oh, please call me Marilee."

She led them into the living room.

Greg smiled as he observed Renee engaging with his mother. He'd had a feeling they would get along well. He remained quiet to give them a chance to talk and get to know one another.

When Marilee went to check on the meal she was preparing, Renee asked, "What exactly did you tell her about me?"

"I told my mom I was crazy about you," Greg responded, deadpan. He couldn't resist teasing her a bit. "That I'd found the woman of my dreams."

Renee's brows rose in surprise. "You really told her that?"

He laughed. "No, I just told her how much I've enjoyed getting to know you and how gifted you are as a designer."

She relaxed visibly. "Your mother seems like a really nice lady."

"Yep, she's a sweetheart. She was an amazing woman, raising me without help from a father. She had a lot of support, though, but Mom always made sure she was there when I needed her. She never missed a school event, ceremony, parent-teacher conference or any of my games. She always put me first."

"I think that's really wonderful," Renee said. "My parents weren't very supportive of my dreams, but they did the co-parenting thing very well."

They stayed long enough to have an early dinner with Marilee.

Greg enjoyed seeing his mother—it had been too long. He vowed to come home more often once it was decided he was getting out of the military. Maybe she would consider moving to the island... But that was a topic for another day.

"I can't believe you're leaving in three days," Renee said when they were heading back to Polk Island. "The ten days flew by quickly."

Greg sighed. "I feel the same way."

"When do you think you'll be able to come back?" she asked, staring straight ahead.

"I'm not sure... I have a training class coming up. But I hope you were serious about coming to visit me."

"I am." Renee grinned. "It's been a while since I last traveled to North Carolina."

He gave her a sidelong glance. "So, you're really coming?"

She nodded. "How about in a couple of weeks?"

Greg tried not to let his excitement show. "Really?"

"Yes… Well, I need to take care of some things, but Memorial Day weekend, I can visit. Will that work for you?"

"I'll put it on my calendar."

Renee laughed. "Make sure you do."

When Greg pulled up to her condo, Renee asked, "Are you coming in?"

"I'd love to, but I need to pack."

She nodded, and he thought he saw a flicker of something cross her face before she smiled brightly. "I'll see you in the morning."

He smiled back at her. "I'll call you when I get to Trey's. You can talk to me while I pack up my stuff."

Greg waited to make sure Renee was safely inside before he drove away. He almost turned around a couple of times. He wasn't ready to leave her side, but he really did have to prepare for his trip, and she most likely had work of her own to complete.

Before they'd left his mom's house, she'd whispered in his ear, "Renee's a keeper. She's definitely the one for you." He'd thought about it the whole way home.

Mom had confirmed what he knew was already his heart.

RENEE WAS UP a little before six o'clock. She was meeting Greg at the café at seven so he could get on the road around eight or nine.

She climbed out of bed and rushed into the shower.

By a quarter to seven, Renee was in her car.

Greg was already there by the time she arrived.

"Good morning," Renee greeted as cheerfully as she could. She wasn't ready for him to leave, but she knew he couldn't stay.

She sat down across from him in a booth near the window.

"Hey, don't look so sad," Greg said.

One of the waitresses walked over with two cups of coffee. "Morning. Misty said that you both look like you could use these."

Renee smiled. "She's right." She took a sip of her coffee as the waitress retreated to grab menus. "I'm trying not to look sad," she said to Greg. "I had a great time with you, and I'm not ready for it to be over." She hoped she wasn't saying too much, but it was the truth.

"Honestly, I'm not ready for it to end, either," Greg confessed. "But I have something to look forward to—you're coming to visit me next month."

She nodded. "This is true. In the meantime, I'll keep busy by working on new designs and preparing for Fashion Week in September. I hope you'll be able to go to New York with me." He was, after all, one of her first sponsors—and he'd been a big support in other ways. She'd love to have him there.

"It shouldn't be a problem," Greg assured her. "I don't plan on missing your big debut."

They kept their conversation light while they ate.

When they were done, Greg reached over, covering Renee's hand with his own. "This has been one of the best vacations ever."

She nodded, then dropped her gaze and stared out the window. "I didn't think it would be this hard to say goodbye."

He gave her hand a gentle squeeze. "We don't have to say goodbye."

She met his gaze again.

"We will just say, *I'll see you later.*"

Greg paid the check, and they walked outside. When they got to his car, they embraced.

Looking up at him, she said, "I'll see you later."

He pulled out of the hug, and she wished they could stand there holding each other for a moment longer. "Yep... You sure will."

He got into his car, and she stood there on the sidewalk, watching as Greg drove away. She stayed until his car was no longer visible. A lone tear ran down her cheek.

Renee walked down the street to her boutique, unlocked the doors and turned off the alarm. Kayla arrived shortly thereafter.

The shop didn't open until ten, so she and Kayla did a quick walk-through to make sure every item was in its proper place and arranged neatly.

Jade arrived at nine thirty.

"Good morning, ladies," she said in her singsong voice. "Today's gonna be a good day. I can feel it."

Kayla laughed. "You say that every day."

"And it works," Jade replied, putting her purse on one of the shelves beneath the counter.

"I love all the good vibes." Kayla folded a scarf and placed it on the right display stand. "Keep them coming."

"Yes, we need all the positive vibes we can

get," Renee said. It would help distract her from missing Greg so much.

Jade joined them on the sales floor. "What do you need me to do?"

Kayla quickly shared information for a sale starting on Friday and lasting through the weekend, then gave Jade instructions on what to mark down.

"You're really great with the employees," Renee told Kayla as they made their way to the office they shared.

The woman shrugged good-naturedly. "It's not hard, because you have such a wonderful team."

"I feel very fortunate," Renee said with a smile.

"Is your friend still in town?" Kayla inquired. She turned on her computer and waited for it to boot up.

"He left this morning, and I already miss him. At least I have enough work to keep me busy," Renee said. "We have to make sure everything is set for Fashion Week." The show wouldn't give her much time to miss Greg.

"Speaking of which... I emailed you the quotes for the reception we're hosting after the show. I also made some suggestions for the menu."

Renee smiled. "Great. I don't know what I'd do without you."

"I hope you never have to figure it out."

Renee spent the rest of the day in her office, working on several sample pieces. Every now and then, she glanced at the clock. Greg had texted earlier to let her know that he was about an hour away from home.

Kayla walked into the office and sat down at her desk. "You've been commissioned to do a ball gown for the governor of Georgia's wife."

Renee nearly dropped the cup she was holding. "Excuse me… What did you just say?"

"The governor of Georgia—his wife wants you to design a ball gown for her. *Mrs. John Waterstone.* She's coming up tomorrow to meet with you. Her secretary emailed some ideas of what she wants."

Her business was booming. "This is my first political VIP," Renee said with a grin. She wasn't complaining by any means; she was grateful for every customer. Her long-term goal of owning her own fashion-design house was becoming a reality.

For the rest of the day, Renee returned her attention to her work. Greg texted her to let her know he'd made it home, and despite the urge to call him or chat over text, she knew she had to focus on her next commission.

She didn't leave for home until it was after eight o'clock, even though the shop closed at six.

Renee made a salad for dinner and ate it as she sat out on her patio, eyeing the long stretch of beach. There were a few people walking along the ocean shore. The skyline was layered in shades of red, pink and blue.

It was a beautiful evening and the perfect ending to her day. She was so happy about her new client that she felt like celebrating. Like dancing. She wished that Greg was still here so she could tell him her news in person.

Renee picked up her phone and called Kayla instead. "I want to celebrate. Are you busy?"

"I was about to order a pizza."

"Come over here," Renee said. "I'll order pizza and some champagne."

"I'll bring the champagne. I have some in the fridge."

"Great. See you soon."

Kayla arrived shortly before the pizza.

When they finished off the food, they danced and sang to the music playing in the background.

They toasted one another with a glass of champagne.

"To Renee Rothchild Designs…" Kayla said as she tapped her flute against Renee's.

"We're movin' on up. Cheers!" She still couldn't believe how far she'd come in the last few years, and she wanted to celebrate each achievement as it came.

Kayla stayed another hour before saying, "We have a lot to do tomorrow, so I'm going to head back to my place. This was fun."

"Thank you for celebrating with me," Renee said. Kayla was a wonderful employee, but she was also becoming a great friend. It felt good to know she could celebrate her wins in her other friendships and take her mind off Greg.

CHAPTER EIGHT

RESTLESS, AND WITH Greg still dominating her thoughts, Renee walked over to the treadmill sitting by the window in her guest room.

She turned it on and began a steady, slow pace.

Maybe this will work this man out of my system.

He'd been gone for days now, but she couldn't seem to shake him from her head. Spending time with him had definitely shifted things for her—she'd always liked him, but now she realized just how much he meant to her.

She didn't stop jogging until she reached her personal goal of five miles. Her energy was depleted, but that didn't stop the thoughts of Greg from looping in her mind. Renee could barely walk after the intense workout, but she managed to drag herself to the shower.

Half an hour later, she was back in her pajamas and sitting on the sofa, watching television.

Misty called and they chatted until Renee started yawning, but she didn't climb into bed until shortly after midnight. Inspiration had hit, and she sketched out the ideas floating around in her head. Her body was tired, but she refused to stop until she translated the images in her mind to the iPad. Only then could she relax and try to sleep.

Renee considered calling Greg to catch up but changed her mind. She needed to put some distance between them. She was tired but not exactly sleepy. She decided to try the mindfulness techniques her therapist had taught her. She hoped to clear her mind enough to silence the white noise, as she called it. She hadn't had a restless night like this in a while.

She sat up and grabbed the novel she'd been trying to read for the past couple of months off the nightstand. Not even the story could keep her interested. Images of clothing, models, magazine covers, Greg...all raced through her mind.

Stop it. Now.

Renee eyed the painting of the rain forest in Hawaii, focusing on her happy place and remembering the good times.

The racing thoughts gradually came to a halt. The visuals slowed down and eventually dissipated. Renee was finally able to clear her mind. She could now get some rest.

It was during these times that she hated being alone.

THE MORNING SUN kissed Renee's skin, and the island breeze swirled around her as she jogged along the strip of beach, enjoying the scenery of her surroundings. She inhaled the freshness of the ocean scent. She felt a sense of freedom anytime she went on a run. She figured it was because she found the ebb and flow of the water calming.

Whenever Renee was out on a jog, she felt her mind was clearer. She was able to relish the feel of the wind and cool droplets of ocean water against her skin. Sounds of laughter, talking, dogs barking… She noticed it all.

Memories of her time with Greg still danced in her mind. Renee liked that he was genuine, so caring and supportive—all the qualities that threatened to shift her feelings from friendship to something more.

Renee made her way back to her condo. When she walked inside, she noted the fresh sea scent and smiled. She picked up a framed photograph off the fireplace mantel. It was of her and her brother, Howard, Jr., exploring a sandy beach on horseback during a trip to Jekyll Island off the Georgia coastline.

Another happy place.

Renee and Greg had discussed Jekyll Island. Turned out this was one of his favorite places as well. They shared a lot in common, which served as the thread that drew them closer. They bonded over similar interests and even opposite tastes. Renee didn't have much interest in sports, but she'd watch a game with Greg—even bet against him. She loved bowling, and even though it wasn't a game he really enjoyed, he'd played a couple of times with her.

Greg often went out of his way to please her. No man had ever treated Renee like that, and initially, she hadn't been sure what to make of him. *It makes him a good friend.*

He would be a catch for any woman, and Renee often wondered what her reaction would be if Greg started dating someone. He had the freedom to. She'd made it clear when he'd asked her out that she wasn't interested. Whenever she thought of him with someone else, she experienced something akin to jealousy. Yet she didn't have the right to be.

Renee strolled into the kitchen to make avocado toast and a cup of herbal tea.

She sat at the counter, eating while surfing through channels on the television to distract her from her feelings.

Greg was a bright spot in her life, for which Renee was grateful. He was the only man outside of her family who'd vowed to stand by her side, no matter what, and had done just that. He had proven his loyalty and never once made her feel devalued. It was quite the opposite—he constantly reminded her that she was special.

GREG WALKED OUT of the hotel from his meeting with Edward Morris, the recruiter who'd reached out to him a couple of weeks ago. He was only mildly surprised to find that the position they were offering was with the CIA as a paramilitary operations officer.

He'd been informed that the position would require him to lead and manage covert-action programs, which intrigued him.

Edward Morris had told him the job would require a nontraditional work schedule, with frequent overseas travel and a five-year contract. That had given him pause.

Five years.

"As I mentioned during the phone call, I've

already made plans to relocate to South Carolina," Greg had reminded him at their meeting.

"To do what, may I ask?"

"I plan to work in a museum," Greg responded after a moment. Even as the words came out of his mouth, he realized this sounded quite unadventurous compared to the position the CIA was offering him.

Edward had stared in clear disbelief.

It'd been an honor to serve and to keep this country safe. Greg had truly enjoyed serving in the Marines and as a Raider, but he also knew the cost that came with military service. His father had paid that price.

"This job I'm offering you is different, and I believe you'd enjoy it so much more, Staff Sgt. Bowman," Morris had said. And Greg couldn't disagree with him. He'd promised the man he'd give it serious consideration.

It was a great opportunity, and the salary wasn't bad at all. It was a whole lot more than he'd make working with Trey. But money wasn't everything. He'd invested wisely and had a nice savings. Greg's decision wasn't based on financial gain; it was based on basic survival. He wanted to have a family. His chances for that to happen were much higher if he worked a regular job where he could still have a balanced home life.

Still, he wanted the advice of someone he knew would give him an unbiased opinion. Greg sat in his car and made a phone call.

"Hey, Mom… You busy?"

"Not at all," she responded. "What's going on, son?"

"I just left a meeting with a recruiter. I was offered a nice job, but it requires a five-year contract, lots of travel and unpredictable hours."

There was a pause on the other end. "You might as well stay in the military if that's what you want to continue doing. It just sounds like you're risking your life all over again."

"I considered that myself," Greg said.

"Do you want to take this job, son? Because you sound conflicted to me."

He sighed. "I told the recruiter I'd think on it."

"So, you *are* interested," his mom said. "Are you able to tell me who you'd be working for?"

"No, ma'am."

"I thought so."

"Renee wouldn't date me because I'm in the military," Greg said. "She's definitely not going to have anything to do with me if I take this job offer."

"Son, this is about what you want. Renee will either accept your choice or she'll move on."

His mother was always straight to the point in her advice.

"You don't understand. Renee has chronic panic disorder. She's been completely honest with me—she can't handle the stress of all the secrecy surrounding my career so far. I'd lose her for good." Greg knew a friendship with Renee was better than nothing with her—but if he moved to Washington and was traveling all the time, he wasn't even sure if that was safe.

"Hon, you should choose the life you want—for *you*. Not for someone else."

"That's just it. I want a family, Mom. You did a wonderful job raising me—but as much as I love you, you could never fill the void in my life. I missed not having a father."

"I know, son. I saw how it affected you. All I can say is that your decision must be what *you* want. It would be a shame to wake up one day and realize you made the wrong choice. Take your time and be sure."

They talked a few minutes more before ending the call.

Greg sat there, pondering his conversation with his mother. He decided not to mention anything to Renee for now. It was unlike him; usually when he got news like this, he'd call her first. Now, though, he felt the weight of guilt in keeping secrets from her.

CHAPTER NINE

THE FRIDAY BEFORE Memorial Day, Renee traveled to Camp Lejeune to spend the weekend with Greg, as promised. She had been looking forward to this trip since they'd planned it. Now the day was finally here.

He embraced her as soon as she got out of the car. "I'm so glad you're here. How was the drive up?"

"It wasn't bad at all," she responded, reveling in the feel of his arms. She had been thinking about hugging him since that day he'd left Polk Island. "It only took a little under five hours, but I stopped and had lunch."

He gave her a tour of the main level, then said, "Let me show you your room." Greg picked up her luggage.

Renee followed him up the stairs to the second level. "I put you in the guest room on the other side of the hallway. I want you to feel comfortable. It has its own shower and everything."

"Thank you," she responded. "Thanks for letting me stay here. I was fine getting a hotel, though."

"It's okay—you're not putting me out. Plus, we're responsible enough to stay in the same house." He winked.

She knew he was teasing, but a small shiver ran down her spine at the thought of holding Greg again.

After she was settled in the guest room, they left the house because Greg wanted to give her a tour of the military base in Jacksonville, NC.

"This is like a home away from home with all the comforts," Renee observed as they entered the parking lot of the commissary. "I didn't realize that there were fast-food restaurants on some bases until Trey mentioned it."

"We're considered heroes, but we are people, too," Greg said. "We need things that lift us up. If we're going hard all day doing difficult tasks, then every other part of our lives should provide some comfort."

"That makes sense to me. It's reality," Renee stated. "You go into battle, putting yourselves on the line for the sake of this country. Many have died in the name of duty. I can see why a place like this needs to provide a sense of normality."

"I've never really looked at it that way," Greg responded. "But you're right. This place does provide normalcy."

After the tour of Camp Lejeune, they decided to go back to his place.

They settled down in the living room.

"Greg, I have to ask you something. What are we doing?" she asked. This felt different to her—it was more than two friends hanging out. Somehow, they'd crossed that line from friendship to…what? Renee didn't have a name for it. But deep down, she'd been very lonely until Greg had entered her life a couple of years ago.

"We're friends…but I also believe that we're exploring how we feel about each other," he said carefully.

She nodded. "I see."

He seemed to be searching within the depths of her gaze. "I'm sure you must know by now how I feel about you, Renee."

"I do and I also care for you, Greg. I've never denied that. But you're aware of why we can't get involved. I was very clear about it."

"That's no longer an issue."

Renee regarded him with somber curiosity. "Am I missing something?"

"I just want you to be open to us continuing to get to know one another."

She eyed him a moment before replying, "Okay…" She'd always been open about learning more about him.

Greg peered down at her. His hazel eyes had darkened to a smoldering warm color. He'd been blessed with naturally thick lashes while she was forced to rely on a good mascara.

"Are you sure?" he asked.

Renee nodded. "Yeah. I can do that." Greg wasn't pressing her to become romantically involved—he simply wanted her to open up to him more. She trusted him as much as she could for now. Besides, after his last visit and meeting his mother, she yearned to learn more about him as well.

She adjusted her position on the sofa. "So what do you have planned for the weekend?"

"Tomorrow we're attending a Memorial Day barbecue in Wilson Park, but that's not until three o' clock. We can do whatever you'd like before then."

"I'd like to do some shopping," Renee said. "I think I saw a mall in Jacksonville."

"There is," he responded. "I'll take you there."

"What about museums?"

Greg smiled. "Yep. Do you want to visit a museum?"

"Yes, and any art galleries in the area," she responded.

"No problem."

Joy filled Renee, flowing from head to toe. She loved that they could fall back into this easy way with each other, that they had so many shared interests. Like any other person, she craved love, wanted to feel important—she wanted to feel special. The truth was that Greg made her feel all those things. Just in the brief time he'd been in her life, Renee felt he knew and understood her more than Kevin ever had. He was willing to give her the time she needed, to earn her complete trust in him.

A hint of doubt about Greg's intentions tried creeping in, but she quickly tossed the thought from her mind. She didn't feel he had any ulterior motives—it was just the way her mind worked. Worst-case-scenario thinking based on the past behaviors of previous guys she dated. However, she and Greg weren't dating, she reminded herself.

Nothing was going to ruin this weekend for her.

"I THINK I'D rather just stay here and cook," Renee announced Sunday afternoon. "We've been out all day, and I'm a bit exhausted."

That amused Greg. "Maybe that's because you insisted on a five-mile run this morning."

She chuckled. "You're probably right. Plus, I've been staying up later than usual, working on the collection for Fashion Week." Even during a weekend away, Renee couldn't let things slip at work. He appreciated her dedication, and he'd been honored by her invite to join her for the show in New York.

"We can order some food for pickup if you're not up to cooking," Greg said.

"I don't mind," she responded. "I'm actually in the mood for a home-cooked meal. And if you want to eat, you need to help."

"I can do that."

Arms folded across her chest, she asked, "What do you know how to cook?"

"You like spaghetti carbonara?"

"I do, but—"

"I got this," Greg interjected. "I can make the sauce."

"Naw," Renee said. "You boil the spaghetti."

"I make a fantastic carbonara sauce."

"Uh-huh…" Renee uttered. "You don't have

any cream for the carbonara sauce," she said as she peeked into the refrigerator.

"Oh, we don't need cream for that," Greg responded. "It would overpower everything."

Leaning against the counter, Renee asked, "So how are we supposed to make the sauce?"

"I'll show you. You need eggs and Parmesan cheese. It's this combination that makes for a creamy sauce."

Renee put the ingredients in a bowl.

"Now, whisk until it's smooth and silky," Greg instructed. "Instead of bacon, we're going to use pancetta."

"Oh wow… My mother used to add heavy cream to make her sauce," Renee said. She narrowed her eyes at him. "You never told me you could cook."

He chuckled. "A man's gotta eat. My mom made sure I learned to survive."

Greg put the water on to boil for the spaghetti.

After she finished the sauce, Renee made a garden salad while Greg placed slices of French bread smeared with garlic butter into the oven.

Thirty minutes later, they sat down to eat dinner.

She sampled her meal. "Okay, I have to give

it to you, Greg—you're a pretty good cook, if this is any indication."

"Thank you," he said with a smile.

After they finished eating, they cleaned the kitchen, then settled down to watch a movie together.

When it was over, Greg and Renee talked until the early-morning hours before falling asleep on the sectional sofa.

He woke up around four o'clock.

Renee's head was resting on his chest as she slept.

It was so easy being with her…no drama or having to keep his guard up. Renee never put any undue pressure on him to be anything other than his authentic self. Because of this, Greg felt the weight of not telling her about the CIA offer. He hated keeping this secret from her, but the last thing he wanted was to scare Renee away.

It was Memorial Day.

Renee planned to get on the road right after they finished eating breakfast to get back to Polk Island before dark.

"Any idea when you'll have to deploy again?" she asked while slicing into her spinach, mushroom and tomato omelet.

"I won't have to," he responded. "I'll be in training. The rest of my team has already left."

Renee looked up from her plate. She was curious, seeing the change on his face. "Why didn't you go with them?"

He decided this was the perfect time to come clean to Renee about getting out of the military. The weekend helped confirm what he'd been thinking—he *was* ready to settle down. His feelings for Renee were real, and he wanted to see where they would lead.

"Because I'm not reenlisting," Greg responded. He picked up a piece of toast and bit into it.

Renee released a gasp of surprise. "When did you decide this?" she asked, clearly trying to put all the pieces together. "You've never said anything about getting out of the military."

"I've been thinking about it for a while," Greg admitted. "I didn't want to say anything until I was sure of my decision. I didn't want to mention anything prematurely." While the decision might seem unexpected for Renee, he felt confident he'd put enough thought into it. He'd been considering it since before his trip to Polk Island.

She seemed to be assessing him closely. "Are you really getting out?" Renee asked.

He nodded.

He could see that despite the confusion, Renee was barely able to contain her joy.

Greg smiled. "I'm glad to see you so happy."

She finished off her juice. "This is so great because I won't have to worry about your safety. Now I can *really* focus on getting my collection ready for Fashion Week."

"Renee…" He paused for a minute, grasping for the right words. "I want you to trust that no matter where I am, I'm never going to put myself at unnecessary risk."

"If you're getting discharged, then it won't be a concern anymore."

She seemed so happy and relieved… He hadn't realized just how much it bothered Renee whenever he went on deployments. There were moments when he'd note the worry lines when they FaceTimed before he left, but for the most part, Greg didn't know the extent to which she worried over him. It was touching.

"I'm coming down to the island in a couple weeks," Greg announced. "I've spoken to Trey about taking a job at the museum, and I also need to start looking around for a place to live."

Renee's eyes grew wide with her surprise. "You're moving to Polk Island?"

"I am. It doesn't make sense not to live there if Trey and I are working together. I could live in Charleston, but I really like the island and the residents."

She folded her arms across her chest. "You better not be playing with me, Greg."

"I'm not. I'm planning to move to the island to work with Trey."

She met his gaze. "This is so exciting. The two of us living on the same island. I'd get to see a whole lot more of you." *That's the idea. Enough to become more than friends...* He didn't say it, of course.

"Any idea when you'll be discharged?"

"Looking to be out by mid-September. That's the end of my contract."

She nodded. "Well, I'll be busy with Fashion Week, so I won't be counting down the days."

Greg took her hand in his and said in a teasing tone, "I hope when you're all famous and stuff, you don't forget about me."

Renee burst into laughter. "You'll never have to worry about that. You'll be right by my side."

After they finished eating, Greg took her luggage to the car.

She followed.

"This is always the hard part," Renee murmured. "Saying goodbye."

He turned to face her, his warm gaze delving into hers, drawing her in and making her thoughts drift away. "Remember, we're not saying goodbye."

"That's right. I'll see you later."

Greg pulled her into his arms, holding her close. "You're so special to me, Renee."

He felt her lean into him, and he wondered if she knew she was doing it. "Are you trying to make this harder than it already is?" she asked. "You keep saying things like that… I'll never leave."

Her nearness made his senses spin out of control. He wanted to kiss her, but instead, he said, "Now, you need to get on the road. Let me know when you make it home."

"I will," Renee said, pulling away. "I don't want you worrying about me."

RENEE ALLOWED THE memories of the weekend to keep her company during the drive back to the island. She felt a thread of guilt over the way she'd responded to being in Greg's arms.

It was as if their connection had short-circuited all the hormones she'd placed in cold storage. Especially after he'd shared his news with her. The idea of having Greg on Polk Island with her, out of harm's way, caused hope to expand in her chest.

When Renee made it back to the island, she didn't feel like going to her empty condo, so she went to Trey's house.

Once she arrived, she sent a quick text to Greg letting him know that she'd made it safely and stopped to visit with Trey and Gia.

"Want something to drink?" Trey asked from his chair on the porch when she got out the car.

"Do you have Pepsi?"

He grinned. "Always. Should be some in the fridge."

She went inside the house to retrieve one, then returned to the porch.

Renee sat down beside him, admiring his neatly arranged flower beds.

"How was your trip?" Trey asked.

"Great," she responded. "Greg and I always have a good time together. While I was there, he told me that he wasn't going to reenlist…" She took a long sip of her soda.

"And?" Trey prompted. "Hey, don't leave me hanging like this, cousin."

"And he's getting out," Renee announced. "He said he's moving here to the island, and he'll be working with you…" Looking at her cousin, she said, "I have a feeling you already knew about all this."

He beamed at her. "I couldn't say anything."

"I understand that," Renee said lightly. "I don't expect you to betray Greg's trust."

"So does this change anything for the two of you?" Trey asked, clearly trying to appear casual about it.

Renee pretended not to understand what he was asking. "What do you mean?"

"Have you decided to give my boy a chance? He's a good man, Renee."

"I know that. Greg being in the military was a huge issue for me, but that isn't the whole issue." She leaned forward, elbows on her knees. "You've seen me have a full-blown panic attack. It's crippling, and not everyone can deal with it. They don't understand the fears I have to deal with—all they see is that I'm being irrational. Greg thinks that this won't be a problem for him but I'm not so sure."

He turned to face her. "You may not want to hear this, but I'm gonna say it anyway. You need to stop trying to figure out the end game in every situation because that's not how life works. No one could've told me that I'd survive everything I've been through."

"Trey, you went through a lot and you're better for it," she interjected. "But you don't live with panic disorder. It's a horrible feeling."

"I had a taste of what you deal with. Enough to know that you have incredible courage and strength," he said softly. "I admire you, cousin."

"I don't know why," Renee responded. "It's not like I've mastered keeping my fears under control. There are days I feel like I'm barely hanging on by a thread." She took a deep breath and prayed for the tightness in her chest to go away.

"But you're still fighting. You haven't stopped trying. You don't give up."

She leaned back, suddenly frustrated. "I'm still angry with myself because I let Kevin do a number on me. He really had me thinking I was losing my mind."

"He's not someone you need to ever listen to, Renee. The best thing he ever did was call off your engagement. He did you a huge favor."

She agreed with that.

Renee stretched, suddenly feeling exhausted. "I guess I'd better head home."

"Why don't you just stay here tonight?" Trey suggested. "We haven't had a movie night in a while."

"Well, you have a wife now."

"She's invited," he responded with a chuckle. "C'mon, I miss our quality time. I know you're trying to get ready for Fashion Week, find a building and all that, but I miss you."

Touched, Renee teared up. "I miss you, too."

"Don't you go crying on me."

She wiped her eyes. "You know I'm emotional. You can't get all sentimental on me like that."

Trey ambled to his feet. "C'mon… Let's go find something to watch."

"I'm picking the movie," Renee said.

"My house, my television. I'm choosing," Trey countered.

When they walked inside, Gia was seated on the sofa, remote in hand. "I'm picking what we're watching."

Renee glanced at Trey, then burst into laughter.

CHAPTER TEN

RENEE HAD BEEN peeking out the window every few minutes for the exact moment when Greg arrived. Her insides jangled with excitement when she spied his car.

She did a quick check in the mirror while he parked and retrieved his weekender bag, then rushed to open the door.

Renee stepped aside to let Greg enter the condo.

Leaning into him, she welcomed his warm embrace.

"It's been a long two weeks," Renee murmured.

"Yep, it has." Greg gathered her in his arms and held her snugly. "I'm so glad to see you."

Burying her face in his neck, Renee inhaled softly.

His fingers loosened a fraction, but he didn't release her. His eyes, dark with golden flecks, were unreadable as they held hers.

Taking Greg by the hand, she led him to the

living room. "It was hard to get my work done because you were on my mind all day long. How was the drive?"

"Not too bad. There were a couple accidents on the highway that slowed traffic down a bit, but not for too long."

"I kept thinking that there had to be something wrong with my watch."

Greg laughed. "I know what you mean."

Renee gestured toward the sofa and said, "Give me a few minutes to set everything up, and then we can eat. I was late leaving the boutique."

"Take your time. We have all evening."

Ten minutes later, Renee led Greg into the dining room.

He eyed the beautifully decorated table. Vibrant flames flickered from the cream-colored candles, casting a soft glow on the succulent display of roasted chicken, macaroni and cheese, homemade muffins and steaming broccoli. "Everything looks delicious."

"Thank you." Renee sat down in the chair he had pulled out for her. He eased into a seat facing her.

After giving thanks, they dug into their food.

Renee smiled when Greg closed his eyes as

he chewed. She was pleased to see that he enjoyed the meal.

Over the past couple of weeks, she noticed the subtle shift in their relationship. They talked every day since her trip to North Carolina. He'd surprised her by having flowers delivered to the boutique her first day back at work. There seemed to be a new awareness between them.

After dinner, Greg helped with the cleanup. None of the men she'd ever dated in the past entered a kitchen unless it was to get something to eat or drink.

Later, curled up on the sofa with Renee in his arms, Greg acknowledged, "The roast chicken was good. You're a wonderful cook."

"You're so good to me and so supportive. I'm glad you enjoyed dinner." She quirked a brow. "The truth is, I was hoping to impress you with my culinary skills, especially after the carbonara sauce you made."

His eyes latched on to hers, serious despite her joke. "Well, you did. I'm definitely impressed."

Renee gave him a sidelong glance. "Okay. I need to know if you're for real."

Greg threw back his head and laughed.

"I'm serious," she said. "You seem almost

too good to be true. I've never met a man like you."

"I'm for real," he responded. "To tell the truth, I was feeling the same way about you. I mean, I've never met a woman I considered perfect for me—not like you are."

His words thrilled and surprised her. "No one's ever treated me the way you do. I hate to say it, but it's kind of strange. Do you know what I mean?"

"I do," he replied. "I'm not going to change, if that's what you're worried about."

Moving closer, Renee lay her head on his chest.

"You're everything I ever wanted in a woman," Greg said softly. "The reason I'm telling you this is so that you know where you stand with me. I want a *real* relationship with you...and I'm not looking for anything casual." He paused a moment, then said, "I have to ask. How do you feel about me?"

He looked almost afraid of her response.

Stroking his cheek, she murmured the truth she'd been grappling with these past couple of weeks. "I want a real relationship with you, Greg, but I'd like for us to take our time." Renee watched the play of emotions on his face. She could feel the warmth of his breath on her cheek as he held her close.

His mouth covered hers, leaving her lips tingling with longing. Greg planted kisses on her shoulders, neck and face.

Renee had never been as happy as she was in this moment in time, and she didn't want it to end.

GREG MADE IT up the steps and fought his way through the large hanging plants Renee had convinced him to buy during her last visit. The short weekend trips, which he and Renee alternated taking when they could, always ended quicker than Greg would've liked.

It felt like one of them had just arrived, and then it was already time for the person to head back home. She said plants always made a porch look more appealing. When he'd told her he planned to sell the house, Renee made several suggestions to draw buyers. He had to admit, the house looked much nicer than it had before.

Greg opened the front door and broke into a smile when his nostrils caught a whiff of the unmistakable aroma of roux floating from the kitchen. His mom was making gumbo.

"Is that you, son?"

"Yes, ma'am." Greg sat on the sofa and removed his shoes. He'd spent his day in training. He thought of his team, whom he'd grown so close to, and he wished for a moment that he'd been able to join them on their most recent mission.

But he couldn't. Because he was getting out of the military.

He'd served his country just as his father had done, and it was still a little strange to be moving on. Following in his father's footsteps had made him feel like he could continue to have a close relationship with his dad, even though he'd passed. Being in the Marines had made him feel like he could spend more time with the father he missed. He hoped that wouldn't change once he was a civilian.

September twentieth couldn't come soon enough. Greg was ready to start his life on Polk Island and take his relationship with Renee to the next level.

Although Greg looked forward to his discharge, he couldn't stop thinking about the job offer from the recruiter.

The house had been listed for sale. If by some chance he did decide to take the CIA job, he still wanted to purchase property on Polk Island. He loved it there. He'd already had a couple of people come to view the home. Except for packing up the place, everything else was set for his move to Polk Island.

Greg padded barefoot to the kitchen.

The rich, spicy smells coming from the large cast-iron pot on the stovetop filled his nostrils, prompting his mouth to water. "Hey, pretty lady."

"Hello," his mother said, turning her gumbo pot.

Greg planted a kiss on her cheek. "Thank you for making my favorite. Now I'm gonna have to make sure my friends don't find out about it. They tried to eat it up the last time."

She chuckled. "You can't eat all of this by yourself."

"I'm going to eat my fill, then freeze the rest," Greg responded.

He walked over to the pantry to retrieve the rice cooker and a bag of rice.

"How much rice do we need?"

"Let's start with five cups," his mom said.

He placed the pot on the counter, then filled it with the required amount of water.

"Why don't you rest after your day?" his mother suggested. "I'll have dinner ready before you know it."

"I'm glad you're here, Mom. I've missed you."

Smiling, she said, "Go on. Rest while you can, because you're cleaning the kitchen."

"That's not a problem," Greg responded. "My dishwasher does a great job."

When they sat down to eat, Mom asked, "When are you going back to Polk Island?"

"Renee's actually coming here in a couple of weeks."

His mom nodded approvingly. "I like the two of you together."

Greg broke into a grin. "So do I, Mom. Whenever we're together, it's like we've never been apart."

She chuckled. "You've got it bad…"

He wiped his mouth on a napkin. "I wouldn't say all that."

"Son, I'm telling you—I know the look. I had it, and so did your daddy." She paused a moment, then said, "There isn't a day that goes by that I don't miss that man. He set the bar so high… I'll never meet anyone who will come close to what he meant to me."

"You know Dad never would've wanted you to be alone."

So many dreams were lost when his dad had been killed in action.

It was also his father's dream to see his son graduate from Howard University. When Greg was in high school, his mother had tried to convince him to go to Howard instead of joining the Marines, but Greg refused.

His mom initially hadn't been happy with Greg's decision to join the Marines, but she'd supported him, nonetheless. And she supported his decision to get out, too.

"My heart still belongs to your father, son," she said. "It wouldn't be fair to another man."

"Mom, have you ever tried to open your heart for someone else?"

She eyed him. "Not really. I've tried going out a couple of times, but they wanted to take the relationship further than I desired, so I just stopped dating altogether. I'm too old for games and slick talk."

"I can understand that. I feel the same way."

"What have you decided about that job?" she asked. "Did you tell the recruiter you're not interested?"

He dipped his spoon into his gumbo. "Not yet."

"Have you asked yourself why?"

Her question gave him pause—he had, and he couldn't figure out why he was keeping the option open. "I'm not taking that job, Mom. I just haven't turned it down officially."

"Maybe it's because you want to have other opportunities if things don't work with Renee. You have a backup plan."

"I don't know if I completely agree with that."

"Then what is your reason?"

At the moment, Greg didn't have an answer for her.

"THIS ARRIVED IN the mail," Kayla said as she entered the boutique office and handed an envelope to Renee.

"This is the information for Fashion Week," she said, opening the oversize packet.

Reading through the contents, Renee announced, "Our show is scheduled on Wednesday at three o' clock—right after Tanya Taylor." She felt the stirrings of anxiety within her. "Our spring/summer collection has to be everything."

"It will be, Renee," Kayla reassured her. "Your designs are fabulous."

She started to feel the edges of panic reaching for her. "Why did I do this? Michael Kors, Tanya Taylor, Christian Siriano… I'm just *me*.

I have a store. They have huge houses, international customers—"

"Your designs are just as beautiful as their collections. Don't start doubting yourself now. The new collection is brilliant. *Women's Wear Daily* has been hinting that it will be the talk of Fashion Week." Kayla softened her voice and added, "I just hope you're ready for all the orders we're going to receive from stores around the world."

Renee released a short sigh and nodded. "You're right. I'm just out of my comfort zone with this. I was fine designing custom pieces for my customers, but this is so much more."

"You're in the big leagues now, and you deserve to be there. You have to believe this for yourself," Kayla encouraged.

"Thank you for saying that. I guess I need a reminder every now and then."

"Your designs are phenomenal. I'm not just saying this because you're my boss, either. I mean it."

"Kayla, thank you," Renee responded. "I feel the same way about your work."

"I'm honored to be part of this."

Renee removed a dress from its protective covering and laid it on the oak table in her office. Examining it with a critical eye, she reached for a piece of fabric lying nearby and fashioned it into a pleated collar around the top of the dress. The garment was part of the collection she'd designed for her show.

"That's a nice touch," Kayla said. "That bright green trim is a nice contrast to the pastel pink of the dress. I'll look for some green shoes to match and a handbag."

Nodding and smiling in satisfaction, Renee handstitched the material in place, then returned the dress to the garment bag. "No purse," she called to Kayla. "See if you can find a nice shawl in pink and green with a touch of yellow or blue."

Renee went through and studied each piece, tweaking hemlines, changing or adding buttons, fabrics or trims. This new spring/summer collection had to be a Fashion Week hit—she would accept nothing less. The Renee Rothchild Designs fashion show would be the talk of the industry if she had anything to do with it.

Renee was happy about Greg's decision to join her in New York for Fashion Week in September. She also was eager for him to meet her parents at that time. She'd mentioned Greg a few times to them over the past year.

"Something's put a smile on your face," Kayla observed aloud as she walked back in.

Renee eyed her assistant. "I was just thinking about Fashion Week. We're going to have so much fun—we're going to be crazy busy, too, but I love the energy during the event."

"I know what you mean. I can't wait until we do Fashion Week in Milan. Now *that's* an experience."

"I'm sure," Renee responded. "It's my goal to do a show there next year hopefully for the fall/winter collection."

"I agree. We'll be too busy filling orders this year, and you'll want to pace yourself."

Once again, gratitude swept through her that she'd found such a great partner in Kayla. She navigated to the office door and then out to the sales floor. "I thought I was a big dreamer…"

Following her, Kayla responded, "How does that saying go? *Let your faith be bigger than your fear.*"

"I guess I'd better get to work, then," Renee said. "I'm running next door to grab some tea, then I'll be in my office the rest of the day if anyone needs me."

Kayla nodded. "I have a meeting with Sophia McCray and her mother at two o'clock for the fitting of her wedding dress."

Renee gave her a grateful smile.

"I wish I'd known you when I was planning my wedding," Jade said. "Finding the perfect dress was a nightmare for me. I had to buy a gown off the rack—it worked, but it wasn't *the one*."

"When—and if—I ever get married, I'm going to have you or Kayla design my gown," Lucy stated. "I don't want anything fancy. Just simple but elegant."

Renee smiled. "We got you."

She left the boutique and headed next door.

Misty was at the counter when Renee walked inside. "What time is Greg scheduled to arrive?" she asked without preamble.

Renee smiled. "Around sevenish. I need you to do something for me."

"What is it?" Misty asked.

"I hope you have some garlic-fried chicken."

"I'll make a fresh batch just for you."

"Great!" Renee exclaimed. "I'll need enough for my employees and some to take home. Greg loves it."

"I can have it ready by five o'clock."

"Perfect," she responded. "I almost forgot. I came here for some of your ginger-and-honey tea. I'll take a large."

Renee hummed softly to herself as she waited.

When Misty returned with her drink, she asked, "Have you spoken to Aunt Eleanor?"

"I called her earlier, but she didn't answer. Is everything okay?"

Misty released a sigh. "Leon had to go over this morning to help Rusty calm her down. She was getting a bit combative because she wanted to drive. She wanted to come to the café to work."

Renee had always known her aunt to be working at the café before having to retire a few years ago. "She loves coming here."

Misty nodded in agreement. "I know—but when she does, she wants to cook, and her doctor doesn't think it's wise for her to do so. Rusty took her to a senior center, but she didn't want to stay."

"Trey told me that he hired a companion for her, but Auntie ended up firing the woman. She accused her of trying to seduce Rusty." Renee bit back a smile. "It's not funny, but Aunt Eleanor isn't letting anybody near her man. He and Gia found someone else and, thankfully, Auntie approves of Marie."

"Gia's mom visits with her weekly. Patricia takes her to lunch, shopping and sometimes to the gym or a park when Marie isn't available. Aunt Eleanor doesn't remember the trips. She thinks Rusty just keeps her locked up in the house."

Renee sighed sadly. "At least she's got a family who loves her dearly." Renee suddenly felt guilty that she hadn't been around to visit much—she'd been so busy with work lately. "And at least her sisters are coming to visit her next week. My dad's looking at his schedule to see if he can come down as well." These types of scenarios made Renee realize how much she desired to share her life with someone special. She was glad her aunt had found Rusty after Uncle Walter had died, and she wanted her own happily-ever-after. No matter how corny some thought it to be, Renee believed in love. She just hadn't found it with her last relationship and couldn't make the same mistake twice.

It suddenly struck her how far she'd come since then. She was finalizing her showcase at Fashion Week, and none of this would be happening if she was still with Kevin. Once she'd left him and New York behind and moved to the island, her creativity had soared.

It was why, despite her excitement over Greg, she knew she couldn't afford to be distracted from her work so close to her Fashion Week debut.

"She'll like that," Misty responded.

"I'll have Jade or Lucy pick up the chicken. I need to get back to work. I want to have as much as possible done before Greg gets here so I can focus on him."

"Tell him Leon and I said hello," Misty told her.

Renee grinned. "I sure will."

Back in her office, she drank her tea while going back through the new designs. An image of Greg rose in her mind again, and Renee indulged herself, but then it was back to work.

When Kayla strolled into the office, Renee pulled an eggshell-colored gown with a polka-dot tulle trim off the clothing rack. "This is our showstopper. It's your best work."

A huge grin spread across Kayla's face. "Are you serious?"

"Yes. This dress is stunning. Nothing compares to it." Renee returned the wedding dress to its bag and hung it back on the rack along with the others. She selected another outfit, a scarlet-colored jumpsuit, and inspected the fabric. "I think we should use feathers around the top. What do you think?"

"Hmm…" Kayla murmured. "Let's spice it

up a bit more with some tulle instead of the feathers."

"We could add some polished gemstones for sparkle," Renee added.

Kayla smiled and nodded in agreement.

When Kayla left the office, Renee attempted to focus on the clothing, but images of Greg— with his close-cropped dark hair, hazel eyes and handsome grin—threatened to take up permanent residence in her mind.

Focus.

Renee went to her desk, picked up a sketch pad and made some changes to a drawing.

Kayla returned briefly.

"Can you take this sketch to the sewing room and give it to Bella when you're done? I want her to add the finishing touches right away."

"Sure."

"Thanks, Kayla. Would you also let Jade and Lucy know that I've ordered them dinner for tonight? I appreciate their willingness to stay late to do inventory."

Her assistant nodded. "I don't have any plans for tonight, so I'll stay and help them."

Renee smiled. "Thank you."

She sent up a prayer of thanks for having such a wonderful set of employees. They were honest, hardworking and dependable. Since opening the boutique, she'd only had to fire one employee, a part-timer who'd been stealing.

Shortly after five o'clock, Renee had a huge box of garlic-fried chicken and fries from the café spread over the oak table in her office. Not quite a family-size bucket but close. Kayla and the other employees sat opposite her, eating while Renee put away the drawings of a new collection she was working on. She was already sketching out some ideas for a fall/winter collection.

"Have you done something different to your hair?" Jade asked as she peered at Renee's head. "I've been trying to figure out what's different about you all day."

"I just lightened it a little." Renee's hand shot up to fluff her curls.

"It looks good."

Kayla nodded in agreement.

"Whatever happened with that handsome soldier?" Lucy asked, picking up her chicken.

Renee tried and failed to suppress a grin. "Greg's coming for the weekend. I'm leaving in a few. I'd like to get home and shower before he arrives."

"Ooooh…" they said in unison.

"Stop it," Renee uttered, pointing a finger. "Boss's orders."

Her employees burst into laughter.

THE SMELL OF garlic greeted Greg as soon as Renee opened the door. He kissed her before asking, "Is that what I think it is?"

She chuckled. "Yeah. Misty's garlic-fried chicken. I know it's your favorite, so I brought some home."

Greg followed her to the kitchen.

He kissed her once more, then strode to the stainless-steel sink and washed his hands. "Thank you. I've been dreaming of that garlic-fried chicken for days."

Renee made plates for them. "How was your drive?"

"It was fine. No real traffic jams or accidents."

He pulled out a chair for her at the kitchen table, then sat down across from her.

"You know, Trey claims that he probably won't get to see you. He thinks I'm keeping you hostage. I suppose I have to do better with sharing."

Greg laughed. "I don't know what it is about this island, but when I cross the bridge, I just get this sense of peace that takes over. When

I become a resident, Trey and I will be spending a lot of time together."

"I know what you mean about the tranquility here," Renee said. "Some of the locals call Polk Island their little piece of heaven on Earth. I have to say, I feel pretty much the same way. Leaving New York was the best decision I've ever made. I've learned that I'm not a fan of chaos or chaotic settings. At least not for the long term."

Her words made Greg consider what his adult life had been like during his time in service— a string of chaotic settings. He recognized that he was also searching for a place of peace. This was what made Polk Island so attractive to him.

He reached inside the carton and pulled out a piece of chicken. "I always assumed that you loved New York. I know you go back there to visit often."

Renee handed him a small tray of fries and a biscuit. "I did. But as I grew up, I soon realized that I'm more of a small-town girl. Don't get me wrong—I do love New York. I also love Los Angeles and Dallas, but I don't want to live there. I visit New York often because my parents and my brother live there."

"I felt that way about Oceanside when I was stationed at Camp Pendleton," Greg said. "I liked visiting LA, but I never wanted to call it home because it was just too busy for me. I guess you and I have that in common."

"Sounds like it," she responded before popping a French fry in her mouth.

It felt so natural for Greg to be here with her. The day he returned to Polk Island to stay couldn't come soon enough for him.

CHAPTER ELEVEN

GREG MADE ALL these trips to the island because he wanted to build a solid foundation for his relationship with Renee. He loved her unique, melodious voice; her natural beauty; her courageous yet humble spirit. Every time he was around her, she made his day a whole lot brighter.

She'd called earlier saying she'd arranged a trip to the International African American Museum in Charleston while he was going to be in town.

He knew how much she loved history. She always put a lot of thought behind any plans she made for them, often including museums. His own love for history was born out of his desire to better understand the world and gain a greater appreciation for current events.

Lately, Renee hadn't mentioned triggers or having panic attacks. Greg was relieved because he wanted her to stay calm so that she was able to focus on Fashion Week. She was still in the midst of preparations. During this visit, he'd chosen to stay at the Polk Island Hotel instead of with Trey and Gia. He didn't want to become an unwanted fixture in their home, even in the short term—not while they were expecting.

It didn't matter where Greg stayed. He still spent most of his time on the island with Renee.

They began the next morning with a five-mile jog on the beach, which left Greg feeling like his legs were going to collapse right from under him. Still dressed in his running shorts and T-shirt, Greg stood behind the kitchen island, waiting for the coffee to brew, while Renee flitted around the room, whipping up a huge breakfast.

He watched as she set out the food. "This looks delicious and…extremely healthy."

Renee laughed. "Wheat-grain pancakes, turkey sausage, fresh fruit and avocado toast—that's for me. I don't eat pancakes."

They listened to music while they ate.

A song came on that must have been one of her favorites because Renee started swaying in her chair and singing.

Greg was surprised when she got up suddenly and started to dance.

"All right, now... I'm loving the entertainment," he muttered.

He soon joined in, enjoying this side of her. She looked free from the stressors in life as she made the kitchen her dance floor.

They sang and danced their way through cleanup.

Later, they spent the evening bowling, one of her favorite pastimes.

Renee was a much better bowler than he was, but Greg didn't care. He enjoyed making her happy.

When they left the bowling alley, Greg said, "Trey texted to invite us to dinner tomorrow night. I haven't responded yet because I wanted to check with you first."

"That's fine," Renee responded. "He's your best friend. I knew he'd want to see you. I really don't mind sharing you with my cousin." She grinned. "Oh, and thank you."

He met her gaze. "For what?"

"I know bowling really isn't your thing, but you play anyway. Your thoughtfulness doesn't go unnoticed."

Greg touched his mouth to hers.

Renee turned her head toward his, and he brushed light kisses against her jaw. Whenever he kissed her, he felt as if his world was suddenly about to spin out of control. But it was a good feeling.

"I don't want this night to ever end," she whispered.

"There will be many more nights like this," Greg assured her.

AFTER HER RELATIONSHIP with Kevin had ended, Renee vowed to never give another man her whole heart, but Greg was slowly tearing down the walls she'd erected. She wasn't ready to open the gates and let her emotions overflow. Despite the wonderful time they'd been having, Renee held part of herself back. She didn't want to risk another broken heart by rushing into a romantic relationship. One reason was because Greg hadn't been officially discharged from his duties with the Marines. The other was questioning whether he would be truly happy as a civilian or wake up one day filled with regret.

She forced the question out of her mind at the sound of someone ringing her doorbell. Greg was picking her up for dinner at Trey's tonight, and she planned to enjoy herself.

Later, when Greg pulled in front of Trey's house and parked, she noted the cars that were lined up and down the street.

Greg must have, too. "Looks like he's turned it into a party."

Renee agreed. "Sure looks like it. He broke out the grill, too. I can smell it from here."

"I thought this was just going to be a small get-together."

"I know my cousin. This *is* small for him," she stated. "It hadn't always been—not when he'd first returned home from his military service. But slowly, with Gia's help, he'd become his old self. You'll need to be here when we get together with the DuGrandpre clan and the North Carolina Rothchilds. Trust me, you'll see the difference."

Renee led him up the path along the left side of the house.

Greg opened the gate for her, and she walked in ahead of him.

The backyard was packed with family members and a few close friends of Trey and Gia.

Renee gasped in surprise when a tall, muscular man wiping his hands on a towel approached them. She'd had no idea her father was in town.

She stepped up to him and hugged him. "Dad, I didn't know you were here. You told me you weren't going to be able to come back to the island for a few months." At least, that was the answer he'd given her when she'd called to find out if he was able to spend some time with Aunt Eleanor.

Her dad threw the towel over his shoulder. "I wanted to surprise you," he said to Renee, although his eyes were focused on Greg.

She cleared her throat noisily, then swallowed. "Dad, this is Sgt. Gregory Bowman. He and Trey have been friends since they were in boot camp. That's how we met." She glanced at Greg, suddenly shy. "And this is my father, Howard Rothchild."

"Nice to meet you, sir." Greg extended his hand, and Renee felt instantly at ease when her father returned the gesture with a welcoming smile.

They exchanged pleasantries for a moment longer before her dad strode away, back to the grill. Renee turned to Greg and said, "I had no idea you'd be meeting my dad this soon."

He shook his head. "It's fine. It was bound to happen one day. Besides, we're not children anymore. There's no reason to be afraid of your father."

"True, but I'd like to have been just a little more prepared." Renee had planned to wait a few months until she felt they were building a solid relationship. She'd never made a habit of introducing guys to her family, especially if the relationship was going nowhere.

"Why?" Greg asked.

"I hadn't really told my parents about you." She flushed suddenly. She'd mentioned him as a friend but not that they were becoming more. "I was waiting until you got out of the military."

He looked confused. "Why would that matter?"

"It doesn't," Renee said. "It's just... Normally, I don't tell my parents about anyone until we've been dating for a while. This is still new. I wanted to process it first."

He nodded. "I suppose I can understand that."

"I hope you do," Renee said. "It's not that I'm ashamed of you or anything like that."

Greg took her hand and brought it to his lips. He planted a kiss there. "Sweetheart, that thought never entered my mind."

She smiled, grateful—and not for the first time—for his understanding. She glanced over at her dad again. "He keeps looking at me. I guess I shouldn't put this off any longer."

"I'll be over here when you get back."

"You're welcome to join us. He should get

to know you better." She tugged on his arm. "I think we should start now."

"Naw," he uttered. "I think this conversation should just be between you and your father."

"You're absolutely no help at all, Gregory Bowman."

RENEE AND HER FATHER went inside the house and sat in the sunroom to have a private conversation. "How long do you plan to be in town, Daddy?"

Amusement danced in his eyes. "Are you in a hurry to get rid of me?"

"No, not at all," she interjected quickly. "I'd just like to know why you didn't tell me you were coming."

"I told you... I wanted to surprise you." Looking past her out the floor-to-ceiling glass panes, he said, "However, I think I'm the one who got the bigger surprise."

Renee glanced over her shoulder toward the patio, then back at her father. "I would've eventually told you about Greg. Everything is still new with us."

He seemed to be studying her closely. "I thought you didn't date military men. Or have you changed your mind about that? To be honest, after Kevin, I wasn't sure you would ever tear down that wall you erected. Don't get me wrong… I'm happy to see this isn't the case."

"I didn't think I would find anyone, but Greg has been such a dear friend to me. My stance on dating military men hasn't changed. Greg's getting out soon and we're taking it slow."

He gave her a wistful look. "You look happy."

Smiling, Renee nodded. "I am, Daddy. I'm very happy and at peace. No drama or chaos."

He laughed. "You all set for Fashion Week? It's coming up pretty quickly."

"Don't remind me," she muttered. "Oh, I might as well tell you that Greg's coming to New York with me."

Her father nodded. "Well, I look forward to getting to know him."

"He's a nice man."

He embraced her. "I've heard nothing but good things about him."

Surprised, Renee pulled away. "From who?"

"My sister," he responded.

Aunt Eleanor… Renee should've known that her aunt would tell her brother about the man who was dating his daughter. She made a mental note to give her mother a call during the week. She didn't want her to hear about Greg from anyone else.

"So, what do you think about the boutique?" Renee asked. "Did you get a chance to go by there?"

"Very nice," he responded. "You've done well. I'm proud of you."

She did a double take, trying to hide her surprise. "Are you really?" Her boutique had made money the first year it opened, and it had grown, but she hadn't heard a word of praise from her parents.

Her dad looked stunned by her question. "Of course. Why would you ask me that?"

"Because it's not what you and Mom wanted for me. I always figured you'd be happier if I'd become a lawyer or some corporate guru."

He shrugged. "What can I say, baby girl? I was wrong. You found your niche, and it's working for you. I want you to be happy, Renee."

She'd wanted to have this conversation with her father for a while now, and she was happy they could be honest.

The next conversation would be with her mother. "I love you, Daddy."

"I love you, too. And you tell Greg that I got eyes all over this island."

Renee chuckled. "C'mon…we should join the others."

CHAPTER TWELVE

IN SEPTEMBER, GREG and Renee checked in to the Alexander-DePaul Hotel in New York City. Renee wasn't overly fond of airplanes, so she was relieved when the plane had finally landed and they were making their way into Manhattan. Their rooms were right next to each other. His was a standard room, while Renee and Kayla were sharing a two-bedroom suite.

After putting away his luggage, Greg joined Renee in her room. "Wow…this is a nice suite. Does it come with a butler?"

She chuckled. "If so, I haven't seen him. However, I just saw the shower in my bathroom, and it can hold at least three people." She glanced at her itinerary, bubbling with excitement about the week to come. "TM Sports and Mason Eye Wear are kicking off the festivities by launching an immersive two-day shopping experience in the middle of Times Square," Renee announced.

"Swag," Kayla blurted out while clapping

her hands. "I *love* Fashion Week. Mason Eye Wear usually gives away limited-edition sunglasses every year to commemorate the occasion."

Renee nodded. "And Karim Adduchi is hosting a master class tomorrow morning that I'd like to check out."

"While you're doing that, I think I'll sleep in and then do some sightseeing," Greg stated. "Just text me if you need my help with anything."

Renee smiled. "You're sweet to offer, but I think we've got it covered. However, keep your phone close by and charged." She wanted Greg to enjoy himself whenever he could—it meant a lot that he was here with her.

"What's on the agenda for today?" he asked.

"I need to check out the venue and meet with the models to go over the schedule and rehearsal."

Kayla glanced at her phone. "We'll have some time after touring the venue to grab something to eat before the model meetup. Jade will be here to do inventory and make sure we have everything."

"When does her flight get in?" Renee asked.

"In about thirty minutes."

Jade had been in Ohio to attend her sister's

wedding, which was why she hadn't been with them on the flight from Charleston.

"We're meeting with the event planner at three o'clock," Renee announced as she checked her schedule on her iPhone. "After that, we will come back here. I'd like to meet with everyone regarding the show."

Kayla made notes on her iPad as Renee talked, her mind running a mile a minute.

"We need to stop by the venue so I can check out our backdrops. The tents are already up. I want to make sure the set is put together correctly. I need to meet with the models, the hairstylist and makeup artist." Renee reviewed her list. "We need to make sure that we have all the accessories for each outfit—if not, let me know so we can buy them." She wanted her show to be as near perfect as possible.

Kayla finished her notes. "I'm going to check on the shipment of gourmet chocolates we're giving out to the attendees. I got a delivery notification that the order just came in."

"Great," Renee murmured. "I can check that off my list. What about the wine? Has it arrived?" She'd ordered miniature bottles of specialty wines from a winery in Italy.

"It's here. They're all going into the gift

bags, right?" All the guests attending the after-party for her show would get one.

She nodded. "You and Jade can start putting the bags together. My brother will be coming by to help as well."

"I don't mind helping," Greg offered.

Renee smiled in gratitude. "I know you were going to do some sightseeing, but do you mind coming to the venue with me?"

He nodded, squeezing her hand briefly. She wanted someone with her when she saw it for the first time. This was all so surreal.

"I'll see you when you get back," Kayla said.

A moment later, she walked out of the suite with Greg and down the hall to the elevators.

"I love the pop-up shops," Renee said as they made their way out of the hotel. "Only this time, I'm not here as just an attendee. I'm a *designer*." She gave a short laugh. "I'm sure I sound like a silly kid right now."

"I love it." Greg chuckled.

As they made their way outside, they saw the huge white tents that would house different events in several locations. The streets were crowded with cars, a sea of people moving about briskly on the sidewalks. The venue for the main runway buzzed with excitement. A few pedestrians tried crossing the busy streets with complete abandon, a move that suggested they trusted the drivers to be disciplined enough not to run them over. They weren't on Polk Island anymore. But the hustle and bustle matched Renee's feelings.

Renee switched her tote from one shoulder to the other as she led Greg to the tent assigned to RRD.

Her footsteps slowed. "I still feel like this is nothing more than a dream."

"It's not." Greg took her hand in his own. "You've got this, sweetheart."

A wave of heat brought a flush to her cheeks and a tingling to her belly. She looked up at him. "How can you be so sure?"

"Everything's all set for your show, right?"

"Yeah." Renee let out a nervous laugh. Without thinking, she fanned herself with her right hand. "We've checked everything off our list thus far." Giving his hand a squeeze, she said, "Thank you for being here with me." Having Greg here was such a comfort to her. She'd realized over the past weeks that he helped ground her. And staying grounded, not letting panic take over, wasn't always easy for her.

"This has always been your destiny."

"You always know the right things to say," she responded.

"Renee," Greg said, "promise me that you'll take some time to just relax and enjoy this week. Everything is going to turn out fine."

"You're right."

Her phone rang.

When Renee saw Kevin's name on the caller ID, shock jolted her system. She hadn't heard from him since the day he'd ended their engagement. She wasn't the least bit curious to find out why he was suddenly reaching out to her.

She ignored the call. The last thing she needed was to hear his voice.

She then received a text.

I was hoping to get a chance to talk. I'd like to at least meet for drinks. Congrats on the fashion show.

No. Definitely not. Renee chose not to respond.

"Everything okay?" Greg asked.

She nodded.

Just ignore him. Renee was not going to allow Kevin back into her life.

She and Greg walked inside.

Models in colorful wigs stalked up and down the runway, covered in very spangly, glittery creations, as a tall woman stood yelling at them. "Every eye will be on the clothing. You're here just to make the clothes look good. Remember that. We are here to sell the clothes." She went on to lecture them: "You damage it, you buy it."

Renee and Greg eased out of the room. "I need to see where our show will be held."

They found a full-figured woman with blond hair at a desk, attaching rhinestones to a white swimsuit. She looked up when they approached.

"You're obviously not one of the models," she said as she tilted her head back, eyeing Renee from head to toe. Renee was dressed in a pair of khaki pants, a red T-shirt and sneakers. She'd wanted to be comfortable because she knew she'd be doing a lot of walking. The other woman's cheekbones were so sharp, they looked like they could put out an eye. Renee found herself leaning back against Greg, just in case.

"No, I'm not. I'm Renee Rothchild."

The blonde's expression changed immediately. "Miss Rothchild, my apologies. What can I do for you?"

"I just need to see the room where my show will be."

"Salon B," she told them.

"Thanks so much. Have a great rest of your day."

Renee and Greg waited until they couldn't be overheard before saying anything.

"Did you see how she switched her attitude when you gave your name?" Greg asked.

Renee shrugged in nonchalance. "I'm not at all surprised. She probably doesn't feel appreciated. And I've heard how rude some of the designers are to people they believe are nothing more than underlings."

"Is that why you were so nice to her?"

She grinned. "I'm nice to everybody, Greg."

When they walked into the room, she found workers busy putting together the set. Renee had chosen a rustic theme for her fashion show, which she hoped would make her brightly colored designs pop. Her vision was coming to life. The stage and catwalk were surrounded by oversize vases filled with branches and drenched in twinkling lights that matched the colors of her collection. The wooden boxes underneath some of the vases were covered in silks, satins, damask and crepe fabrics. Renee glanced over at Greg. "So, what do you think?"

"I like it."

"You guys are doing a great job," she told the setup crew.

Renee and Greg left an hour later, once she was sure that the setup was running smoothly and well in hand. They walked across the street to have lunch.

He opened the door to the restaurant and followed behind Renee as the hostess showed them to a table.

"Can I start you off with an appetizer?" the server asked after handing out menus and placing glasses of ice water in front of them.

Renee studied the menu. "I think I'll forget about lunch. You can just bring me a slice of chocolate-strawberry shortcake."

Greg chuckled. "I second that."

She checked her phone. "My brother just arrived at the hotel. He's with Kayla and Jade. They're getting ready to stuff the swag bags."

When the server returned, Greg said, "As much as we'd like to start with dessert, we have a lot of work to do, so we need to eat real food." He eyed Renee playfully.

Renee reluctantly agreed. "I'll take the jambalaya."

"We'll still have five orders of the chocolate-strawberry shortcake to go, but for now, I'll have the grilled catfish."

Renee passed the server her menu, folded her arms on the table and looked Greg directly in the eye. "Five orders?"

"I don't know about you, but I'm not sharing mine with Kayla, Jade or your brother. That's why I ordered them their own."

Renee grinned. "You think of everything."

Greg's phone started to ring. He glanced at it, put it on silent and put it away.

She glimpsed a spark of something in his eyes, but it disappeared as quickly as it had come. "Everything okay?"

"Yep. Why do you ask?"

"You just had this strange look on your face at that phone call."

"It's nothing to worry about," Greg stated. "I'm on vacation. I'll deal with it when I get back home."

They returned to the hotel in time for Renee to meet with her event planner to finalize the details of the reception.

Greg went to help the others fill the swag bags.

He still seems too good to be true.

That was how it had felt when she'd accepted Kevin's proposal—and it turned out she was right. It wasn't that Renee was looking for Greg's flaws—she'd just learned from experience that everybody's true colors were revealed eventually. She gave herself a mental shake. Right now, her complete focus had to be on her show, so she pushed away all other thoughts.

After her meeting, she walked over to where the others had gathered. Looking around, she asked, "Are the bags packed already? Where's my brother?" She hoped Greg and Howard's introduction had gone okay, but she hadn't been able to make it herself.

"Your brother had to leave," Greg said. "Something to do with his job. He said he'll call you in the morning."

"And the bags are done," Kayla replied. "Jade and I are going to take them over in the morning to the hotel."

"Okay." Renee breathed a sigh of relief. "That's another item to check off my list."

"What do we need to do now?" Jade questioned.

"Nothing. You and Kayla are free to enjoy the city."

"There's a party tonight." Kayla turned to Jade. "My boyfriend's working late so, Jade, you can be my date." The two women left together, leaving Renee alone with Greg.

AFTER SAYING GOODNIGHT to Renee, Greg returned to his room. He was glad they'd been able to spend a relaxing evening together after her busy day. They'd sat out on the balcony of her suite long after dinner, watching the night sky and sipping hot tea. Now he lay awake in bed, staring up at the ceiling. Sleep evaded him as he thought about what had happened earlier while he'd been putting his luggage in his room and then again at lunch.

He'd been contacted by Edward Morris, who was requesting an answer, but Greg still couldn't decide what answer to give.

The CIA position wasn't that different from the military, so there wasn't a way to put a spin on it that would please Renee. She wouldn't be comfortable with this job, and it would be the end of their relationship. Greg didn't want to lose her. His feelings had continued to deepen and intensify as he spent more time with her, especially seeing her now in her element at Fashion Week. Her passion for her work was written all over her.

But what would he be giving up by choosing to stay with her?

Will I really be happy working in a museum? Or should I accept this position, which will keep me away from home and have me facing short-term deployments or multiyear assign-ments in various locations? Am I ready to just be a civilian?

But what about Renee? I can't disappoint her. The last thing I want to do is have her triggered by the type of job I take.

The timing was all wrong.

Greg knew what he wanted to do, but he needed to be sure he was doing it for the right reason. For now, his focus had to be on help-ing Renee through Fashion Week. He had two weeks left before his military discharge, and then he'd be a civilian. Then he could decide what he was going to do next. Maybe he could still work for the CIA. He could see what other positions were available within the agency.

RENEE WAS UP early the next morning, pack-ing for the day. She ordered room service and had just enough time to eat a bagel with cream cheese and a couple of strawberries.

She jumped at the sound of a loud knock on her bedroom door.

Renee walked briskly across the floor, her heels tapping a steady rhythm.

"Good morning," she said when Greg en-tered the suite. "I didn't expect you to be up so early. You're on vacation. You can sleep in."

"I came here to support you, and this includes helping out in any area I can." She needed all the help she could get. The excitement of arriving in New York had worn off, and she'd awoken feeling a little overwhelmed. "Did you sleep okay?" he asked.

"Yeah," she responded. "Well, not really. I couldn't shut down my mind." She pointed to the food. "Have you had breakfast?"

"I'm fine," Greg said.

Renee grabbed her tote. "I'm ready. We just need to stop by Jade's room and grab her."

"Where's Kayla?"

"On a conference call. She'll meet us there."

Renee and Greg left the suite.

"The cocktail party tonight is hosted by the Fashion Network," she announced. "It's always a great event."

Smiling, he said, "I'm looking forward to it."

She eyed him. "Are you really having fun?"

"I am."

"Wait until the Fashion's Night Out event. Last year, I scored so much stuff… You wouldn't believe the prices."

"So you're saying I might be able to find some great gifts for Christmas and birthdays?"

"Definitely," she said with a grin.

Jade walked out of her room just as Renee

was about to knock. "Good morning," she greeted.

They returned her greeting as they headed to the elevator.

When it came, they stepped inside and rode down to the lobby.

Out of nowhere, Renee began to feel strange.

Is it my imagination, or is it getting hot in here?

Her face flushed with heat, and she felt dizzy.

Renee glanced over at Greg, who stood just inches away. He must have seen something in her eyes because he asked, "Are you okay?"

She suddenly felt as if she couldn't breathe. *Why now? Why am I being tortured this way?*

"Renee, sweetheart…"

She couldn't respond because she was trying hard to keep her sanity intact. She didn't want to suddenly freak Greg and Jade out by having a panic attack. It was a humiliating, deflated feeling.

Greg was instantly by her side. "Slow down your breathing, babe…"

Renee couldn't tear her gaze away from him—he was her happy place, and she needed to focus. She had to find a way to regain control of her thoughts. Beads of perspiration formed on her forehead.

"I'm in control," she whispered. "I won't stop breathing…"

"That's right," Greg said. "You're fine. You're the one in control."

Renee reached out, taking his hand in her own trembling one. She was helpless to halt her embarrassment.

Slowly, she regained her composure.

Jade pulled out a bottle of water from her tote. "Try to take a few sips, Renee. It hasn't been opened."

"Th-thank you," she managed as she fanned herself.

Renee's racing heart had slowed down to its normal rhythm by the time they reached the lobby.

She walked quickly toward the exit, needing to feel the air on her skin.

"Feeling better?" Greg asked in a low voice as he gently wiped the sweat from her brow.

"I think so," Renee responded. But shame washed over her. She was embarrassed that Greg and Jade had witnessed her attack.

He hailed a taxi for them.

During the ride to the venue, Greg and Jade seemed to want to give her space to decompress and gather herself before their day started.

By the time they arrived, Renee felt more like herself. "Thank you both for everything. I think I just got a bit overwhelmed."

Jade embraced her. "No explanation needed. Just let me know if you start to feel uncomfortable, and I'll escort you somewhere private. You have me and Greg. One of us will always be by your side."

"She's right," he interjected. "You can tell everyone I'm your personal bodyguard."

Her eyes filled with unshed tears. "I appreciate you both. More than you know."

Jade pointed behind her. "I see a coffee shop. I'll get you some herbal tea. It should help calm your nerves."

When she walked away, Greg hugged her. "It's going to be okay, sweetheart."

Instead of repudiation, Renee saw genuine concern for her in his gaze. Her eyes strayed to his lips. "I'd rather be kissing you right now. That would certainly make me feel better—but it's not a professional look."

He chuckled. "Maybe we'll make the cover of one of the magazines covering Fashion Week."

She gave a short laugh. "That's not exactly

the way I want to be featured. No shade, but I'd rather the article be about my designs."

"Everything is all arranged for the party," Kayla said when she walked up to them. "The set designer is on the way. He wants to make sure you're pleased with everything. He's concerned whether you want more lighting."

"Thank goodness," Renee uttered. "They were doing a great job yesterday, but I need it to be perfect for the fashion show."

"It will be," Kayla reassured her. She gave her a concerned look—she must've sensed Renee felt a bit off. "Just relax. You should be enjoying yourself."

Renee shook her head. "Until the fashion show has taken place, I won't be able to fully relax."

Jade returned with the tea. "Here you go."

Renee accepted it, trying to draw comfort from the warm paper cup.

She checked her phone. "I just got a text. I need to meet with a sponsor in an hour. I'll need you to finish up with Bart regarding the stage. Just send me a photo, and I'll determine if more lighting is needed. Hopefully, this meeting shouldn't take longer than an hour."

"No problem. See you later," Kayla said.

Renee looked up at Greg. "Do you mind staying with them? I won't be gone too long."

He smiled down at her. "Not at all."

GREG KEPT A close watch on Renee. He was worried about her after witnessing her panic attack in the elevator that morning. He decided at this point to stay by her side instead of going off on his own to explore the city. There would be other times for that. He felt Renee needed him more.

She'd gone through the rest of the day seemingly fine, but she was quieter than usual. He didn't say much while Kayla and Jade were around, but he checked in with Renee from time to time to see if she needed anything.

Every so often, she would walk over to him for a hug. No words were needed.

That evening, Renee passed on dinner, opting to order room service. She and Greg ate in his room.

"Are you sure you're okay?"

She nodded. "I just have a lot on my mind right now."

"Are you feeling anxious about the show?"

"Somewhat," Renee responded. "I think I'll feel better after a hot bath and a good night's sleep."

"I'll make you some tea," he said.

"Thank you."

After she drank her tea, Renee told him, "I feel like taking a walk around Times Square. Are you in the mood to join me?"

"Sure."

"You're such an indulgent man. I'm a very lucky woman."

He hugged her close and kissed her. "I want to see it through your eyes."

"I kind of consider this the essence of New York," Renee said as they exited the hotel. "We're right in the center of all the happenings."

Greg glanced around. "I can see that." He slowly took in the neon lights, huge billboards, theaters, museums. There was a lot going on in this area. "This looks like a very lively place."

"It is. When I was younger, I used to beg my parents to bring me here every New Year's Eve for the ball drop. It was fun, exciting…" She looked around wistfully. "I loved coming here and trying different restaurants. I loved the energy and the atmosphere. But that was when things seemed less scary to me. After the panic attacks started, eight years ago, I found that I stopped going to a lot of places, like the

Macy's Thanksgiving Parade, the New Year's Eve celebration—it was just too crowded for me."

"How do you feel right now?" he asked. "We can go back to the hotel."

"I'm fine. That happened at the very beginning of the attacks. They don't bother me like that anymore—apart from the random ones that come on, like today. Besides, I love everything about Times Square."

"It's nice here. Looks a bit overpriced," Greg said. "But that's just my opinion. There's something to be said about the bright lights and an ocean of people milling about. I do have to admit, there's a lot about New York to love. I'm fascinated by the history alone."

"There is a lot of fascinating history here. You should do some sightseeing while you're here. My team and I can manage. I know you mentioned you've been here before. Have you ever been to Harlem?"

He nodded. "I had a friend who grew up there. I went home with him one year and had a blast."

"I bet you did." She grinned. "You probably left behind a trail of broken hearts."

"Actually, I was the one who ended up with the heartache."

She looped her arm through his. "Tell me about her."

"She was beautiful, but she didn't want to settle down with a 'country boy,' as she called me. I thought we were happy—at least I was. But as it turned out, we were never on the same page." Greg shrugged nonchalantly. He was young then and hadn't thought about it in a long time. "People leave, and we survive."

"That, we do," Renee murmured.

She held Greg's hand as they navigated back to the hotel located near Forty-Seventh Street. As they walked, he glanced up, admiring the midnight blue sky and the bright city lights.

The perfect backdrop for two people in love.

"I HATED THAT you and Jade had to witness the attack in the elevator." Renee didn't want to admit it, but she'd been feeling strange about it all day, and she wanted to be honest with Greg. "It was embarrassing for me, on top of all that's going on."

He turned to her. "I'm glad we were there. I can't imagine what it would've been like for you to be alone." He stopped walking. "Renee, whenever you're feeling like that—don't try to hide it from me. I want to know… I want to help, even if it's just holding your hand or lightly massaging your back. I'm all in, sweetheart."

His words sent her spirits soaring.

She glanced up at him. "You really are too good to be true," Renee teased softly. She wasn't really joking, though. Greg had managed to wash away the dread she'd felt all day long with the sweetness of his words.

They returned to the hotel and shared a dessert in the restaurant before calling it a night.

Kayla was out with Jade, so Renee had the suite to herself.

After a nice long bath, she climbed into bed.

While she was reviewing the full Fashion Week itinerary, her phone vibrated. She almost answered—until she glimpsed the name on the caller ID.

Kevin.

"Why do you keep calling me?" she whispered into the empty room.

Renee rejected the call and blocked his number. Hopefully, that would end Kevin's attempts to contact her. She wouldn't mention any of this to Greg because she didn't want him to get involved. She could handle Kevin.

He was her past, and she refused to let him collide with her future.

CHAPTER THIRTEEN

THE NEXT DAY, Renee felt like her normal self. She and Greg were meeting her mother and stepfather in the restaurant downstairs for breakfast. Her brother, Junior, was supposed to join them. She was a bit nervous about Greg meeting her mother. Charlotte Rothchild Wiggins had her own ideas of the type of man her daughter should be with… She'd approved of Kevin, though, which called her credibility into question.

Greg was in the hallway when Renee strolled out of her room.

She kissed him. "Good morning."

"Did you sleep well?" he asked.

Renee smiled. "I did. I took my meds and slept like a baby."

They walked down the hallway to a waiting elevator.

When they reached the lobby, Renee saw her mother enter through the revolving door, followed by her stepfather.

"My mother, Charlotte, and her husband, Reginald Wiggins…" she said to Greg before rushing over to greet them.

"I'm so glad y'all came." She embraced her mother first, then her stepfather.

"It's so good to see you," her mother responded. "I can't believe you cut your hair so short. I thought maybe you were thinking of a bob or something."

"It looks great on you," her stepfather quickly interjected. "The style fits your face."

She gave Reginald a grateful smile, then introduced them to Greg.

Her mother eyed him up and down. "So, this is the young man I've heard so much about. Staff Sgt. Bowman, I've been wanting to meet you for myself. To see if you live up to the hype, so to speak. Renee's father can be over-generous in his compliments at times."

Renee's eyebrows rose a fraction. "Really, Mom?"

"I'm sorry. I didn't mean to embarrass you, sweetie."

Greg stepped forward. "Mrs. Wiggins, I know you don't know me, but I'm a simple man, and I am crazy about your daughter. I recognize that she's not only beautiful but also brave, intelligent and gifted," he said. "She's a very special woman, and I'm honored she's allowed me in her life."

Renee broke into a smile. She liked that he was so direct, especially with her parents.

Her mom initially seemed taken aback but recovered quickly. "My daughter is very special indeed. You seem like a nice man." She glanced between them. "I have good instincts about stuff like this."

Her brother, Howard Jr., arrived minutes later. "Sorry I'm late. I have a new assistant, and we're still trying to work out a rhythm."

She let out a short sigh of relief as she watched her mother and Greg interact as they made their way into the restaurant. They only had to wait a few minutes before being seated. Her mother didn't interrogate Greg while they waited to order, for which Renee was grateful. After the server came and wrote down their selections, they discussed several topics while waiting for their food to arrive.

Renee glanced over at her brother.

He smiled and winked.

She was happy that this experience was going so smoothly. Renee took this as a sign that greater things were to come.

After breakfast, it was time for her and the team to get busy.

"I'll see y'all at the show," Renee said to her family before she and Greg got up to leave.

"That wasn't so bad," he said as they left the restaurant.

"No, it wasn't. I had no idea what to expect from my mother. She can be a little extra at times."

They didn't return to the hotel until ten hours later.

Renee glanced around her suite. The lighting was a warm, flattering shade of gold against muted mustard-colored walls, and it put her at ease after a hectic day. She settled back against the luxuriously soft couch with a throw pillow on her lap. She leaned against Greg, saying, "I don't know about you, but I'm exhausted. I'm actually too pooped to party."

He wrapped an arm around her. "Isn't there an event you have to attend tonight?"

"Yeah. The host is one of our sponsors." Renee stifled a yawn.

"Lay down and take a nap," Greg suggested. "I'll call you in an hour."

She made herself comfortable on the sofa. "Thanks. That's all I need…an hour-long power nap."

As promised, he called, waking her up one hour later.

She felt so much better and more energized.

Kayla walked out of her bedroom, dressed and ready to go. "I was just coming to make sure you were up."

"I am."

"*Focus* magazine throws some of the best parties," Kayla said as she sat down in a nearby chair to strap up her shoes.

"I know," Renee responded. "Do you think Greg's having a good time? I invited him to come as a guest, and now he's unofficially a member of the team."

"As far as I can tell, he's enjoying himself. Besides, he just jumps right in, doing whatever needs to be done."

Renee smiled. "I want to do something special for him. To show my gratitude."

"I think Greg's perfectly satisfied just being by your side," Kayla said. "Spending time with him is most likely gratitude enough."

"This is some party," Greg murmured as they entered the huge ballroom at the Ritz-Carlton. He circled the room with Renee, who occasionally stopped to talk to VIP guests. She looked like she belonged here. Greg pulled out a chair for her to sit down in after getting their food. Kayla and Jade were already seated and eating.

"So, what do you think, Jade?" Renee inquired. "This is your first experience at Fashion Week."

"Oh my gosh! I hope I get to come again. I've seen celebrities, models that grace the pages of magazines. This is incredible."

Renee beamed at her enthusiasm. "I felt the same way my first time, too."

When the music began playing, Jade started bouncing in her chair. "All right, now... I love to dance."

"I guess you'll be my dance partner," Kayla responded. "This DJ is good."

They got up and walked to the dance floor.

"Would you like to dance?" Greg asked.

"Sure," Renee said. "The music is sounding pretty good."

Greg rose to his feet, took her by the hand and led her toward the sea of people moving their bodies to the rhythm. He loved watching her dance. The cadence of her movements mesmerized him and held him captive.

When the music slowed down, Renee said, "I think I need something to drink." She fanned herself as they made their way back to the table.

Greg left to get ice water for her.

"You two looked good out there," he heard Kayla say as he turned.

He smiled when Renee said, "I think so, too."

Greg was enjoying himself thoroughly. Outside of the one episode, Renee hadn't had another attack. Tomorrow was the day of her fashion show, and Greg wanted it to be perfect for her. She deserved to shine. He was going to go out of his way to make sure everything went smoothly. He grabbed two waters from the bar and returned to their table.

Greg liked seeing her so happy. She sat there, talking and laughing with her employees. When photographers came around, they smiled and posed for pictures. Renee was in her element for sure.

In that moment, Greg knew he was treading through dangerous territory. He was falling hard for Renee, and he knew she cared for him—he just wasn't sure of the depth of her emotions. She was still a bit guarded when it came to letting him in.

It was why he still hadn't mentioned the job offer to her—she would completely shut down, especially if he dropped it on her during Fashion Week. Greg knew he would walk away from a job that risked a future with Renee.

But was it the right thing to do? The question still nagged at him. Should this job decision—one that could change his life and give him fulfillment—be based on his feelings for Renee? What if things didn't work out between them?

Then what?

Greg couldn't shake the question all night, though he continued to put on a happy face for Renee and her employees. They didn't stay out past midnight because Renee was exhausted.

Back at the hotel, they walked through the lobby to the elevator.

"I'm tired, but I really had a lot of fun," Renee said as they walked the long hallway to their rooms.

"So did I," Greg responded. "This whole trip has been fun and educational for me."

She paused outside her suite. "I invited you here to experience Fashion Week. Since you've been here, you have done nothing but work. I appreciate everything you've done, Greg, but I want you to have fun."

"I'm having a blast," he responded. "I can't just stand by and not do anything to help you."

She reached up and gently pulled his face to hers. "You're really too good to be true. I'm convinced of it."

She eyed him for a moment. "You look like

something's weighing heavily on your mind… Are we okay?"

Should he tell her about the job? No. Now wasn't the time. "We're fine… I just can't help but feel like you're holding back your emotions," he said instead, which was also the truth. "You must know that I'm not here to hurt you. You *can* trust me with your heart. You can trust me with anything. I hope that I've proven this to you." Guilt flowed through him at his deflection. He hadn't been completely forthcoming.

"It's nothing to do with you," she responded, taking his hand in her own. "After what I went through with Kevin… I don't have the mental or emotional capacity to go through anything remotely close to that again. That's why I'm being so careful, Greg."

"I'm not out to break your heart."

"I know that, but…" Her voice seemed to falter. "Just give me some time."

"I'll give you all the time you need," Greg promised. "But I'm not going away." He kissed her. "It's late, and tomorrow's the big day."

"I guess I'll see you in the morning, then."

KAYLA ARRIVED AT the suite just as Greg was leaving.

"How was the Sargenti party?" Renee asked.

"So much fun." Kayla held up a bag. "I got you some swag."

"Why, thank you." They sat side by side on the sofa, going through the items in the silver gift bag.

"Oh, before I forget... Lucy said some guy named Kevin keeps calling the boutique for you. He says you two are friends, and he wants to connect with you while you're here in New York."

Renee couldn't believe what she was hearing. "He called the boutique?"

"Yes. Do you know him?" Kayla inquired. "He left a phone number."

"Oh, I have his number—I just don't intend to use it."

"Ookaay..."

"Kevin is my ex-fiancé. We broke up, and he ended up marrying someone else." She and Kayla hadn't started working together until after that time, so she hadn't known about him. "I have no idea why he suddenly wants to talk to me now. Back then, he didn't think I was a good match for him and his political aspirations."

Kayla sat back, looking surprised. "Maybe he's no longer married or has a political career."

"Doesn't matter to me." Renee shrugged. "We're not good together. I had to learn that the hard way."

Kayla nodded. "What happens if you run into him this week? If he's trying to reconnect with you, he might show up somewhere."

"I'll simply say hello and keep it moving," Renee responded with a tight smile. She prayed Kevin would have the good sense to stay away from her. "Please make sure he's not on our list for the fashion show or the reception. I'd like my events to be drama free."

Kayla picked up her iPad. "Let me check the list right now."

"Thanks."

Renee made some tea to help ease the tension she was feeling. She couldn't understand why Kevin was being so persistent. He'd never had any interest in her personal goals. In fact, he'd tried to persuade her to give up the dream of being a fashion designer. He had never been supportive.

"The only Kevin on our list is Kevin Reynolds, and he's a singer."

Renee released a short sigh of relief. "Good."

"You know, he may be coming around now because you're the new face in the world of fashion design."

That was true—people like Kevin were always trying to use others. "Whatever the reason, I'm not interested in seeing or talking to him again." She was glad to have Greg with her. She knew if Kevin tried anything, she'd be protected. Her father and brother weren't too thrilled with him, either. They didn't like the way he'd ended their engagement. She hoped Kevin would give up and just let her be.

THE SUNNY WEATHER matched Renee's mood. She'd slept well and was up early to get her day started. The moment she'd been waiting for had finally arrived. Models would walk the catwalk in front of an impressive list of industry VIPs and fashion journalists, best-selling R & B and hip-hop artists, and a few Hollywood A-listers as well.

"Wow, you're in a good mood this morning," Kayla observed as Renee practically bounded into the living area of the suite. "I need some of whatever you have in that mug. Right now, I just want to crawl back into my bed."

"I'm excited about this afternoon!" Renee exclaimed. "I'm nervous, too, but I feel like something big is going to happen."

"I feel the same way." Kayla walked over to

the Keurig to make a cup of hot tea. "This is your moment, and I'm so glad to be part of it."

"You're a fantastic designer in your own right. Why haven't you tried to start your own label?" Renee had often wondered this, although losing Kayla would be difficult.

"I'm not ready for something like that. I enjoy what I'm doing right now. This is where I want to be."

She could understand that. "When you're ready to go on your own, please come talk to me," Renee said. "I'll do what I can to help you."

"I appreciate that." Kayla grabbed her mug. "We have about forty-five minutes to get dressed and get out of here. I've scheduled one final walk-through with the models before they go to hair and makeup."

"I don't have to worry about hair." Renee chuckled and fluffed her short curls.

Kayla was all business. "You're the last one to get your makeup. Your jumpsuit is pressed and already at the venue. Where are your shoes?"

"They should be there as well," Renee said. "They're in the black crate with the accessories. I put them in there myself so I wouldn't forget them."

Thirty minutes later, she was dressed in a pair of black jeans, a black shirt and a pair of combat boots with silver detailing. She walked out of the bedroom.

Kayla joined her minutes later. She was also dressed in all black. Her long dark hair was pulled back in a ponytail. "Ready to go?" she asked Renee.

"I am."

Greg was dressed and ready when she knocked on his door.

"This is it!" she said.

He kissed her. "It's going to be perfect. Just remember to breathe."

Renee nodded. That's what she'd been telling herself all morning.

RENEE STRODE PAST a refreshment table laden with yogurt, soda, muffins and plenty of coffee and tea. She headed to a room designated for hair and makeup. Models dressed in robes stood nearby, chatting and checking their phones while waiting in line for hair and makeup stations to open.

She entered the room and asked, "Is everyone all set? We need to get the models ready."

Renee left Jade with the list of models.

"Make sure they don't leave this area. We don't have time to waste."

Kayla and Greg were in another room, attaching accessories to the outfits they belonged with. Renee removed a dress from one of the plastic bags and felt a surge of pride in her handiwork.

"It's a piece of art," Greg said.

She turned around to face him. "I appreciate the compliment. My inspiration came while I was in Santorini, Greece, watching the sunset. The designs are all hand-painted."

Jade opened the door and entered the room. "Sorry for interrupting, but Nia's needed in hair and makeup, and she hasn't arrived yet."

"She was in another show," Kayla stated. "She should be arriving anytime now. Nia's been doing this for a few years. She'll show up in time."

Renee agreed. "I've never known her to be late or miss a show. That's why I chose her."

Jade released a sigh of relief. "That's good to hear. I was about to freak out."

She left the room as quickly as she'd entered.

"I'd better go down there to make sure we don't have any issues," Renee said. She needed to reassure herself. It just wasn't like Nia to not show up. She was a professional—still, anything could've happened...

Renee inhaled deeply and shook the thought from her head.

Not today. Everything is going to work out.

By the time she made it to the room, Nia was reading something on her phone while one of the stylists combed out her hair. She looked up and waved at Renee.

She smiled and waved back. "All the other models are here and accounted for?" she asked Jade.

"Yes," the woman responded.

"Okay. You can start sending them down to the clothing room to get dressed."

Two hours later, it was time for the show to begin. Seeing her collection backstage for the first time was surreal. She was somewhere between bursting into tears and feeling totally numb. Her chest swelled with pride and her pulse raced with excitement. The models were lined up, and the music was playing.

Greg embraced Renee. "Showtime, sweetheart."

She took several deep, calming breaths. *This is what I've been waiting for. I'm ready for this. I am.*

Renee stood backstage next to Greg as Nia,

who would start and end the show, strolled down the catwalk, wearing a black jumpsuit with snakeskin-leather straps, a belt and matching shoes. Renee chewed on her bottom lip and resisted the urge to peek out at the attendees.

"Go, go…" she heard the producer say to the next model. "C'mon, let's get out there."

A moment later, the third model walked out in one of the hand-painted designs, followed by another wearing something similar.

Nia wowed in the showstopping bridal gown Kayla had designed.

All the models walked the catwalk once more; then Nia escorted Renee, who'd changed into the vivid purple jumpsuit she'd designed just for this moment.

The room erupted in applause.

Smiling, Renee waved at the buyers, fashion editors and others in attendance, then gestured for Kayla to join her onstage. She couldn't put into words how it felt to walk the catwalk with her models during the finale. Her eyes filled with unshed tears. Holding back her emotions, Renee beamed and gave a final bow to the attendees before exiting.

Her parents were waiting for her backstage along with Greg.

Both her father and stepfather handed her a bouquet of roses while her mother embraced her, saying, "Honey, I'm so very proud of you. I know that I never believed this was a good career choice for you, but I can admit when I'm wrong."

"We were both wrong," her father offered. "Like your mother said, we're extremely proud of you."

She'd waited a long time to hear those words of support from her parents, but the truth was that they were no longer necessary. It was enough that she'd proven to herself she could do this. Renee hugged her mother, then her father. "Thank you both for being here today. I hope y'all plan on coming to the reception tonight."

"I wouldn't miss it for the world," her mother said.

"I'll be there as well," her father stated. "You did a fantastic job, baby girl."

She smiled at them. "I have to get going, but I'll see you tonight."

She and Greg walked away.

"What's wrong?" he asked.

Renee looked at him. "It kind of bothers me that they're suddenly so supportive now. They never wanted this life for me. Always thought fashion was a waste of time."

"What they think shouldn't matter now."

Renee smiled inwardly. Greg was what she could only describe as her person. Her *soul mate*. "You've always had faith in me. In the fashion show. My parents know me better than you do but didn't trust that I'd succeed. My dad and I talked about it when I saw him last, but I still need to have a conversation with my mom."

"You have a host of people who *do* believe in you," Greg reminded her. "Don't forget that. Your cousins flew in this morning for the reception tonight—to celebrate with you. They knew your show would be a hit. Focus on all the good and the people who came to support you. As for your parents—better late than never."

Renee broke into a smile. "Thank you for the pep talk. You're right—I just had a great show. Let's make sure everything is packed up so we can get out of here. Once I get back to the hotel, I'm taking a long, hot bath and a nap before the reception."

She hugged him. "Thank you, Greg. Thank you so much for being here for me. I can't tell you what it means."

He looked at her with such tenderness that she felt it all the way to her soul, and Renee knew she was done for. There was no escaping Gregory Bowman now.

CHAPTER FOURTEEN

THE FASHION SHOW had gone off without a hitch. Greg had never seen anything like it—it was almost magical. Seeing the look on Renee's face had been worth it all. She'd done a fantastic job, and her hard work had paid off.

Now it was time to celebrate her success and the official launch of her own design label.

Greg eyed his reflection in the full-length mirror. Renee had selected the tuxedo he was wearing. He'd never spent so much money on an item of clothing, but he didn't want to embarrass her—not that anyone would be paying attention to him. This was her moment to shine.

And shine she would. Just as she had during the fashion show.

He loved seeing her in this space. She truly loved her job and didn't allow fear to hold her back. He felt a tinge of sadness at the thought of leaving his own job, especially his unit, but he consoled himself with the thought of serving his country in other ways. He'd miss the other Raiders—his brothers- and sisters-in-arms—but Greg would keep in touch with them. His father had chosen duty over love and lost his life. He wanted to choose a different path.

Greg stole a peek at the clock on the nightstand.

He paced as he waited until it was time to meet Renee and Kayla in their suite. He was excited and hopeful about the party tonight.

There was a knock on his door.

He opened it to find Trey and Leon standing there.

Greg ushered them inside. "Glad you guys came up. Renee is going to be happy to see you."

Leon sat down on the edge of the bed. "Misty and Gia have been reading about the show. They've been sending us links to articles. Sounds like Renee Rothchild Designs is becoming a full-fledged design house."

"It is," Greg confirmed. "She did a fantastic job."

"We heard you helped out a lot," Trey said. "Are you thinking of leaving the museum and working for the design house?"

They broke out in laughter.

"Naw… She was really nervous and anxious," Greg said. "I just wanted to do what I could to alleviate some of that. I will say this… I never knew how much work it could be to put on a show like this."

Trey and Leon nodded at that.

"We heard you met Aunt Charlotte. How was that?" Leon questioned.

Greg shrugged. "It went fine."

"She and Renee get along okay?" Trey inquired.

"Yep. Everything is all good."

Leon checked out his reflection in the mirror. "Standing next to you, I feel a bit underdressed."

Greg laughed. "You're wearing a tux, man."

"Yeah, but it doesn't look as expensive as the one you're wearing."

"Nobody should spend this much money on a piece of clothing." Greg pulled his jacket closed. "I do look good, though."

"I look like one of those male models," Trey interjected. "At least, that's what Gia would have me believe."

Their laughter rang out around the room.

"Yeah, baby bro," Leon said. "All our wives say that about us. And we tell them the same thing. It's called love."

"I believe Gia," Trey stated.

Greg chuckled. "Let's get out of here. It's almost time to leave for the reception. We're meeting Renee and her team in ten minutes."

"How do I look?" Renee asked, twirling slowly in a turquoise gown Kayla had designed and presented to her last night.

"Fabulous," Kayla told her.

"This dress is gorgeous. I don't know how you found the time to do this for me."

"You designed the gorgeous pieces that Jade and I are wearing, so I thought I'd do the same for you."

Jade executed a slow turn in the dress Renee had created for her, saying, "I feel like a princess. Renee, you're the best boss ever. I've worked in retail for years, and no one has ever treated me the way you treat your employees."

Renee warmed at Jade's kind words, but then her stomach began to flutter with butterflies. "I'm getting nervous."

She sat down, placing her hand to her chest. She exhaled and inhaled slowly.

"No, no, no… There's nothing to be anxious about," Jade said. "Kayla and I triple-checked everything." She rushed to the mini fridge and returned with a bottle of water. "Here, drink this."

Renee took a few sips. "I'm fine. Just got a bit overwhelmed."

Her heartbeat slowly resumed its normal rhythm.

She finished drinking the water and felt much calmer as they prepared to leave the room.

Renee broke into a grin, and all her anxiety vanished at the sight of Leon and Trey with Greg. She knew some of the DuGrandpre cousins would be in attendance tonight as well, especially since they were also sponsors.

She hugged each cousin. "I'm so glad to see y'all."

"You look absolutely stunning," Greg murmured.

Renee smiled at the compliment. "And the three of you look like models. Y'all should be on the cover of a magazine." Her words sent the men into a round of laughter.

Kayla and Jade exchanged a look of confusion.

"Don't mind them," Renee said. "It must be an inside joke." Her phone vibrated. "Perfect timing," Renee said. "The limo just arrived."

During the drive, she pushed away the anxious thoughts that tried to force their way into her head. She couldn't afford to let them overtake her now. There was no reason. The show had been a success, and a lot of the same VIPs were rumored to be attending her party tonight.

Renee wasn't prepared for all the media attention but was comforted with Greg and her cousins by her side. She felt safe.

As soon as they entered the ballroom, Greg ran into someone he knew. After introductions, Renee and her employees excused themselves. Kayla and Jade went to their assigned swag stations while she navigated the room, pausing to greet and chat with the guests.

Renee glanced over her shoulder to locate Greg a little while later and found he was right where she'd left him. She was just about to make her way over when she heard a familiar voice.

"Renee."

She turned around to face the one person she never wanted to see again.

Kevin.

Her stomach plummeted. "What are you doing here? How did you get in? I know you weren't on the invite list." She managed to get the words out, though she nearly choked on the questions.

"A friend of mine had an extra invitation, so I convinced him to give it to me." He glanced around. "Congratulations on your success." Then he openly assessed her from head to toe. "Wow, you look beautiful."

"Thanks," she murmured.

"You don't look happy to see me."

Arm folded across her chest, Renee asked, *"Should I be?"* She thought ignoring his calls would've suggested that she didn't want to reconnect.

"Are you saying you haven't missed me?" Kevin asked.

"No, I haven't, honestly. I've been busy with my boutique and now my design house." She took a step back, feeling awkward. "How's married life treating you? And your political career?" She paused, then said, "You know what? Don't answer that because I don't really care."

"Wow. I guess I deserve your anger. For the record, I'm no longer married, and I decided to focus more on my first love—photography."

"Good for you," Renee said tightly. "I really should be going."

He moved to block her path. "There's no

need for any of this," he said with a sigh. "I came here tonight to make peace with you. I actually came to apologize."

Her head swam—why was he pulling this now? "Kevin, I don't want your apology."

"I owe you that and more." He glanced around to see if anyone was listening to them. "I realized I was insensitive to you back then. Ever since we broke up, I haven't been able to get you out of my mind."

Renee gave a short laugh. "You've got to be kidding me. What's really going on here?"

"I'm serious. I've missed you like crazy." Kevin hesitated, then said, "I still love you."

"Okay, now I know you've lost your mind or you're on something."

"Why would you say that?" he asked.

She sighed impatiently. "You don't love *me*. And even if that were true, it's too late, Kevin."

"Are you seeing the dude you came here with?"

She took another step back. "That's none of your business."

"Maybe after the party, you can send him home and we—"

Renee cut him off with a slash of her hand. "I already have plans, and I've had enough of this conversation. Since you went through the trouble of sneaking into my party, I hope you enjoy it, Kevin."

His eyes narrowed. "Is this what you're doing now? Playing the *victim*?"

She sent him a sharp glare. "I'm nobody's victim."

"Really? That's what you did the whole time we were together. When things didn't go your way, you'd conveniently have a panic attack. Do you do that with him?"

Renee jerked back, resisting the urge to slap him. She knew Kevin was trying to bait her into making a scene, and she needed to avoid that at all costs. This night would launch her career to new heights. She took a steadying breath. "Why did you come here tonight?"

"You think you're some big shot now that you had a little fashion show, but you're the same insecure girl that I knew." His voice took on that deadly tone she remembered from all those years ago. "You're not going to be able to keep any man until you grow up. Stop living in the past and acting so afraid of everything. Trust me, it's not attractive. Nobody likes a woman who can't keep it together over little things."

Filled with white-hot fury, she curled her

fingers into fists. *"Walk away now before I call security and have you forcibly removed."*

Renee strode away without waiting for a response. She was so angry, she could barely contain her rage. She stepped outside the ballroom to find a place to cool down.

She wasn't gone long, and then she stepped back inside, forcing herself to look calm, and joined Greg at a table.

"Who was that guy I saw you talking to earlier?" he inquired. "You seemed upset. I started to come over, but Trey told me to just wait."

Renee didn't detect any jealousy in his query—only concern. "That was Kevin. He claimed he came to apologize. He wasn't invited." She glanced over her shoulder in time to see her brother escorting him out of the ballroom.

"Don't worry, dear. Kevin won't be back," her mother interjected as she strode over.

Renee nodded in gratitude. She glanced over at Trey and Leon.

They were both watching her, studying her, likely to see her reaction and determine if they felt the need to join her brother.

"I'm fine," she told them. "And I'm going to enjoy my party." She stood up and turned to Greg. "Why don't we get something to eat? I'm paying a lot of money for this food. We need to enjoy it."

Greg offered her his arm as they walked away. "So why do you think Kevin came tonight if it wasn't to apologize?" he asked in a low voice. "You think he has another motive?"

Renee decided to be honest with him. "Kevin told me that he still loves me."

Greg released a slow sigh. "Maybe he does."

She looked him in the eye. "I'm not interested in rekindling anything with him. He was lying. The minute I made it clear I wanted nothing to do with him, he reverted back to his old self."

"What did he say to you?" he asked, again out of what looked like concern. "Do I need to have a conversation with him?"

"He's not worth it, Greg. Enough about Kevin," Renee responded, smiling up at him. "It's time to party."

Greg grinned and, after snapping up some passing hors d'oeuvres, led her to the dance floor.

"Excuse me." A young woman approached them when they had finished dancing. "I'm with *Fashion Forward* magazine. I'd love to interview you for our upcoming issue."

Renee beamed, unable to contain her excitement. *Fashion Forward* was a well-respected magazine in the industry. "I'd be honored."

She made plans to meet the woman the next day for lunch. When the woman walked away, Renee embraced Greg. "I have an interview tomorrow."

He laughed. "I'm proud of you."

"This will be my third one." The RRD show was garnering the interest she'd hoped for.

"This is a great party," Kayla said when she walked up to them. "I've gained a good five pounds already."

Renee grinned. "I'm right there with you. I've been munching all evening."

"I'm heading over to the chocolate fountain. Jade said the white chocolate is heavenly."

"Enjoy." Renee glanced around. "I see a few buyers I haven't greeted yet. We should say hello."

Straightening his bow tie, he asked, "How do I look?"

Laughing, she responded, "Perfect. C'mon…"

She took Greg's hand, and they made their way across the room to make sure they personally greeted everyone in attendance.

Kevin's hurtful words tried to infiltrate her thoughts, but she continued to block them. She refused to let him ruin this night for her.

CHAPTER FIFTEEN

RENEE WAS COUNTING down the days until Greg was out of the military and back on the island. For good. No more going back and forth.

Six days.

She was already planning a special surprise for him. Renee had invited his mother to spend a few days on the island. She thought it might be nice to take Marilee on a tour of Charleston since she had mentioned she'd never been there before. They could also take her to Hilton Head.

Renee strolled into the boutique, humming softly to herself.

"Your show was a hit!" Lucy exclaimed. "You're blowing up all over social media. All the fashion sites are talking about you. The phone hasn't stopped ringing all morning."

Jade walked out of the stockroom. "I read online that RRD hit a home run during Fashion Week. I told you that you'd knock it out of the park."

She was speechless. "I'm still in awe over all that's happened."

"Okay, boss lady," Jade said. "You're the real deal, so it's time to act like it. You have a bunch of phone calls to return. We're good out here. You go on to your office and be the boss fashion designer that you are."

Renee chuckled. "Yes, ma'am."

Smiling, she headed to her office.

She was joined by Kayla half an hour later, who asked, "Did you know that RRD is trending on Twitter?"

"I saw. I just got off the phone with one of the buyers from Willingham Department Store in Massachusetts. They loved the collection. They're interested in both the couture and ready-to-wear collections." Renee was still recovering from the phone call—she couldn't believe it.

Kayla squealed in delight. "Yesssss."

She grinned. "They're going to test them in four of their stores. If sales are good, then our clothing will be in the entire chain."

Kayla pumped her fist. "This is just the beginning. I keep saying this."

Renee agreed, feeling like getting up and dancing. But there was so much to do. She held up a handful of notes. "These are all calls

I need to return. We really need to find a building soon to expand. Actually, let's make an offer on the one we saw in Charleston. It's perfect, and I don't want to keep waiting and risk losing it."

"I'll call them right now."

"Offer twenty thousand below their asking price," Renee said. "The other buildings in that area didn't appraise for more than that."

Kayla eyed her for a moment. "You really seem to be in your element."

"I just love what I do," Renee responded.

She spent most of her morning on the phone with buyers and reporters.

Renee took a break at noon to grab something to eat. She left the shop and went next door to the café. As she entered, everyone dining there broke out into applause. She stopped in her tracks, flushing. "Thanks, everyone."

"We got us a local celebrity," one of the patrons said. "You done put Polk Island on the map of the fashion world. We real proud of you, Renee."

She smiled and sat down in one of the booths.

Misty came out of the kitchen and joined her. "Hello, Miss Rothchild."

"Don't you start…"

"Right now, you're the talk of the island, Renee. It's well-deserved recognition."

"Everyone here has been so supportive of me." She teared up at the warm welcome and looked away.

Misty patted her hand. "What would you like?"

"I'm in the mood for your chicken-salad sandwich on a croissant."

"Coming right up," Misty said.

She returned a short time later with a plate of food. "I heard you saw your ex."

Renee gestured for Misty to join her. "Yeah, he had the nerve to show up at the reception. Before that, he'd called me until I blocked his number. He found the number to the boutique and called there, leaving messages for me."

"What did he want?"

"Kevin said he wanted to apologize—but not only that, he had the nerve to say he still loves me." Frustration still simmered in Renee when she thought about their last encounter.

"How do you feel about that?" Misty asked.

"Indifferent." Renee shrugged. "Kevin showed his true colors not too long after. He told me I was a drama queen and that I needed to grow up."

Anger flashed in Misty's eyes. "He's a jerk. I hope I never meet him."

"It's not likely you will," Renee stated. "My brother made him leave the party."

"That's good." Misty nodded. "So, what are you working on now? Have you already moved on to a new collection?"

"Not yet," Renee replied. "I've been playing with several ideas, but nothing's concrete. My focus is on purchasing a building large enough for a design house. I've already got orders coming in." She took a bite of her sandwich, chewing slowly. Misty's food was always delicious.

"I knew you'd been looking for a place. Have you found anything?"

"Yeah. We put an offer in this morning." She smiled. "This is really happening."

Misty reached across the table and squeezed Renee's hand. "And you're ready for it. Your parents must be so proud."

A thread of unease unfurled in her. "I told you how they weren't very supportive at first. But they came to my show and talked about how proud they were of me."

Misty gave her a knowing glance. "You would've liked for them to have told you this much earlier, before the successful show."

She nodded. "Exactly. My boutique made money the first year it opened and is doing well, but my parents never seemed to notice. It's not that I needed to hear praise…"

"It's okay to admit that you wanted your parents' praise…their support."

"I wanted them to be proud of me. They're always singing my brother's praises. Whenever they would mention me, they would tell people that I worked in retail. That's the way they saw me. I think my mother once told someone I was a seamstress." There was still a grain of hurt that remained, but Renee chose not to dwell on those memories. Her parents were now staunch supporters, and for that she was grateful.

"I'm sorry," Misty said gently.

Renee shrugged. "It's fine. I wasn't going to let them stop me from living my dream. I wanted to be a fashion designer or work with one. I was willing to do whatever I had to do to reach my goal." Days after returning from New York, it still hadn't fully sunk in that she'd pulled off a successful show at Fashion Week. All that dreaming and hard work was paying off.

Misty nodded. "Oh, we need to get together to plan a baby shower for Gia and Trey."

Renee grinned. "Just let me know when and where. I'm there."

"Can you believe they decided to wait until the baby is born to find out the sex? I thought for sure Trey would want to know whether he's having a boy or girl. I was surprised."

"It would've made it easier on us when it comes to shopping for the baby," Renee said.

Misty laughed. "Exactly." She soon had to excuse herself to speak with a customer.

Renee finished eating, paid the bill and returned to the shop.

The drumbeat of rain that had started falling lasted most of the afternoon as she worked on a new design in her office. Renee's door was closed, a signal to her staff that she didn't want to be disturbed. Not even Kayla ventured inside unless it was an urgent matter. She appreciated that her assistant respected her space when she was in creative mode.

Renee picked up a couple of fabrics and held them out toward the light. Her lips formed a smile as her eyes traveled back to the vivid orange fabric in her left hand. She laid it next to a navy blue sample in Ponte knit. Renee tacked the fabrics to her sketch.

The ringing of her cell phone pulled her away from her drawing.

"Hello, Mom."

"Honey, I just had to call you. You're all over the fashion magazines. My friend Bonnie called me this morning to tell me how impressed she was with your designs. She works for *Vogue*, you know…"

"I remember her."

"She sent me a copy of what she posted on their Facebook feed. It says, 'The highlight of this year's Fashion Week came the moment Nia stepped onto the catwalk in a stunning black shantung silk-and-snakeskin creation by Renee Rothchild. The fashion industry has been buzzing about her ready-to-wear line for a while now, but this year, Rothchild outdid herself with a dramatic couture collection.'"

"Wow…" was all Renee could say. She couldn't believe she had received this type of praise on *Vogue* social media. "I need to send her some flowers. I don't think a card is enough."

"Your star is shining brightly."

She smiled…but there was no use putting off what needed to be said. "Mom, I need to know something."

"Yes, dear?"

"Why are you being so supportive of me now? When I *needed* your support and your approval, I didn't have it—so what's changed?" She didn't want to remain silent in this situation. For years, her mother had made Renee feel like she didn't approve of her dreams.

"Renee, I only wanted what was best for you," she replied softly. "I must admit that I didn't think you were on the right path. There are so many people who want to be a designer…but only a few actually make it. I didn't want you to get hurt if you didn't."

"You still could've taken a gamble on me, Mom," Renee pointed out. "If you'd talked to me, you would've known that I had a plan. I had options if it didn't work out."

"I'm sorry if you felt I failed you. I only wanted to protect you."

"Isn't this what life is all about? *Trial and error?* Failing at something and learning from it but not giving up?"

There was a pause on the line. "I suppose you're right."

"I have to tell you that it hurt when I didn't have the support of my parents. I put so much pressure on myself to prove you and Daddy wrong. I wanted to show you I could be successful."

"I'm so sorry, honey. I hope you won't hold this against me, because I just wanted to protect you—not kill your dreams. To be fair, I would try to discuss your wanting to be a designer, but when you didn't like what I had to say, you'd shut down. You'd go off to your room and you didn't want to be bothered."

"You're right. I just felt you didn't understand me." She hoped that could change. She didn't want there to be distance between them.

"It wasn't easy trying to get you to open up. The only ones you'd talk to were Trey and Leon. Even Aunt Eleanor could accomplish what I couldn't." Her mother sighed. "I thought maybe you were upset because I'd remarried."

"That might have been some of it," Renee admitted. If she were honest, that had been a tough adjustment. "But I just wanted you to believe in me. I wanted you to trust me."

"I've always believed in you, and I do trust you. I promise to listen going forward."

Renee felt hope swell within her. "I love you, too, and I'm glad we talked about this... I needed to get it off my chest."

"You internalize your feelings, but you don't have to. You can always talk to me about anything."

"Thanks, Mom."

They talked for a few minutes more, then ended the call.

Smiling, Renee returned her attention to her work. The conversation with her mother should've taken place earlier, but she'd simply chosen to ignore her real feelings by pushing them deep into the recesses of her heart. She loved her parents dearly and never wanted to disappoint them—but Renee knew design was her calling, her gift, and she wasn't going to quit.

She thought about her relationship with Greg. He'd said pretty much the same thing as her mother—she needed to open up more about her feelings. She began to wonder if she'd gone about things all wrong. Regardless, she had the opportunity to change things. To free herself from the shadows of her past.

GREG STARED DOWN at the orders in his hands. He read them several times over, until he'd memorized every word. His discharge was on hold.

During the briefing, he was told that a member of his team had been taken hostage and that he had to leave within the hour to join the rest of the unit.

He was supposed to be getting out. Only three more days and Greg was done.

By the weekend, he should've been on his

way to Polk Island. He'd been looking for a place to live. He'd initially planned to find an apartment, but Trey had convinced Greg to stay with him and Gia until he found a house. He hoped to find a property before the baby came.

Renee had texted him a couple of days ago to let him know that she'd placed an offer on a building in Charleston. Greg was ecstatic to witness Renee's dreams coming true. And now, suddenly, *his* dreams were on hold.

He dreaded telling Renee the news. He knew this could possibly destroy everything they'd started to build together.

But she had to be told. There was no other way around it. No point in putting off the inevitable.

He dialed her number.

"Hey, you…" she greeted when she answered. Her cheery tone only served to make him feel worse because he was about to ruin her day.

"There's something I have to tell you," he said gingerly.

"You sound strange," Renee replied. "What's wrong? Did something happen?"

Greg hated doing this to her. He knew no matter how he phrased the next part, she was going to be upset. "I have to leave… I have to join my team. I'm leaving shortly."

"Hold up," Renee uttered. "Greg, what are you talking about? I thought you said they wouldn't send you on a mission since you're getting out."

He could hear the panic rising in her voice. He forced a calm tone as he said, "They don't usually do this unless something bad happens."

"So something happened—something you can't tell me about."

"Everything's gonna be okay. I'll be back before you know it." Hopefully in time for the surprise birthday party he'd started to plan for her. It would be held at a bowling alley in Charleston in October.

"I don't understand. Your last day was supposed to be Friday. *This Friday.*" Renee's voice rose an octave. "Now you're telling me that you're leaving on a mission?"

"I'm sorry, Renee. I just got the orders. Literally." He hated that things were changing so quickly on her—and he wasn't there to comfort her.

"I don't believe this," she muttered. "I should've known this was too good to be true."

He sighed. "I'm not happy about this, either, but you know I don't have a choice in this."

"No, I don't suppose you do." Her voice sounded so flat—not like the cheerful Renee he knew.

"I have to go, but I'll give you a call when I can."

She didn't respond. And he couldn't blame her for not knowing what to say after receiving this unexpected news.

"Just do me a favor and try not to die."

"Renee… I'm so sorry."

The sound of a sob as she disconnected broke Greg's heart. This was the last thing he'd ever expected to happen.

This was the worst thing that could've happened.

The only thing left to do was complete his mission and make it home to her. Greg packed quickly and headed to the airstrip. The only thought on his mind was that he couldn't lose Renee.

"ARE YOU OKAY?" Kayla inquired when she entered the office.

"Not really," Renee responded, dabbing her eyes quickly. "Greg just told me that he's leaving to join his team."

Frowning, Kayla asked, "Can they do that?"

Renee lifted her shoulders in an indifferent shrug. But inside, the pain of Greg's latest news ripped through her. "I don't know."

Kayla seemed to sense that she needed time alone and retreated quietly.

Picking up her phone, she called Trey. "Hey, have you spoken to Greg?"

"Naw, what's up?"

"He's deploying. That's all I know."

There was silence on the line for a moment. "Something must've happened."

"How can they just do that?" Renee asked, fighting for calm. "He's supposed to get out on Friday. It's not like we're in a war, so how can they renege on his discharge?"

"Renee, the military has a stop-loss policy, which is the involuntary extension of active-duty service beyond an ETS."

"ETS?"

"End of Term of Service," Trey explained. "Greg is a Raider. Something's happened— that's the only reason his ETS was extended. They must need him." He sighed. "Cousin, this isn't permanent. There's nothing for you to worry about."

It took all her effort not to scoff at those words. "We have no idea how long he'll be gone. I thought Greg was done with all this."

"I'm pretty sure this is just a temporary situation," Trey said gently. "His discharge will be effective once he returns from this mission."

"That could be a year…two years…five years…" She clenched her eyes shut. The thought of Greg being gone that long… "We don't know. Anything could happen." She was trying not to go to the worst-case scenario, but in this moment, she couldn't help it.

"Just stay calm. Anything can happen anywhere."

She wasn't in the mood for placating words. She was upset. Her imagination continued to fight her for control, filling her head with horrifying images. Renee fought back as valiantly as she could, trying to refocus her thoughts.

"Renee…" Trey prompted. "You there?"

"I'm here," she managed after a moment.

"Slow down your breathing," he instructed.

Renee did as she was told. She swallowed the panic and wiped away new tears.

After their call ended, Kayla reentered and handed Renee a bottle of water—presumably what she'd left the office for.

"Thank you," Renee said, opening it and then taking a few sips.

"Why don't you take a break?"

"We have a lot of work to do. I'll be fine."

She blinked back the tears that threatened to spill down her cheeks. "I'm good."

Kayla nodded but looked concerned as she headed to the door. "I'll be on the sales floor if you need me."

"You don't have to leave," Renee replied.

"I'm sorry this is happening," her assistant said softly.

"This is why I never dated men in the military…because of stuff like this. I allowed him to get close to me because he told me he was getting out. I didn't know they could control his discharge as well."

"I've never known that to happen," Kayla said. "My brother was in the Air Force, and he didn't have a problem when he decided to get out."

Renee leaned heavily on her desk. "Whenever Greg was away on a mission, I was so afraid. We were only friends, but I was worried about him." She remembered the nights she'd stay up, unable to sleep, whenever he'd been deployed. This was even worse. "Kayla, I've let myself fall for him."

Kayla's gaze held sympathy and understanding. "You have to trust and have faith that he'll come home soon. Pray for his safety and that of his team."

She nodded. "I will."

An hour later, Renee decided to go home.

She walked into her condo and sat down on the sofa.

Now that she was away from everyone, she didn't need to be brave or strong. She allowed her tears to fall, venting her disappointment—her anger.

She'd never signed up for this.

CHAPTER SIXTEEN

"I'M WORRIED ABOUT RENEE," Trey said during dinner with his wife. "Greg was deployed today."

Frowning in confusion, she asked, "*How?* These are the last few days on the job."

He shrugged. "There's a clause called stop loss in our contracts. They can extend our service dates. Something happened if Greg was sent to join the rest of his team." Trey knew things like this could happen. And he prayed it was a routine operation for Greg. Still…he was concerned for his friend, and for Renee.

Gia wiped her mouth with her napkin. "Renee's going to be devastated. Do you think I should go over there?"

"Not tonight, unless she needs us," Trey responded. He was worried about his cousin, but he knew Renee well. Right now, she just needed space. Trey wasn't sure what would happen upon Greg's return, but he hoped their relationship would survive.

"I should at least call her," Gia insisted.

"She needs some time to process the news. When Renee's ready to talk, she'll reach out." He looked over at his wife. "But if you do want to help, keep Renee busy and keep her encouraged while Greg's away. Her thoughts will take her to the negative, so it's best to keep her positive and hopeful."

Gia nodded. "I know she's going to be busy with her design company and the orders coming in, so that's a good thing."

Gia had a point. With Renee's business taking off, the timing was ideal. "I just hope Greg's unit can get the job done and get back here before too long," Trey said.

"Me, too." Gia sighed. "Things were going so well for her and for them. This is the last thing that needed to happen."

He agreed. "Renee is a lot stronger than she thinks—she just hasn't realized it yet. Trust me, I had my own demons to fight after I came home." His wife knew only too well what that had looked like. He still woke up from nightmares and suffered from bouts of anxiety, so he understood these things weren't so simple.

"Maybe she should see her therapist more than every other week. That might help."

"It just might," Trey said. "The challenge is getting Renee to agree."

"Leave that to me and Misty," Gia responded.

After dinner, they settled in the living room.

Trey gently placed a hand on Gia's belly. "How's my little one doing?"

"Busy," Gia answered. "Boy or girl, this is a busy baby."

Despite everything that had happened, his heart was already full of love for his family. "When I came home, I never thought I'd see this day. You as my wife, and now we're having our first child…" He grinned. "The first of eight."

Gia lifted a brow. "Excuse me?"

"Yeah, eight children. Didn't we talk about it?"

Gia changed position and placed a pillow between her and the sofa. "We never discussed having *eight* children. We only talked about two."

"So you don't want to have eight babies with me?"

She kissed him. "Trey, I'll have as many children as we're blessed with. Just remember that this is a team effort when it comes to parenting—not just conception."

"Understood, ma'am."

Trey pulled Gia closer to him. "I love you."

She looked up into his eyes. "Ditto." She paused a moment, then said, "I'm sorry, but I have to check on your cousin. I don't think Renee needs to be alone right now. I'm gonna call Misty and see if she'll go over there with me. I won't feel good about this until I see her for myself."

His wife had such a big heart. "You want me to go with you?"

Gia shook her head. "I think it should just be me and Misty. If we need backup, we'll call Aunt Eleanor."

"I guess you got it covered, then," Trey murmured. "Be safe out there."

"I won't be gone long," she assured him.

RENEE OPENED THE front door to Gia and Misty when she heard the doorbell ring. "Hey. I suppose Trey sent y'all over here to make sure I'm okay."

"Trey didn't send us, but Misty and I did come to see how you're doing," Gia said.

She stepped aside to let them enter the foyer. They followed her into the living room, where they sat down. Renee pointed to the bottle of red wine. "I was about to have a glass. As for how I'm doing…I'm okay. I know Gia can't have any—but what about you, Misty? You want a glass?"

"No, I'm good. Renee, we'd understand if you're not okay," Misty said. "This was totally unexpected."

"It doesn't matter either way." Renee poured the dark liquid into her empty glass.

"How many of those have you had?" Gia inquired.

"I had a glass last night and now I'm having another tonight." She glanced up at her friends. "I'm not over here drowning my sorrows in alcohol if that's what you're thinking. I have too much to do for that."

"How is your anxiety?" Misty asked gently.

"Higher than usual, but I've been able to manage the attacks by trying to stay busy. It's not easy, because I can't stop worrying about Greg. It's hard not knowing what's going on. I can't watch the news because it'll only make it worse."

"We're not here to intrude," Misty said. "We just want you to know that you don't have to deal with this alone."

She pasted on a smile. "Thank you both."

"Trey says that Greg should be back soon,"

Gia said. She propped a throw pillow behind her back for support.

"He doesn't really know that for sure." Renee shrugged. "We have no idea where he is or how long he'll be gone."

Gia's voice was gentle as she said, "What we all know for sure is that Greg cares for you. For that reason, he will do everything possible to come home to you."

"I know that," Renee replied. "But is it enough? It's not like he's in complete control of his life." She had a bad feeling; she felt it all the way to the depth of her soul.

"I understand what you're feeling," Misty put in. "I feel anxious whenever Leon has to put out a fire. Remember when they went to Los Angeles to help with that huge firestorm out there? I was scared for him."

"You never said anything," Renee said.

"I didn't want to give voice to the *what-if* scenarios. I couldn't let my children see me fall apart. I didn't watch the news about it. I just focused on the positive—my faith that Leon was coming home to me and the children. And like you, I kept myself busy. You have to remember that this is something that was beyond Greg's control."

"That's exactly the problem," Renee uttered.

"His life is not his own, and I don't want to deal with that." Then again...he could've volunteered to join the mission. Maybe he wanted one last adventure before becoming a civilian. She didn't voice the thought aloud, but it was there.

"My dad was military," Gia said. "It wasn't a bad life."

Gia had opened up about her dad in the years they'd been friends.

"Were you ever worried about your father?" Renee asked. "Did you worry if he'd come home whenever he was deployed?"

She nodded. "Yeah, I had moments like these, but my mother would tell me to have faith, and of course, we'd pray for his safety and all the troops."

Renee shook her head. "Well, it's not that easy for me." She needed to know Greg was safe. She didn't want to spend her life worrying about him.

"I know, sweetie," Gia said softly. "That's why we're here. What can we do to help?"

Renee teared up. "I hate being this way. Always living in fear like this."

"This may be hard to hear, but the way you live your life is a choice," Gia stated. "Choose to focus on your designs, the boutique and the new building. Have faith that Greg is safe, and he'll return before you know it."

She nodded. "That sounds like something my therapist would say."

"What do you think of seeing her on a weekly basis for a little while?" Misty asked.

Renee let out a harsh laugh. "Why? Do you think I'm losing it?"

"That's not what I meant," Misty said.

"Just know that Trey and I are here for you," Gia interjected. "Misty and Leon, too. We're not going to let you go through this alone—but you must *talk* to us or your therapist. Don't suffer in silence."

"I hear you," Renee responded. "I keep hearing Kevin's voice saying that I'm overreacting, and right now, that's the last thing I need." Deep down, she knew her family, friends and coworkers had been so supportive of her.

"This is a judgment-free zone," Gia responded. "Renee, you know that. We'd never do that to you. Kevin's opinions are irrelevant."

She knew they wouldn't judge her. Renee wished Kevin hadn't suddenly reappeared in her life. It had taken a session with her therapist to get him out of her head again. He'd never once tried to understand her disorder or her triggers, and that had left her doubting herself for a long time.

They talked for another hour before Misty and Gia left.

Renee walked them to the door and locked it behind them.

She went back to the sofa and drank her wine while staring at the painting over the fireplace.

Her happy place.

"I'M SURPRISED I'M just now seeing you," Renee announced when Trey entered the boutique. "Gia and Misty came over last night. Now you're here. Is Leon going to show up at any moment? Are y'all two planning to gang up on me?"

"I wanted to see for myself how you're doing. I've witnessed one of your panic attacks and even dealt with a few of my own… Sometimes being alone is your worst enemy."

She was touched by his thoughtfulness. She knew Trey's return to civilian life and coping with anxiety and PTSD meant he understood her in a way few others did. "I don't mean to be so grouchy, Trey. I'm angry."

He nodded. "I understand. But what's behind that anger, cousin?"

Renee led him to her office so they could talk in private. When they were seated, she said, "Greg worked so hard to join the MAR-SOC unit. I have to wonder if he's really ready to walk away. Maybe he wanted to join his unit."

Trey's brows rose in surprise. "You think he volunteered for the mission?"

Renee nodded. "There's a part of me that believes Greg could've found a way to stay behind if he'd really wanted to."

He shook his head. "The military doesn't work that way. Greg had no choice. Trust me on this—he was ready to get out and start a life with you."

"He's out there somewhere... Anything could happen to him," Renee uttered. Unsettling thoughts of him being hurt had continued to barrage her since their last phone call, when he'd told her he was leaving. "Last night, I dreamed I was in a wedding dress, and I was at the airport—inside some hangar. The plane arrived, and after everyone got off, Greg was carried off the plane in a casket. I became hysterical..."

The memory of her nightmare induced the tightening of her chest, making it hard for her to breathe normally. The familiar edges of fear reached out for her, and Renee found herself lost in time and space. Her brain triggered her fight-or-flight response.

"Renee... Renee, sweetheart, look at me," Trey instructed. "That dream wasn't real. It didn't happen. There's no danger that we know of. Nothing to fear."

A tear rolled down her cheek. "I don't know why, but I just have a bad feeling about this mission."

Trey got up, walked around the desk and hugged her. "Why don't you come spend a few days with us? I don't want you to be alone."

Renee nodded. "Maybe I'll do that. I don't think being alone in the condo is good for me." Maybe all the stress of Greg's leaving was causing her to unravel a little.

After she was composed once more, she looked at Trey and said, "You've known Greg a long time. Do you really believe a man like him will be happy living on Polk Island and working in a museum?"

"Greg is the type of person who knows what he wants," her cousin responded. "His decision is more about him than you."

She slumped back in her seat. "I keep telling myself this, but I guess it's the timing. It just seems he didn't come to this decision until after we met. I don't want to be the reason because he may regret it one day."

"I've had this same conversation with Greg," Trey insisted. "He told me the same thing he told you—he decided to get out because he is ready to settle down."

Another lone tear rolled down her cheek. "I just want him to be safe. He's been so supportive of me, and here I am, having a tantrum over something he can't control. I don't deserve a man like him."

"Yes, you do," Trey said, patting her on the shoulder.

With the arrival of her patternmaker, their conversation came to a sudden end. She needed to pull herself together and focus on opening her fashion house.

"I'll see you later," her cousin said.

She nodded. "Okay."

Renee was grateful to have something to keep her busy at work. She didn't like the direction in which her thoughts were going. She was also grateful to have Trey and Gia, and their offer for her to come stay with them, so she wouldn't have to deal with everything alone.

At the end of the day, Renee stopped home

long enough to pack a few things, then headed to Trey's house.

She felt much better being in a house with someone else. Maybe the quietness of her condo had added to the turbulent thoughts she'd been having. Normally, the sounds of the ocean from her windows calmed her—but not lately.

Renee didn't like feeling like this; she resented feeling weak and afraid of the unknown. Living in this abyss was torture.

I'm not going to let this get the better of me. I just have to find a way to make it stop—these terrifying and negative thoughts. If I don't, I'll lose everything.

CHAPTER SEVENTEEN

GREG SAT ON the edge of his bunk, cleaning his gun. He was miles away in the jungle, yet his thoughts were of Renee and how she was faring.

"You haven't had much to say since you arrived, Bowman," his fellow Raider Holloway said. "What's up?"

"I was supposed to be discharged. I made plans with my lady," Greg admitted.

"Hey, I understand. My wife is not too happy right now—but this is our life. She knew it when we got married." The man shrugged. "However, if things go as planned tomorrow, we'll be stateside before you know it."

Greg nodded in agreement. "I hope so." Holloway patted him on the shoulder before leaving the tent.

He lay back on his bunk, imagining everything about Renee. He couldn't help but visualize running his fingers through her short curly hair, kissing her lips, the sound of her laughter.

He hoped their rescue mission tomorrow would produce the desired results and his unit could head back home. This particular part of the job didn't appeal to him at all. He didn't like being in the thick of all the lush foliage. The jungle was filled with insects and creatures he'd never seen and didn't care to see ever again in life.

But he was here to help his team retrieve one of their own—a brother. They were miles away from their target but would be ferried in closer at dawn. Satellite photos showed their target was heavily ringed by men with automatic weapons.

He couldn't wait to return stateside. To Renee.

This mission didn't sit well with him. Greg couldn't explain it, but he had a bad feeling. He hadn't shared his thoughts with the team, not wanting to set the others on edge, but his whole body was on alert to every sound, smell and touch. Even when sleeping, the tiniest noise woke him up.

He sighed, wishing the mission were already over. Until then, he'd just have to take it one day at a time.

RENEE AND HER employees were working tirelessly to get the new design space in Charleston ready for operation as quickly as possible. Sewing machines and other equipment had arrived almost daily for the past two weeks. The office furniture had been delivered yesterday.

Rusty, Trey and Leon had volunteered what free time they had to help with setting up furnishings and equipment.

Today was the first day Renee and Kayla would be in their new offices. She'd promoted Jade to manager of the boutique and hired two additional sales staff. Renee would be focusing more on her fashion house in Charleston, but she knew her boutique was in good hands with Jade as the store manager. She was also excited to focus on her couture collection, but she wasn't going to push aside her ready-to-wear pieces—that was where she'd gotten her start.

Kayla gathered all the employees into a huge empty room, where a light breakfast buffet was being served. One of the main attractions of their new building was the cafeteria.

"Welcome to Renee Rothchild Designs," Renee greeted her new team. "I'm excited to have you here with me on this journey." She shared her vision and mission statement for the company before inviting them to enjoy the assortment of breads, muffins and other breakfast items set out before them. She was in a state of euphoria after addressing her team. Her goal of owning her own design house had come to fruition. Everything was perfect.

Renee walked down a long hallway on the top floor to a large corner office painted a platinum gray, with orange accent pieces on gray antique furnishings. She loved it. Kayla's office was the second largest and was across the hall. She'd chosen to paint her office a vivid green, with blue and yellow accessories. Her desk and bookshelves were white. All the administrative staff would be working on the fourth floor as well.

The second and third floors would house the manufacturing and quality control departments, while the first floor had a lobby area complete with receptionist, private VIP meeting rooms, a room with a built-in runway and the cafeteria.

"This is just the beginning," Renee told Kayla.

Kayla glanced around. "It's perfect for RRD."

"The orders are coming in," she informed

her assistant cheerily, "so we don't have any time to waste."

"We're on schedule," Kayla stated. "We should have the initial shipments out in a couple of weeks."

Renee felt a wonderful sense of accomplishment. She'd turned her boutique into a successful business; her debut at Fashion Week had been a hit; and next year, she would not only have two shows in New York but also a show in Milan.

If only Greg was here to share her excitement and her joy. She missed him. There were times when fear would try to rise, but Renee forced it away. She refused to let panic rob her of her peace. She just had to trust that Greg was safe and would return home soon.

Despite that hope, Renee wasn't sure what would become of their relationship. The past few weeks had shown her that Greg would never truly be free of the military—and despite her efforts to keep her panic attacks under control, it had been a constant struggle for her. She could force it away, bury herself in work, but anxiety was always near the surface. As much as it pained her, it might be best for them to go back to being just friends. They had a lot of talking to do when he returned.

THE HELICOPTERS OF Task Force 202 flew into a nearby area and turned their noses toward an abandoned prison, where the hostage was being held. It had taken eight days to locate him, but they finally were nearing the run-down building to retrieve and bring him home. Unable to land, Greg and his teammates began to rappel down the ropes hanging from the helicopter doors.

As soon as the men made it safely to the ground, the helicopters were caught in a crossfire from the front. Insurgents hidden in the prison opened fire with automatic weapons. Greg expected that they wouldn't be welcomed, so they were prepared to respond with their own guns.

The helicopters also rained down heavy small arms and machine gunfire at the targets.

When the helicopters left the area, it was suddenly silent.

The Raiders covertly made their way toward the target at ground level. Another unit was coming from behind the prison. They had the place surrounded and waited for the cover of darkness.

There was only a limited amount of time to successfully extricate the hostage. Under the dark of night and under heavy camouflage, the Raiders forged ahead toward the prison, locked and loaded.

The unit reached their target, and seconds later, the fireworks began.

Greg and his team were able to infiltrate and retrieve their teammate, who looked as if he'd been beaten and tortured. He was weak but still physically able to keep up with the unit.

They moved quickly through the jungle, rushing to the designated spot for retrieval.

Greg knew Holloway was on his right.

Suddenly, the air was knocked out of Greg as a round of gunfire went off when they neared the pickup spot. Greg heard more bursts as his unit began firing back.

Then he heard a loud blast as a missile launcher hit its target, reducing the prison to a mound of rocks and debris. Fighting to breathe, he tried to regain his balance. As he looked up, he felt a rush of relief when he laid eyes on the helicopters that would take them to safety.

GREG SAT ON the plane with his team on the way back to the States. He was happy to finally be going home. The operation had taken longer than expected, but the day after the extrication, they were heading back.

It hadn't been an easy mission by any means.

He'd nearly been shot during the rescue. Greg had never been that close to death in the past—close enough to see his life flash before his eyes.

There was one person he had to thank for saving his life.

Greg glanced over his shoulder at the black body bag in the back of the plane.

Sgt. Ernest Holloway. Married less than a year, and his wife was now a widow. He'd died while protecting Greg.

He would never know how Holloway had known that there was still a shooter somewhere. It didn't matter, really. Holloway's instincts had led him to sacrifice his own life for a brother. His unit returned heavy gunfire, making sure the insurgent following them was dead. They'd made sure it was safe for the helicopters to land long enough for retrieval.

He rubbed his eyes, trying not to linger on the horrible images, the thought of his friend dead. This mission had made everything clear for Greg. Putting himself at risk in dangerous surroundings was assuredly not the life he wanted for himself. He just wanted to return to Polk Island and to Renee's arms.

But before he could do that, he had to say goodbye to a brother.

CHAPTER EIGHTEEN

GREG WAS FINALLY STATESIDE. He hadn't called Renee to let her know because he didn't want to tell her about Holloway. He also wanted to ensure there would be no more delays with his separation from the military.

Jaw clenched, he glared at the sleek lines of the flag-draped, bronze-colored casket.

He stood shoulder to shoulder with his teammates as an image of his fallen brother flashed through his mind. The last thing he'd seen was the look of determination on Holloway's face, just before he pushed Greg down and a bullet went through his head. They had followed the rules to the letter and still lost a teammate while extricating another.

Overwhelmed by the memory, Greg glanced down at his hands and tried to imagine the sound of the ocean. He was struggling to find peace. The imagery wasn't helping, especially when he could hear the heartbreaking sobs coming from Holloway's wife. Her tears made him feel worse.

Holloway would be remembered as a hero, but Greg would've preferred to have his friend grow old with the love of his life. To have a house filled with children; to be remembered as a wonderful soldier, husband, father and grandfather. That was what he wanted for Holloway.

The pastor's words about honor, bravery and sacrifice were meant to be encouraging, but they rolled over Greg, not making much of an impact. The pastor then spoke of Holloway's sense of humor, the way he always seemed to have a kind word for anyone and of the Bible Holloway carried with him on every mission. Greg didn't know that his teammate had prayed before and after every mission. He'd carried two photos with him—one of his parents and the other of his wife.

A loud blast sounded in the air as seven guns exploded in succession. Once, twice...twenty-one shots.

Faces implacable, the honor guard shouldered their guns and stood as tall and rigid as the ancient oak trees surrounding the cemetery in Columbia. The entire platoon was in attendance—the men Holloway had served, fought and trained with. His friend had always said he'd lived a good life and was prepared to offer up the ultimate sacrifice for his country without regret.

Holloway was a true hero, and he deserved the honors that were bestowed upon him.

Later tonight, they would celebrate him, their brother, as was tradition. Greg wanted nothing more than to get on the road and head to the island, but he owed Holloway. He would wait and leave first thing in the morning.

He stared at the casket for a moment, then shifted his gaze to the trees again when the captain began the ritual of folding the red, white and blue flag.

As the pastor continued to offer his final words of comfort, the captain gently placed the folded flag into the hands of Holloway's wife.

She gently moved her fingers over it.

Greg's eyes watered when she suddenly lost it, her slender shoulders shaking as she sobbed into that triangle of fabric. His attention remained on that flag and Holloway's widow until the service ended. The people around him began shifting, preparing to leave.

He didn't move.

He couldn't.

Greg's gaze traveled back to the casket.

"Goodbye, brother," he whispered. "And thank you for your sacrifice."

ALL WEEK, RENEE had been looking forward to a girls' night out with Gia and Misty at their usual place, the Polk Island Resort.

"*Tonight* is a celebration," Misty stated. "Congratulations, girl, for opening your own design house. That's huge, and we're all so very proud of you." Renee couldn't contain her grin. It felt good to be celebrating something positive.

"Yes, we are," Gia agreed. "Shelley wanted to come, but she isn't feeling well. She's been so sick with this second pregnancy. She didn't even have morning sickness with her daughter." Gia's friend Shelley, a local history teacher, often joined them on their ladies' nights.

"You look like you're doing much better," Renee said.

"I am," Gia confirmed. "I'm happy to finally be in my third trimester."

The server came to take their drink orders.

"A round of ice water with lemon, please," Misty told her. "We'll be ready to order when you return."

"You guys can order drinks if you want," Gia said. "It won't bother me."

Renee settled back in her chair, feeling more relaxed than she had in a while. "How are you handling being pregnant and working with your clients?"

"I do what I normally do—instruct them on how to do their routines. If I need assistance, I have one of the interns work with me."

The server returned with glasses of water, then wrote down their other drink selections.

Gia picked up her glass. "I don't know about y'all, but I'm hungry."

Renee chuckled. "So am I. I worked through lunch today."

"Have you heard anything from Greg?" Misty inquired.

They asked her occasionally, and she tried not to get sad thinking about him. "To be honest, I try not to think about the lack of communication. I just keep telling myself that he's fine. No news is good news, as they say."

Misty gave her a tender smile. "I know it's hard, Renee."

"I don't like these secret missions and the lack of information." She shook her head. *"I hate it."*

Gia reached over and took her hand, giving

her a light squeeze. "Hopefully, it'll be over soon."

Their server and a helper arrived with a tray carrying their entrées. After they left, Misty blessed their food, and they dug in. The warm meal made Renee feel a bit better.

"So any idea what you'd like to do for your birthday, Renee?" Gia asked.

"I haven't really thought much about it," Renee said after she'd finished chewing.

"Well, we have to celebrate." Misty grinned.

Renee gave them a polite smile, trying to let the women down gently. "I'd rather focus on my business."

Gia sliced into her smoked salmon. "Your birthday's tomorrow, and you're usually very excited about it. I know what we should do to celebrate—we should go bowling!"

"Gia, you're pregnant," Renee uttered. "So you won't be able to bowl. What's the fun in that?"

"C'mon… Trey and Leon can give you all the competition you want," Misty said. "And I can bowl, too."

Renee and Gia burst into laughter.

"What's so funny?"

"Misty, you throw the ball. You're supposed to *roll* it," Renee said, laughing at her friend's technique—or lack of it. She smiled. "I just wish Greg was here. He's not very good, either, but he's good for the laughs."

"You never know… He just might surprise you," Gia responded.

Renee wasn't about to get her hopes up about Greg's return. Playing with her glass, she responded, "I doubt he'll be here for my birthday. He didn't think he'd be gone a week, and it's going on the third week and he's still not back."

"Have faith in Greg," Gia encouraged. "He wants this discharge as much as you do."

Renee took a sip of her water. "That's not the problem."

Gia wiped her mouth with her napkin before asking, "Then what is it?"

"I've done a lot of research about this stop-loss policy." She'd probably spent too many nights at home reading up on it, when she wasn't working on her designs. "I've learned that Greg can actually be recalled back into the service at *any time*. As much as I care about him, I don't think I can be with a man who doesn't have control over his own life. Greg tries not to show it, but he loves his job. He belongs with his brothers-in-arms. Deep down, I really believe that he'll come to regret it if he goes through with the discharge." The last thing she wanted was to hold him back from something he loved. She cared for him too much to do that.

Misty and Gia exchanged a look of confusion but didn't respond. Thankfully, the topic soon turned to happier things, and they finished their night in good spirits.

Later, at home, Renee secured all the doors and windows, then turned on the security system.

After jumping into the shower, she slipped on a pair of pajama pants and a long-sleeved top. Then she climbed into bed.

Renee checked her phone and sighed in frustration. Nothing from Greg—but then, she hadn't really expected to hear from him. She tried not to be upset, because it really wasn't his fault. She hoped the operation went well and that no one had been harmed.

"HAVE YOU MADE any special plans for today?" Kayla inquired after they'd finished a meeting with their patternmaker.

"No, I haven't," Renee responded. "Just going to pretend this is nothing more than another day."

Frowning, Kayla asked, "Why would you

do that? Birthdays are special. They're to be celebrated."

An image of Greg formed in Renee's mind. "The one person I want to celebrate with isn't here with me. He did send me a text at midnight wishing me happy birthday. I didn't see it until this morning." She'd been so happy to hear from him, yet it reminded her of how empty her days felt without him. Now she just wanted to get through today as painlessly as possible. Her fashion house had kept her going these past few weeks—kept her positive—and she intended to stay focused on that.

"But you have a lot of friends and family on the island to help you celebrate your birthday, Renee," Kayla insisted. "You really should at least go out to dinner or something."

Picking up her tote, she said, "I'll think about it. But honestly, I'm just not in a party mood."

"I hope you'll change your mind."

I doubt it. But she smiled at her assistant anyway.

On the way home later that day, she made one stop after crossing the bridge to the island.

She parked in front of the boutique and got out of her vehicle.

"Happy birthday," her staff yelled in unison when she stepped inside.

"What in the world is going on?" she asked, looking at the beautifully decorated cake and brightly colored gift bag on the counter. "Jade called me and said I needed to come to check on some items that had been damaged…" Renee looked around at her employees, then back at the manager. "Did you just say that to get me here?"

Nodding, Jade said, "Guilty. This is your *born* day. I couldn't believe it when Kayla said you were working. You should've at least taken the day off."

"I came by here to see what was going on with the ready-to-wear pieces, and then I'd planned to work from home the rest of the day."

Lucy sighed. "I hope you don't expect me to work on my birthday next month."

Renee laughed. "I don't." She heard the door open and glanced over her shoulder. "Hey, Gia."

"Happy birthday, beautiful!" Her friend grinned. "Ooh, what a lovely cake."

"Thank you," Renee said. "It's from my thoughtful employees." She looked back at her staff, touched that they'd thought of her today.

"I saw your car and stopped by to make sure we're on for bowling tonight," Gia said.

"Is this your low-key way of trying to celebrate my birthday?" Renee teased. "Because I'm really not in the mood for a party," she continued honestly.

"It's just bowling, and I refuse to take *no* for an answer."

"Gia…"

"You're coming with us."

Renee gave in. "*Fine*. But I'm only doing this because you're pregnant and I don't want to hurt your feelings."

Gia beamed. "Whatever works."

Jade and Lucy burst into laughter. "Doesn't look like your family's letting you off the hook," Jade said.

Renee sighed. "No, they're not." She pasted on a smile. "At least I get the pleasure of beating them all tonight at the bowling alley."

Jade waved that off. "You're gonna have the best time tonight. I can feel it."

Renee picked up her keys, saying, "All right, Miss Optimistic All the Time. I'm heading home for the rest of the day."

Renee spent a peaceful and productive afternoon at home, and four hours later, she was back in town and parking her car near the entrance of the bowling alley. She got out and headed for the door.

As soon as she walked inside, Renee was directed to one of the private rooms. *What? Why are we bowling in a private room?*

She opened the door.

"Surprise!"

Renee jumped.

She was both shocked and overjoyed to see everyone gathered here, including her employees. Even her parents had flown in.

"Oh wow…" Renee uttered as her heartbeat slowly returned to normal. Her gaze bounced around the room at all her family and friends. "I definitely wasn't expecting this."

"Happy birthday, cousin!" Trey yelled from where he stood.

She smiled at him. "I told y'all that I didn't want a party," she whispered when Gia walked up to her.

"We only helped out," she whispered back. "This isn't on us."

Renee glanced over at Leon's wife. "I bet this was Misty's idea."

Trey chuckled. "Nope, she didn't do anything but make your birthday cake."

"I'm pretty sure Aunt Eleanor didn't plan this party," Renee stated with her arms folded across her chest. "If it wasn't Leon or Misty… and if it wasn't you or Trey…then who is responsible for all this?"

CHAPTER NINETEEN

"THE PARTY WAS my idea."

Greg was pleased that he'd been able to time his entrance perfectly. He glanced over at his mother beside him and smiled before returning his attention to Renee.

She stared up at him as if in shock—mouth open, a look of complete surprise on her face. "I can't believe it. You're here… *You're back.*"

Embracing her, Greg whispered, "I told you I wouldn't miss your birthday."

She clung to him as if her life depended on it. "I'm so happy to see you. How are you here? When did you come home?"

He kissed her.

"When did you get back?" Renee asked a second time, still looking a bit dazed.

"I returned stateside last week, but I had to take care of something before coming to the island."

She looked around. "How were you able to pull off this party?"

"I couldn't have done any of this without Trey and Gia's help." He smiled. "I was hoping I'd be here in time, but I didn't want to wait till the last minute to plan it."

She shook her head. "I had no idea about any of this."

Greg chuckled. "That's the point."

Renee turned to his mother. "It's so nice to see you again, Mrs. Bowman. Thank you for being here tonight."

The woman squeezed her shoulder. "I wouldn't have missed this for the world."

Renee placed a hand on Greg's cheek. "I can't believe it."

He relished the feel of her soft hands on his face. He'd missed her lips…heck, he'd missed everything about Renee. Greg hadn't been sure what her reaction to his return would be, but it came as a relief that she seemed very happy to see him.

"I could stand here holding you in my arms like this all night, but this is supposed to be a bowling party."

Renee chuckled. "I'm still processing."

"Let's bowl," Greg said. "Maybe I'll win a game or two since you're a bit distracted right now."

She lifted a brow. "You can hope." She

turned to her guests. "Let's get this game going."

"Greg, you're a brave soul," Trey said when they walked past him. "Renee is the bowling champion in this family."

"After me," Leon proclaimed.

Laughing, Renee dismissed his words with a wave of her hand. "Whatever."

Greg chose his ball. "All right, sweetheart. Be gentle."

RENEE WAS OVERJOYED to see that Greg was home safe. A small part of her wanted to be angry with him for not letting her know he'd returned last week, but now that he was back, she decided it didn't matter. He was safe.

After beating him at two games, Greg gave up and they decided to let someone else play. He and Renee walked over to the buffet table to get food.

She sat down facing him. "I still can't believe you're here." She dipped a drumette into ranch dressing. "This is the best birthday present ever." And she meant it. Despite the hardships of the past few weeks, her relief at seeing Greg again overtook everything else.

"I'm glad to see that you're enjoying your party," he said.

She cleaned her hands on a wet wipe. "You're here and my family's here, so yes— I'm having a blast. And the food is delicious."

He glanced at the spread. "I asked Misty to select all your favorites."

She smiled. "You're always so thoughtful."

He held her gaze. "I didn't like leaving you so abruptly," Greg responded. "But I didn't have a choice. That's all over now. Outside of taking my mother back to Hinesville, that's it. I'm here to stay."

Her chest expanded at his words. "Are you serious? You're here to stay?"

"Yep. I'm a civilian."

Renee wanted to shout for joy but managed to contain herself. There was still the idea that he could be recalled back into service. She tried to dismiss the thought, but it stayed in the back of her mind.

While she ate, Greg excused himself and went over to speak to Trey. The two men left the room, likely to catch up.

Gia eased into the booth across from her. "If I get any bigger, I won't be able to fit in one of these." She chuckled. "Anyway, you look very happy."

"That's because I'm ecstatic. Greg just told me that he's home safe—for good. He's a civilian now." Renee wanted to be happy, to believe him, yet she sighed. "But we both know that status can change at any time."

"Only good thoughts." Gia patted her hand. "It's your birthday."

Renee pushed her empty plate to the side. "I know. I have to change my thought behavior. I'm trying."

"I know you are, and it's going to take time. But this is your night, and I want you to enjoy it. Relax and just have a good time."

Renee nodded, then glanced around. Greg and Trey were still gone.

"If you're looking for my husband and Greg, they're probably outside chatting," Gia offered.

"Maybe I should go look for them," Renee said. "If we let them, they'll spend the entire night talking." And she wanted to have more time with Greg to herself—she'd missed him so much.

She got up and headed toward the exit.

Outside, Renee spotted them near Trey's SUV. She was close enough to hear Greg's deep voice say, "I buried a brother last week."

"I'm sorry," Trey murmured.

"You don't understand," Greg said, swiping a hand over his face. "He pushed me out of the way, and the bullet hit him. If he hadn't—I'd be the one dead. Holloway saved my life."

Renee felt her body go numb. He had almost been shot. Someone had died saving him.

She pressed a hand to her chest, her stomach suddenly sinking. Renee went back inside. She knew without a doubt that Greg was never going to tell her about this. This was why he hadn't let her know when he was back in the States. He'd had to attend a funeral. They'd vowed to never have secrets between them. Right now, there was a huge one staring them in the face.

Why hadn't he told her? Maybe he didn't think she was strong enough to handle this sort of news.

Feeling numb, she walked back inside the building.

"Did you find them?" Gia asked.

Renee put on a bright smile. "You were right. They're outside, yapping away."

Greg returned to her table not too long after. "Sorry. I didn't mean to be gone so long."

"It's fine. I'm sure the two of you had a lot to discuss."

He must have detected something in her tone because he asked, "Are you okay?"

She pressed a hand to her chest again, trying to calm herself. "Yeah. I'm fine."

There was concern in his gaze as he asked, "Are you sure?"

Renee pasted on another smile. "I'm good. I may have eaten too much. You don't have to worry about me."

After the birthday cake, it was time for her to open her gifts. She was touched by everyone's kindness, but she was also ready to go home. She wanted to curl up in her own space after overhearing Greg and Trey's conversation.

"Come sit over here," Greg told her. He handed her a gift bag.

Renee stole a peek at him, then turned her attention back to the guests. She was doing her best to hide the fact that she was upset with him and kept it up through the gift-giving.

When she had finished opening her presents, Greg helped Renee stand up and turned her around so that she was facing him. For a moment, he just stood there, staring at her with such warmth in his eyes. Finally, he said, "I'm sure you know that I love you, Renee Rothchild."

The words crashed over her. He'd never said it before, but she knew he did. She found herself getting lost in his eyes and struggled to maintain some control over her emotions. "Greg…"

"Please hear me out," he pleaded. "I've loved you from the moment we met, but you made it clear that you didn't date men in the military." Greg paused for a moment before continuing. "You stood your ground and made me wait until I decided it was time for me to get out. Don't get me wrong—I was fine with waiting for you because you're in my blood, my soul, my bones."

Renee gazed at him, her emotions a wild raging river inside her. There was a time when she'd been ready to open her heart to him, but now it seemed far riskier than anything she'd ever done in her life. This was all too much, too fast.

Greg gazed back at her, emotion burning in his eyes. "I have never been a man to beg, but if I have to beg, I will—because you're my life."

Renee's thoughts were whirling as she tried to figure out exactly how to respond. She cared for him so much. He'd become her best friend. A bright and hopeful joy fluttered inside her like a trapped bird trying to break free, but she was afraid to let go because she'd finally realized the truth: she was not the right woman for Greg. And yet she didn't want to hurt him.

Greg pulled out a small black velvet box.

Her breath caught in her throat as he opened it up to reveal a stunning engagement ring.

"I love you, and I want you to be my wife," he said. "You only have to walk into a room, and everything else fades away completely for me." Her eyes filled with tears. "Will you marry me?"

Renee swallowed hard, and a single tear rolled down her cheek. She could feel the eyes of everyone on them. She struggled to control her breathing. She didn't want to embarrass him or break his heart in public. But she couldn't say yes.

It would be wrong.

Greg peered into her face. "Renee?"

She glanced at Aunt Eleanor, whose tears mirrored her own—but for what she supposed were different reasons. Her chest started to feel tight and her breathing shallower. "I need to get out of here."

And she rushed out.

She got into her car and drove away. Renee had no idea where she was going—she just knew she needed to get away from everyone.

Instead of going home, she decided to go to

the boutique. She figured Greg might come to the condo, and right now, she didn't have the emotional capacity to have a much-needed conversation with him.

Making sure she locked the door behind her, Renee went to the back office. She hadn't expected Greg to propose, especially so soon. They hadn't been dating that long; she needed more time. She should've stuck to her decision to not date him. Then she wouldn't be sitting in her former office, crying her eyes out.

What a mess. She was pretty sure Greg would never want to see her again.

CHAPTER TWENTY

"I DON'T BELIEVE THIS," Greg uttered to himself. "She actually turned down my proposal." Right now, he was sinking in a puddle of rejection. His mind was a swirling sea of sorrow and confusion.

"Technically, she didn't say anything," Trey stated.

"Not saying anything and running off is an answer. It tells me that she clearly doesn't want to marry me." Greg's heart was in his throat.

The atmosphere around him had suddenly become shaming. Embarrassing. Excruciating. His chest seized as he tried to ignore the sinking sensation in the pit of his stomach.

"I feel like such a fool right now," he whispered.

"I think Renee just needs time," Trey responded. "I know she loves you."

Greg shook his head. "Naw… I don't think so. I brought my mom here because I knew she wouldn't want to miss it. I need to get out of here, too. I'm going to go for a drive."

"We'll drive your mother back to the house," Trey assured him. "Greg, don't give up on my cousin. Renee—"

"You're not going to like what I'm about to say, but right now, I don't want to hear her name." He couldn't believe what had just happened.

He strode over to his car in brisk steps, unlocked the door and got in.

Greg drove out of the parking lot and onto the street.

Never in a million years did he think that Renee would say no to his proposal. He'd felt sure she was on the same page as him about their feelings for each other. The past few weeks apart had been terrible—for both of them, he'd thought—and he didn't want to be without her again. After Holloway's funeral, after seeing how broken his wife was, he'd bought the ring. He wanted to spend the rest of his life with Renee. His homecoming and discharge should've made everything easier, not more complicated. His heart felt like it had shattered into thousands of tiny little pieces. The word *hurt* didn't come close to defining the pain he felt.

Greg had fought for everything he wanted in his life. Deep inside, he knew Renee was worth the fight. But did she want to be fought for? If she didn't, then he had no choice but to walk away.

Still pondering that question, Greg drove to the beach and parked in the parking lot of the shopping mart. He sat in the vehicle, recalling the memories he and Renee shared, their plans for the future. It had all been for nothing.

How can I stay on this island after this?

He didn't think he could live so close to the woman who'd broken his heart. Maybe he should move to Hinesville.

I gave Trey my word that I'd work with him at the museum, but I can't. Not after this. I'll tell him tomorrow.

WHEN IT CAME to love, Renee knew it was foolish to dream.

Foolish to hope.

It had been foolish to fall in love with someone who was so far out of her reach.

Greg possessed every quality she looked for in a man, and she couldn't remember a time when he hadn't shown her how much he cared for her.

She was surprised to find Greg's mother

waiting outside her door when she arrived home from the boutique. She cleared her throat loudly, then asked, "Mrs. Bowman, how long have you been here?"

Marilee shrugged. "I don't know. I just couldn't let this night pass without having a conversation with you."

Renee unlocked her door and stepped aside for her to enter. They sat down in the living room.

"I'm really sorry about tonight," Renee said. "This is not how I thought this night would end."

"I can truly say, neither did I," Marilee responded. "I haven't talked to my son, but I know Greg is heartbroken."

"Mrs. Bowman, you have to understand that I never meant to hurt him. I had no idea Greg was going to propose marriage."

The woman sighed. "Yet you *did* hurt him."

Renee's stomach clenched at the words. "I love Greg, but I have to be honest with myself about what I can and can't handle."

"I understand," Marilee said gently. "Greg told me about the panic disorder."

"Every time he left on a mission, I was so worried about him," Renee said. "I agreed to date him because he was getting discharged.

Then that didn't happen, and I had so much anxiety with this last mission..." She paused a moment, trying to keep the overwhelming feelings at bay, and then continued. "Right before Greg proposed, I went looking for him. He was outside talking to Trey, and I found out he was almost shot. Another Raider pushed him out of the way. He didn't make it. I panicked over how close he came to dying." Thinking about it even hours later left her stomach in knots. She put her head in her hands.

"I can understand that. I was shocked when he told me what happened, but I had to move past it. He made it home safe, and I'm thankful."

Renee glanced up. He'd told his mother, he'd told Trey, but he hadn't said anything to her. In truth, though, she hadn't given him a chance to say much of anything.

"When I lost my husband," Marilee continued, "I didn't think I'd ever get over his death, but what kept me going was my son and memories of my time with Carl. He was my first love—and to be honest, he is the only man I'll *ever* love. I'm thankful for the time we had together."

"If you had to do it all over again, would you?" Renee asked.

"In a heartbeat," Marilee responded, without hesitation.

She assessed the woman sitting across from her. "Even with losing your husband the way that you did?"

"Renee, it's not the amount of time I had with Carl. I cherish the *quality* of that time together. We didn't waste it—we loved and lived every moment as if it were our last."

She watched Marilee in amazement. She'd never thought of it like that. "I wish I were more like you," she admitted. "I love Greg so much, but I can't handle the stress of the military recalling him back into active duty. I can't just sit without wondering where he is and if he's okay. And then I have to wonder if he's keeping things from me because he's afraid I'm not strong enough to handle them."

"Honey, you can't control what happens in this world. My son could be standing right beside you, and something could unexpectedly take him away from you."

"This is true," Renee murmured. She knew Marilee was right—no amount of worrying about Greg would keep him safe.

"I know Greg loves you, but you have to decide just how much you love him. Is it enough to enjoy whatever time the two of you have left in this world? Or will you allow your fear to keep you apart? If you decide on the latter, I believe you'll always wonder what could've been. You will find it won't be so easy to just sit on the sidelines, watching life pass you by."

She let her shoulders slump. "I do want to talk to Greg, but I'm sure he's too upset to have a conversation with me."

"Give him some time," Marilee advised. "I like you, Renee, and I hope you and my son are able to work things out."

"I want the same thing. I really do. But I'm not so sure it's possible. However, I don't want there to be any tension between us. He's going to be working with Trey. I'd like for us to at least be friends." Even that sounded impossible to her after tonight. It wasn't like she could just stop loving Greg. It would take time to sheath her emotions.

"Well, I've had my say, I should leave you to think about what it is that you want."

Marilee got up, and Renee walked her to the door. "Thank you for being so kind. I really feel awful about the way I handled the proposal."

"Maybe you both still need some time." Greg's mother patted her hand in a nurturing way. "Marriage is a huge decision."

That's the truth.

Marilee had given Renee a lot to consider. Hurting Greg made her feel dreadful. She'd had no idea he'd planned to propose at her birthday party. She hadn't even known about the celebration.

After Marilee left, Gia called. Renee clicked to accept. "Hey, you okay?"

"No, I'm not," Renee answered honestly, her voice breaking. "I embarrassed Greg, and that's not what I intended at all. He probably hates me now."

Gia sighed. "Greg could never hate you."

"Is he with you?"

"No. Trey tried to convince him to go back to the house, but he said he wanted to go for a drive."

She could understand him leaving shortly after she had. "His mother was just here, talking to me."

"I let her take my car to come see you," Gia told her. "I hope it was a good conversation."

"Yes… I hope he's okay." Renee was concerned about him. She didn't think he should be driving around in what she imagined was his current state of mind. "I wish I knew where he was."

"He may already be at the house, but I don't know for sure."

"I feel terrible about this, Gia."

"I will only say this—you and Greg need to talk, unless you're ready to just let him walk out of your life."

Renee agreed. "I owe him a conversation. I'm just not sure he'll ever want to hear what I have to say. His mother just told me to give him some space."

"I don't see him giving up on you so easily," Gia said. "I do think you need to give him time to process what happened, though."

"I'm willing to do that, but I don't want to hold off on apologizing. He deserves it." She ended the call with Gia and went up to bed.

Sleep did not come easy.

Renee sat cross-legged in the middle of the mattress, phone in her left hand.

She called Greg twice.

It went straight to voice mail both times.

She wasn't surprised that he wasn't answering her calls, but she refused to wait another moment to offer an apology. She couldn't shake the feeling of sorrow that he was out there somewhere, hurt and alone.

After the third call, she decided to leave a message.

"Hello, Greg," Renee said. "I want to apologize for the way I responded to your proposal. It was beautiful… Everything was perfect, but in that moment, I panicked. I think we need a day or so to think about things, then we should sit down and have a discussion. I'm willing to do this if you are." She reached for what else to say, then went with the simplest truth. "I'm sorry. I hope you'll call me soon."

She ended the call.

"See you later, Greg," she whispered into the night.

GREG GLANCED DOWN and listened to the voice-mail message she'd left, but he wasn't ready to talk to her yet. The way Renee had treated him was humiliating. His mother had tried to discuss what happened at the party when he got home, but Greg wasn't ready to do so.

The phone rang.

It wasn't Renee. He didn't feel like talking to anyone, so he ignored the call.

Greg had a feeling that Renee wouldn't call again after her last message. She would wait until he was prepared to have that conversation. At this point, he wasn't sure there was anything to discuss. She didn't want to marry him.

The next morning, Greg went downstairs to find Trey and Gia in the living room.

"Hey, y'all," he said.

"How are you feeling?" Trey asked.

"Like a fool."

"Greg, Renee loves you," Gia stated. "I hope you know that. Have faith in that love."

"I'm not sure what to believe anymore."

"One thing's for sure—you and my cousin need to sit down and have a conversation about your relationship," Trey advised.

"Maybe at some point," he said. "But right now, I'm just not ready." He knew his friend was right, but it would do neither him nor Renee any good to rush that conversation, especially while he was still licking his wounds from last night.

Rubbing her swollen belly, Gia shifted her position on the sofa. "Do you really think it's a good idea to keep postponing this talk?"

Greg shrugged. "I don't know what to say right now."

Gia smiled softly. "Maybe you should just listen to what she has to say."

"Gia, I saw her face. Her body language… It was clear to me that she and I aren't on the same page when it comes to us. I have to accept the truth."

Something grabbed at his chest like a sharp talon. Its grip tightened and squeezed. The thought of losing Renee made his insides feel hollow and empty, as if they had been scraped out with something sharp. Greg's chest retracted in another suffocating spasm.

He grabbed his keys. "I'll be back in a couple of hours."

Greg drove to the gym to work off some of his unsettled feelings.

He ran ten miles on the treadmill, pushed a few weights around and did a hundred abdominal crunches, but none of it helped ease his pain.

Greg was angry—with himself, mostly. He shouldn't have pushed her into a relationship before she was ready or proposed so quickly. It had been selfish, and now he was paying the price.

THE NEXT DAY, Greg took his mother back to Hinesville. Upon his return, he drove to the waterfront and sat in the parking lot a few yards from the corner grocery store. He glanced up in time to see Renee walking toward his car with a couple of shopping bags in her hands.

He knew he could not continue to avoid her

for much longer. The island was only so big, and it was futile to delay the inevitable.

He let down his window as she stopped in front of it.

"I wanted to give you some space," Renee began, "but running into you like this… Could we talk?"

"I'm not sure I'm in the right headspace," he admitted. Greg felt like he needed more time.

"Will you at least give me the chance to explain?" she pleaded. "Just hear me out, *please*. I'm not asking you to change your mind about me or anything."

He sighed. "We can talk in the car."

Renee walked over to the passenger side and got in.

"I heard the message you left on my phone," Greg said. "What else is there to say?"

"I know you're angry with me. And I'm sorry for embarrassing you. Everything just happened so fast, and I panicked." She shifted in her seat. "Before the proposal, I went looking for you, and I overheard your conversation with Trey. You can't imagine how I felt learning that you were almost killed."

That surprised him. That conversation was meant for him and Trey. "I was going to tell you about that, but I didn't think that night was the right time or place." He sighed. "As for the mission itself, I didn't have a choice. I had to join my team."

"I know, but your mission triggered me. I'm working to get better. I really am." He knew it was an uphill battle for her. "I told you when we met that I didn't have the emotional capacity to be a military wife."

"I'm a civilian now."

"That's what you say now, but you know that you can be recalled into service."

"It's highly unlikely, but it's a possibility." Greg paused a moment before continuing with the other news he should've told her before. "I might as well tell you that I also received a job offer from a government agency. At one time, it would've been the ideal job for me, but I turned it down."

She tilted her head. "What changed your mind?"

"I realized that I wanted *you* more. I—"

"Greg, if you want to take that job, then do it," Renee said, cutting him off. "I don't want to be the reason you stay on the island."

"Even if it means I'm going to be living in Washington, DC?"

"If it's what you really want to do," she said.

"You should take it." Renee glanced down at her watch. "I need to get going."

She was shutting him out again. "I thought you wanted to talk."

She looked out the passenger window. "I wanted to apologize and make sure you understood what I was feeling and why I responded the way I did."

"Apology accepted," he said. "I'm not sure I handled things right, myself. Maybe we—no, *I* rushed into this relationship. We should've taken more time to learn one another as a couple."

Renee continued to stare out the passenger window. "So…where does that leave us now?"

Greg felt like his heart was breaking all over again, but he had to be honest. "It shouldn't be this hard when two people love one another."

"I agree." She wouldn't look at him…but did her words mean she loved him, too? "I want what's best for you and me both."

What did that mean? "I have to admit that I'm really confused about what's happening between us. How did we get here, Renee?"

She faced him. "You almost got shot. Someone died on your last mission. You went through something traumatic, and you confided in my cousin. You didn't tell me because you didn't think I was strong enough to handle the truth." Her voice rose with every word.

"We were celebrating your birthday, Renee. I didn't want to ruin your night."

"Be honest with me, Greg. Were you really going to tell me that you narrowly escaped death?"

"No. I probably wouldn't have told you," he admitted. "But it's not because I view you as weak. I just didn't want to cause you any additional stress." He knew how important it was that she keep her triggers at bay.

"And you thought keeping secrets from me was the way to go?" she asked.

"I'd say I was right, judging by the way you reacted."

He glimpsed a flash of anger in her eyes. After a moment, she responded, "Sounds to me like I'm not the woman you need, Greg. I have too many issues. So I guess this is goodbye."

Now he felt anger flash through him. He didn't see how a positive outcome was forthcoming. Maybe they were right for each other—but they weren't right for each other *right now*. Greg sighed in resignation. "Goodbye, Renee."

Renee stormed into her condo, barely making it to the bedroom before collapsing in a heap of silent sobs.

She and Greg were over.

The only thing left of her fragile heart was a shadow of its former self. Perhaps it would heal over time—but never completely.

Renee vowed to focus solely on her company moving forward. It cost too much to love; the price was much too high.

From the first moment she'd set eyes on him, Renee knew she had to do her best to put Greg out of her mind. But instead of listening to the warnings echoing in her brain, she'd let her guard down. Although she *knew* he was a distraction she didn't need, she'd allowed herself to fall in love with him.

It's over. It's time to move on.

She didn't want to continue allowing the memories of him to dampen her mood. She still had a boutique and a successful design house—things were going well for her, professionally. Though none of this did anything for the heartache she felt.

Tears filled her eyes once more at the reality that she was losing the one man who'd made her feel safe, loved and special. Renee felt like she wanted the ground to open, swallow her whole and spit her out somewhere on the other side of the world.

He'd been so wonderful and supportive— why couldn't she open her heart to him fully? Why didn't she trust in his love?

CHAPTER TWENTY-ONE

"I SAW RENEE YESTERDAY," Greg blurted out at breakfast the next morning. "We just ran into each other."

Gia's head whipped up. "How did it go?" she asked.

"We broke up."

"You did *what*?" Trey questioned. "How did that happen?"

Shrugging in confusion, Greg responded, "I'm not really sure." The rest of the previous day had passed in a daze for Greg—he still didn't entirely know how they'd ended things or how he felt about it.

"Maybe it was too soon," Gia offered. "You two need to have another conversation. I've never seen two people more in love. Y'all need to stop this foolishness."

Greg sighed. "I told Renee about the job offer—I didn't tell her it was the CIA. Before I could tell her that I wasn't taking it, she told me to take the job." She'd seemed only too ready to tell him to leave and pursue a life away from her. One that didn't include them together. "Renee said she wanted me to be happy. If that were true, she would've accepted my marriage proposal."

"Greg, do you *want* to take this job?" Gia asked.

"No, I don't."

"Did you tell Renee this?" Trey inquired.

"Not really. She kind of ended the conversation at that point. She'd said she wanted to talk, but then she had to leave."

Shaking his head, Trey said, "So you two *still* need to sit down and have an open and honest conversation. I said that earlier."

"We tried and now there is no *us*. It's over," Greg said flatly.

Trey eyed his friend. "Are you going to give up just like that?"

"We both have to want this relationship to work." There was no sense in talking to Renee again when it'd only bring about the same outcome. They both needed time and space. His focus now should be on adjusting to civilian life, making next steps.

Shaking her head, Gia uttered, "I can't believe this."

"Trust me," Greg responded. "I feel like I'm

in the twilight zone." He pushed away from the table. "I'm meeting with Austin DuGrandpre this afternoon. So I'll be heading out around eleven o'clock."

Trey gave him a slight nod.

An hour later, Greg was in the car and driving to the Charleston business district, where the DuGrandpre Law Firm was located. Austin DuGrandpre had called him and asked to meet—it was a bit out of the blue, but he'd enjoy catching up with the man.

He found an empty spot on the street, leaving his car there instead of inside the attached parking deck.

Greg strolled through the lobby and made his way to the elevator. He stood there, humming softly to himself, as if that could force Renee from his thoughts. His heart still ached from their last conversation.

The elevator doors opened.

He was shocked to see Renee inside. She must have gotten on at the garage level. She looked just as surprised to see him.

It didn't help that Renee looked stunning in navy blue slacks and a crisp white shirt that would have looked severe if not for the sapphire-and-silver choker and matching earrings she wore with it. She smelled divine, and

Greg tried to disguise his deep inhalation as a regular breath as he stepped inside.

Did I just dream her into reality? He'd been thinking about her, and now she was in Charleston, on the elevator with him.

They stood staring at each other for a moment.

Well, *he* stared while Renee tried to look past him.

Greg cleared his throat. "Hello."

"Hi," she murmured.

Renee was polite, but the look in her eyes was distant. She'd obviously been trying to avoid him. As if to deter a conversation, she pulled out her iPhone and scanned through what he assumed were emails.

Despite everything, Renee still had the ability to make his heart melt at the mere sight of her. He resisted the urge to pull her into his arms even as his lips yearned to feel hers.

"I'm surprised you're still here," she said after a moment. "I figured you might be preparing to leave for D.C."

"I was never taking that job, Renee," Greg told her firmly. "You didn't let me finish. I'm not the type of person to give my word and then renege on the deal." He didn't mean to sound harsh, but her assumption needled him.

She turned to him. "I thought it was something you wanted to do."

"I'd already turned it down."

She frowned in confusion. "That's not the way I understood it. You said you didn't take it because of me."

"I turned it down right after I got back," Greg said. "It would've been like being in the military all over again, and I'd already told you that I was done with that type of work. After my last mission…I knew I'd done the right thing."

The silence hung heavy between them, so he continued. "As for our breakup, I never wanted that, either." He might as well be honest and lay everything out right now. Clearly, fate was having its way with them—forcing them together in this tight space. "I just thought we needed to take a step back and slow things down a bit. To be completely honest, I thought that was what you needed. I've been clear on what I wanted from the day we met."

She dropped her gaze. "I feel like I've made an unnecessary mess of things," Renee whispered.

"It's on both of us."

She shook her head. "This is my fault. Greg,

I have too many issues. More than you should have to deal with."

"Stop with all the excuses," he uttered. He wasn't going to allow her to become the victim in all this.

"I'm not making excuses. I'm just trying to be honest with you and communicate my feelings," she responded tersely. "But this isn't the right time or place to talk about it."

"You're right." They would run out of floors soon. "But I want to finish this conversation."

Renee met his gaze. "So do I."

After what seemed like an eternity, the elevator doors opened.

"Give me a call," Greg said before walking out.

"I guess we're going to the same place." She pointed to the sign for the DuGrandpre Law Firm. "I'm having lunch with Jadin and Jordin."

Strange coincidence, just like the elevator. "I have a meeting with Austin." He held the door open for her.

Austin was at the front desk, talking to the receptionist. "Renee, I didn't know you were coming with Greg. Good to see you, cousin."

"We're not together," she said. "I'm actually here to have lunch with your sisters." She glanced at Greg. "See you later."

Those few words gave him hope. "For sure."

"ALL THE SHIPMENTS are complete," Kayla said when Renee returned to the office a couple of hours later.

"That's great news," she responded, distracted. Greg was the last person she'd expected to run into in Charleston. Renee blamed herself for this distance between them.

While she still felt a slight resentment toward Greg for not confiding in her about his latest mission, and when he'd returned stateside, she knew he hadn't because he felt she'd overreact. Turned out, he was right. That was exactly what had happened.

She'd never be able to undo the damage done in that moment when she'd run from him instead of talking to him, but it also felt good knowing she'd been honest. She was always looking for reassurances that everything would be perfect, but this could only exist in her head. The reality was that bad things happened; life wasn't something anyone could control. She had to stop looking at the worst-case scenarios and focus on the positive. She had no idea when she'd become a glass-half-empty kind of girl.

Kayla's voice cut into her thoughts.

"I'm sorry...what did you say?" Renee asked her assistant.

"Everything okay with you?"

She faced Kayla. "I saw Greg earlier, and things are still a bit awkward. But we're trying to sort out what happened."

Kayla looked surprised, then said, "I have a feeling everything is going to work out between you two."

Renee smiled. She wished she could be as confident as Kayla about her situation. Greg had taken time to plan a party because he'd wanted to make her birthday special... She'd never wanted to hurt him. Why couldn't she have just taken that leap of faith and said yes to him that night?

The number of items on her to-do list forced Renee to abandon thoughts of that for the rest of the day. She couldn't let her personal life interfere with her business. She'd worked too hard and sacrificed too much to lose the boutique and design house.

"I'm glad to have our first orders to the department stores fulfilled," Kayla was saying. "We've had a busy few weeks."

"Yeah, it's been a bit hectic, but I think we've finally found our rhythm." That, at least, was something she could be proud of.

"Do you want to discuss the ideas for the fall/winter fashion show in February?" Kayla asked.

Images of Greg carrying boxes and helping to fill swag bags ran rampant in her mind.

"Renee?"

She glanced over at Kayla. "Huh?"

"I asked if you were ready to go over some ideas for Fashion Week. The fall/winter collection. We need to discuss a theme for the fashion show."

Renee picked up a pen. "Yeah, let's come up with a theme." She focused her thoughts on work for the rest of the day.

Later at home, she lay back in the tub, eyes closed. She wanted to make things right between her and Greg. He was a good man, and while she felt she didn't deserve him, she couldn't see her life without him in it. Renee had never been one to fight for a relationship. When it ended, she simply walked away and never looked back.

She thought she was protecting herself in doing so. But maybe she'd been wrong.

She'd just slipped on a pair of jeans and a shirt when her phone rang.

She answered it. "Hey, Aunt Eleanor. How are you?"

"I'm fine. I was wondering if you'd come by here on your way home. I'd like to talk to you."

"I'm at my place, so I'll be over in about five minutes," Renee replied.

Why does she want to see me? I guess I'll know soon enough.

She got dressed and walked the short distance to Eleanor and Rusty's house.

Her aunt swung the door open. "I'm glad you stopped by. You've been on my mind," she said. "C'mon in."

"You asked me to come, Aunt Eleanor." Renee wondered if she was having an episode. Glancing around, she asked, "Is Marie here?"

"Naw, just me."

Renee quickly texted Rusty.

He responded that he was on the way home. Aunt Eleanor's companion had had a family emergency.

"Do you remember calling me, Auntie?" Renee asked.

"I call you all the time," she replied. "How are things with you and Greg?"

Renee's brows rose in surprise. She hadn't

expected her aunt to remember what had happened at the bowling alley. She usually couldn't recall what happened a day or hours before. "Why do you ask?"

"I saw him earlier at Trey's house. He looked troubled—heartbroken, is more like it." Aunt Eleanor scanned her face. "Now that I'm looking at you, you got that same look."

"Do you remember my birthday party?"

"Yeah. I was there. It was yesterday, wasn't it?"

Not quite, though it sure felt that way.

"Well, Greg asked me to marry him. I didn't give him an answer. I just ran away."

Aunt Eleanor frowned in confusion. "Why would you do a fool thing like that?"

Her aunt had never been one to hold her tongue. "I can't really explain it, Auntie. I just panicked."

"You love him, don't you?"

"Yes, ma'am. More than I ever thought I could love anyone. But I let fear get between us." She wanted to be open to loving him fully and completely…but she didn't know how.

"Renee, one thing I know is that tomorrow isn't promised to any of us. I can't remember a lot of stuff sometimes. I could worry about the day I wake up and have no memory of this house, Rusty or you. Instead, I just try to get through the day. I have a journal where I write down the good things that happen. I write about the stuff that bothers me, too. But mostly, I *live*. I don't give a thought to the bad things that can happen. I look to make memories. Do you understand what I'm trying to say?"

"I do, Auntie," Renee responded. She wished she could just forget all the bad things happening around her and focus on the good. She wanted to break the chains of fear and finally let go completely. She wanted to enjoy her life.

"If I were you, I'd go to Greg and work things out," the older woman said. "The two of you belong together."

She made it sound so simple. Could it be? Fighting back sudden tears, Renee embraced her aunt. "I love you so much."

"Ahh… I love you, too." Her aunt stood up. "I think I'll give Rusty a break and make dinner." She gave a short chuckle. "I love that man, but his cooking leaves something to be desired. Now, the man can grill and smoke up some meat."

"Why don't I stay and help you?" Renee asked. She knew Rusty didn't want Aunt Eleanor cooking. Even her doctor had advised against it. "I could use some cooking tips."

She'd just taken the baked chicken out of the oven when Rusty arrived home.

"She wanted to make you dinner, so I convinced her to give me a quick lesson. The food might not be as good as hers."

"I'm sure everything is delicious," he reassured Renee with a grateful smile.

"How is she doing with having Marie here?" she asked Rusty while Aunt Eleanor busied herself with plating the food. Her aunt hadn't initially responded well to having someone in her home watching over her. It had taken Leon and Trey to get her to acknowledge that she couldn't be home alone.

"They seem to get along well," Rusty responded. "Eleanor don't like Marie in her kitchen, though. She always says it ain't right to have a strange woman in your kitchen. She thinks she's giving Marie cooking lessons, too."

"Y'all gwine stand there and talk all night, or you gonna come eat?" Aunt Eleanor said from the entryway of the family room.

"We're coming, honey," Rusty told her.

Throughout dinner, Renee thought about the

advice her aunt had given her. It mirrored the advice she'd received from Trey and the others.

So why am I not listening?

GREG SAT IN a booth at the back of the café, going through the real estate section of the newspaper, looking for a property to purchase. He'd decided to eat dinner out to give Trey and Gia some alone time. He didn't like being a third wheel.

He also felt uncomfortable witnessing their displays of love, their complete and absolute happiness as they prepared for the arrival of their first child. Right now, it was just too much to endure for a heartbroken man. Besides, he'd spent the entire day with his friend, going over the Rothchilds' history and artifacts to prepare for his new job at the museum.

A waitress brought his meal to the table.

"Thanks," he said.

Greg glanced around but didn't see Misty, so he assumed she wasn't working tonight. A part of him was relieved. He didn't really want to talk to anyone, especially about Renee. He'd decided to increase his focus on settling down and finding a permanent home.

He circled several listings.

Greg planned to call the real estate agent in

the morning to schedule tours of the ones he selected.

A touch of sadness washed over him. Looking for a house was something he'd hoped to do with Renee. Although at the time, she'd had no idea he was going to propose marriage.

The question of whether to fight for Renee was still at the forefront of his mind. He still wasn't sure if she wanted to be with him, and without that assurance, he didn't think he could move forward. At least she was open to finishing the conversation they'd started in the elevator earlier. He would get his answers soon.

Greg didn't like being in a space of uncertainty. Before he made Polk Island his permanent home, he needed to know where he and Renee stood. While he didn't want to back out of working with Trey, Greg wasn't sure he could face seeing the woman he loved but couldn't have every single day.

He glanced down at the newspaper. *Maybe I should hold off on calling the Realtor until after Renee and I talk.*

If things didn't work out between them, Greg had a backup plan. He could move back to Hinesville like he and his mother had discussed. He could work as a civilian at Ft. Stewart… He had options, but none of them compared to what he'd found on Polk Island.

CHAPTER TWENTY-TWO

RENEE COULDN'T SLEEP, so she'd gotten up early enough to watch the sunrise from her patio.

Dressed in Nike activewear and sneakers, she left around seven o'clock for an early-morning run along the water's edge.

Every now and then, she'd stop and just admire the beauty of the ocean. The lacy waves wafted up and down, almost matching the steady rhythm that echoed in her heart. She welcomed the cool October breeze across her face.

Renee glanced up, watching birds flying above without a care in the world. That was what she wanted—a life where she was only concerned with the day ahead of her. Nothing more.

Fear is a choice.

If this is true, then I choose not to be afraid. I choose to live my life with intention. I choose to embrace each moment of happiness.

Her thoughts attempted to shift toward the negative.

Happiness isn't permanent. Bad things happen. Look what happened in the past...

Renee glanced around her, looking for rocks. She found some of varying sizes and picked them up. She threw the smallest one into the ocean. "I cast out the belief that I am not worthy of my success. I don't need the validation of my parents or anyone."

She tossed a slightly bigger rock into the water next. "I cast out the pain of the past. I've held on to it far too long. It's time to let it go but keep the lessons I've learned to help me make better choices in the future."

Renee picked up the largest of the rocks left and, with all her strength, threw it into the water. "I cast out the irrational fears that have shaped my life and decisions for so long. No longer will I be ruled by fear. I'm taking back my life."

She felt a peace she hadn't felt in a long time overcome her.

Smiling, she walked across the sand toward her condo.

Renee didn't know what her future looked like where Greg was concerned, but she wasn't worried about it. She only had to get through today.

She was surprised to see him at her door when she turned the corner. "Hey."

"I know that I should've called you instead of just popping up. I was heading to the beach for a run, and before I realized, I was here. I'm hoping we can finally finish our conversation."

She unlocked the door. "Sure. C'mon in."

Inside, Renee asked, "Have you eaten?"

"No."

"I worked up an appetite during my run, so I'm going to make something," she said. "We can talk while we eat."

"What are you making?" Greg asked.

"Scrambled eggs, bacon."

"Works for me." He entered the kitchen and washed his hands. "Why don't I help?"

Renee chuckled. "You ain't slick, Gregory Bowman. I know you don't like the way I cook bacon."

"You like yours hard, and I like mine soft." He gave a slight shrug. "No big deal."

She rolled her eyes. "Fine...you're on bacon duty." She hadn't expected them to fall so easily back into friendship mode.

"I came by because I will never stop caring about you, Renee."

"I feel the same way," she responded as she concentrated on the eggs.

Fifteen minutes later, they sat at the kitchen table, eating.

"Greg, I'm really sorry for the way I reacted after you went through the trouble of planning such a beautiful proposal. I shouldn't have run off like that."

He set down his fork. "I wish you'd pulled me to the side to discuss what you overheard. If I'd known, I probably wouldn't have proposed that night."

"I realized I never once said how sorry I was to hear about your teammate. It's terrible that anyone had to die at all." She shook her head. "I heard you tell Trey that he saved your life. The thought that you had been that close to death really scared me. In that moment, it overshadowed the reality—that you'd come home. That you'd made it back to me."

"It was as if he somehow knew what was about to happen," Greg said. "I didn't see or hear a thing. No one on the team did. But Holloway… He must've felt something wasn't right. He pushed me down just as the bullet…"

"How are *you* doing?" Renee asked when it became clear he couldn't finish.

When Greg looked at her, she saw the pain in his gaze. "I was right beside him…the bullet was just that close. It was in that moment that

I knew real fear. I realized that those days for me are over. While I can't control when my life will come to an end, one thing I know for sure is that I want to spend it with you, Renee. That one bullet could've put an end to our story, but it didn't. I have Holloway to thank for that. He was a great guy. The kind of person who loved life. He left behind a wife—they'd been married just a few months."

"I can't even imagine," Renee said as she reached over and covered his hand with her own. "I'm so sorry."

"I don't want *this* to be the end of our story, either. I can't lose you."

Her eyes filled with tears. "You haven't lost me, Greg."

"So…where do we go from here?"

"I've been doing a lot of reflecting," Renee said. "To be honest, I felt like I didn't deserve you. That's why I couldn't say yes. You are such a good man, and you've been so good to me. You always make me feel so safe. I think I was relying on you for that security. I was afraid to just live—that's the best way I can explain it." She shook her head again. "This morning, I realized I've been living so cautiously, I'd forgotten how to enjoy life. When I was a little girl, I did some reckless stuff.

Like, my friends and I used to stop the elevator between floors. We would either climb up or try to swing our bodies to the floor below."

"That's crazy," Greg uttered. "I can't see you doing that at all."

"Hey, *I* can't believe I did it. I guess my point is—when I was younger, I took a lot of chances that could've led to dire circumstances."

"I'm sure we can all say we've been reckless in some way," Greg said. "When Holloway died, I knew it was definitely time to leave the military."

"I can't believe I'm saying this, but I hope you won't let fear hold you back from what you love. You loved being a Raider."

"The truth is that I don't have it in me. MARSOC was my father's dream. He was willing to die for his brothers. I wanted to honor him, but when Holloway died, I realized I'm not prepared to knowingly make that kind of sacrifice. It was time to walk away."

She loved him even more in this moment. It took a lot to be honest in this way. "My respect for you just went up ten levels. You're always talking about how courageous I am, but you're so much braver than me. It takes someone brave to admit when it's time to leave. Especially if staying might put someone else's life in danger."

He nodded. "Don't get me wrong—I loved being a part of an elite squad like MARSOC. I was a bit of an adrenaline junkie, but when I started to seriously contemplate what I'd signed up for... At this stage of my life, having a family is more important to me."

Renee pushed away from the table and stood up. She picked up the empty plates and carried them over to the sink. "I really appreciate you sharing this with me. I should've talked to you that night, but we can't undo the past."

"I don't hold that night against you. I was hurt and embarrassed, but I knew something triggered you—I just didn't know what it was."

She couldn't face him, but she had to say what was on her mind. "I would give anything to not have these issues. It's so unfair to you."

She heard him get up and walk toward her. "Renee, look at me. We all have our challenges."

Her eyes filled with tears. "But I can't seem to shake mine. I even made your getting deployed all about me." She swiped at her eyes.

"Your reaction was normal. Deployments aren't easy on anyone. My mom was worried every time my father left. I didn't realize just how hard it was for her until my own deployments. Waiting for word of my safe return after losing my father... She has incredible faith, but it was still a challenge—she just didn't let worry take control." He put a hand on her shoulder. "One thing I'd like for you to do— erase Kevin's words from your brain. I feel like he somehow triggered you when you saw him in New York."

"Maybe," she responded, finally facing him. "But I'm determined to make some much-needed changes. I'm no longer going to let panic disorder define my life."

Greg embraced her. "I meant it when I said that you won't have to do it alone. If you'll allow me, I'll be right by your side."

She could hear the sincerity in his voice and believed him.

Renee glanced up at him. "I keep thinking about how hard you worked to help make my fashion show a success. We make a great team."

He smiled. "I've been trying to convince you of this for almost three years now."

"I have a confession, Greg—I miss my best friend. Do you think we can try being friends again?" She knew it wasn't what he wanted— he wanted them to be more—but she needed to be true to herself. She needed to start again and take things slow.

"If that's what you want," he responded.

"I do. I need a do-over."

GREG FELT LIGHTER than he had in days.

He and Renee had reconciled, and they'd decided to celebrate getting their friendship back by doing something they both loved. They were looking at houses on the island—he was staying in town and needed to find his own place.

While he drove, she scanned through the listings he'd found that were saved on his tablet.

"These sound nice, but seeing them might tell us a different story."

"I'm hoping to find something soon so Trey and Gia can have their house to themselves."

"I'm sure they enjoy having you there," Renee stated.

"Maybe so, but I don't want to wear out my welcome. Remember, Trey and I will be working together—I don't really want to live with him, too."

She chuckled. "I understand."

He enjoyed hearing her laughter once again. It had been a while, and he'd missed the delightful sound.

They met the Realtor at the first house.

It was located two blocks from the bakery and Renee's boutique.

At first sight, Greg liked the yellow cottage-style house with white trim, but as soon as they walked inside, they were met by walls painted a bright pink. He could see the kitchen, and everything—from the cabinets to the appliances—was outdated. He wanted something move-in ready that wouldn't require renovations.

When his Realtor mentioned a new condo community on the north end of the island, he and Renee drove there and toured the model, which was much more modern.

"It's nice," Renee said, "but it doesn't look like you."

He nodded. "I was just thinking the same thing."

They left the community to check out another property that was only three blocks away.

After leaving the fifth property, Greg decided to call it a day. "They're starting to look alike to me." The condo was really nice, but he'd prefer a house. He could picture the extra rooms being used for an office and a sewing room for Renee. Whatever he found, he hoped it could one day become a home for both of them.

"Do you want to go back to my place?" Renee asked. "We could watch a couple movies and chill." They'd ended up spending the entire day together house-hunting, yet she wasn't ready for him to leave.

Greg's bright grin made his handsome face even more devastating. "I'd like that. Let's stop at the store to pick up a late lunch and drinks."

At the condo, they settled in the living room to watch Netflix.

Renee sat on the sofa while Greg made himself comfortable on the floor with a bowl of popcorn in his lap.

"You plan on sharing?" she asked.

"Oh, I thought this was mine." He glanced up at her. "You didn't make any for yourself?"

"Ha ha…"

Greg handed her the bowl. "Have some."

They watched one movie and fell asleep during the second one.

Renee was the first to wake up.

She smiled.

Greg was stretched out on the floor, sleeping, his head on one of the throw pillows. She was tempted to let him nap but changed her mind. She tapped him gently with her foot. "Hey, sleepyhead…"

He moaned softly and shifted.

"Greg…"

"Huh?" he uttered as he pulled himself up to a sitting position. "I think I need to pick the next movie. That last one put us both to sleep."

Around eight o'clock, Renee's stomach growled. More than a few hours had passed since they'd had lunch.

He looked over at her. "Hungry?"

"I am," she said. "I'm in the mood for hot dogs. Have you ever been to Benny's?"

"Naw, I haven't. Trey has mentioned it a couple times, but he never took me there. Is the food like what the café serves?"

"No, they specialize in hot dogs only—New York dogs, Chicago dogs…hot dogs from across the world."

"I'm down," Greg said.

At Benny's, they sat down in a booth and picked up a menu.

"Alaskan hot dog with cider and caramelized onions," Greg uttered. "Sounds interesting, but I think I'll pass."

"What about the Boston Fenway Dog?" Renee asked. "Or the Vermont Maple Dog?"

"What do you normally get?"

"The Chicago or New York Dog. I tried the Wisconsin Beer Brat Dog, and it was okay but not one of my favorites."

A waitress walked over to take their order.

"I'll have a lemonade and the Chicago Dog," Renee said.

"I'll take the same."

While they waited for their food to arrive, Greg settled back in his seat. "I don't know about you, but for me, this day just keeps getting better and better."

"Same here," Renee murmured. She was glad to have Greg back in her life—even if it was just as a friend. She knew they had something special; but first, she had to work on herself before she could consider anything more. The last thing she wanted was to see the heartbreak that had been etched in Greg's expression on her birthday.

He glanced around, then said, "Talei would've loved this spot."

She chuckled. "Oh, she did. A world of hot dogs and French fries...this was her favorite place to come. Leon and Misty were thrilled to pieces when Talei fell in love with flatbread pizza. Leon's counting down the days until she finds a new food to love."

Greg smiled. "I know. Last time we were all together, Leon said he didn't even want to see another pizza in his life."

"I try to introduce her to new foods whenever we hang out, but that little girl has a stubborn streak in her. She gets it honest, though." Renee shrugged. "Misty can be stubborn."

"I don't know. The entire Rothchild family is obstinate."

She eyed him a moment before saying, "I guess I can't really argue with that truth. It's part of our DNA."

CHAPTER TWENTY-THREE

The following Sunday, Renee and Greg went to Leon's house for dinner.

"Is this just a regular dinner with the family?" he asked. "Or something else? Another pregnancy announcement?"

"I think it's just a meal," Renee responded. "But I'm not sure. In case you haven't noticed, my family likes to spring surprises on you. I guess we'll find out soon enough."

They were the last ones to arrive.

Misty ushered them into the house. "We're just about to sit down at the table."

After washing their hands, Renee followed Greg into the dining room, where they sat across from one another.

Halfway through the meal, Leon stood up at the head of the table, lightly tapping his glass. "Tonight, we have so much to celebrate. First, Trey kept it quiet, but he earned his bachelor's degree a couple of years ago. Today, he received his master's in museum education. Not only did my little brother put plans in motion to open the Polk & Hoss Rothchild Museum but he's also making sure he knows how to properly run it."

Applause rang out around the room.

"We're also celebrating Greg for getting his master's in history. But I heard today that he's not stopping there—he's planning to get a PhD in historic preservation."

Another round of applause, led by Renee, who said, "I'm so proud of you. You, too, Trey."

When the room quieted down, Leon said, "I have one more announcement to make."

Eleanor eyed him. "Well, what is it, son?"

"Misty and I are expecting another baby."

"That's wonderful!" Renee exclaimed. "Congratulations."

"Mighty good things are happening," Eleanor said. "It's a blessing to be above ground to witness this. A blessing indeed."

Misty's mother, Oma, leaned over and kissed her cheek before getting up to embrace Leon. "You promised me many grandchildren, and it looks like you're keeping your word."

He chuckled. "I'm trying."

"I hope she's a girl," Talei stated. "I want a

sister. Leo just wants to wrestle and fight all the time. And he tears up my dolls."

Leo's face scrunched up. "No, I don't."

"You do, too."

"Okay, you two," Misty said. "Let's just enjoy this meal I spent most of the day cooking."

Later, after Renee and Greg had headed back to her condo, he said, "Okay, you lied to me earlier. You knew what this dinner was about, didn't you?"

"I did," Renee said. "It was meant to be a surprise. I was sworn to secrecy, and I only found out the other day."

"Thanks. It was very thoughtful of your cousin to include me." It touched Greg that the entire Rothchild family had embraced him, treating him as part of the family. He wished he'd come from a large family like theirs because of the wealth of support. However, his own family did what they could for him and his mother. If she had chosen to leave Hinesville, he could've grown up with his own cousins. Regardless, Greg maintained contact with them and still visited them whenever he could.

"You're doing great things, Greg. You should be celebrated," Renee was saying. "Now we just need to find your house."

He smiled. *Our house.* He couldn't help the thought that shot through his mind, but if he and Renee wanted something lasting, he knew it would take time.

"Do you miss being in the military?" she asked without preamble.

He turned to face her. "What makes you ask?"

Renee gave a slight shrug. "I'm just curious. You've been trying to settle into a new life on the island. Do you miss your old one?"

"Not really. I have some great memories of my time, but I'm excited about the future. This is what I'm focusing on. That's my past."

She nodded, seeming to weigh his words. "So no residual anything from your last mission?" Renee asked. "Because you did lose a friend."

"I grieve that loss…" He'd thought about Holloway often over the past few weeks. "I sometimes think of how close I was to losing my life, but I try not to dwell on it."

"That's comforting to me," she responded. "It would've been hard to comprehend how you could just distance yourself from something so traumatizing. I appreciate your honesty."

"How about you?" Greg inquired. "How are you feeling about everything?"

"I'm excited about the future, both personal and professional. I'm taking it one day at a time." Renee paused a moment, then said, "It's not always easy, but I manage."

He gave her hand a light squeeze. "Talk to me. I told you that you don't have to do this alone."

She nodded. "Good, because I'm also going to need your help again during Fashion Week in February."

"I like the way you just did that." He chuckled. "I'll do it, but I'm going to need my own staff T-shirt and a custom-designed suit for the party. I'm still paying off the other one."

"It's a deal." She grinned. "I'll even make your suit. I don't think I told you, but Kayla and I have been discussing a menswear collection. Her brother just graduated design school, and he's interested in working with us. I've seen some of his work, and it's really nice."

She never stopped trying to expand her business, and he found that impressive. "What do you think about coordinating a fashion show as a fundraiser for the museum?" Greg asked. If it meant they got to work together, he was all for it.

"I love the idea. We could showcase some of the pieces from the ready-to-wear collection. We can split the proceeds from the sale of the clothing."

He listened intently as Renee rattled off ideas in her excitement. She was in her element, and he'd learned this was when she felt free from all thoughts of fear and worry.

RENEE WOKE UP each morning filled with a yearning to see Greg. She'd gotten used to seeing him daily at the café for breakfast before heading over to her office in Charleston. However, this morning, he and Trey had a meeting to attend and a few errands to run.

Instead of going to the café, she ate at home and went to the office.

Every time she pulled into the parking garage of her building, she could hardly believe all that she'd accomplished. She'd been interviewed several times since Fashion Week regarding her company and her collections.

Humming softly, Renee walked into the building and was met by Kayla. "There's someone here to see you."

"Who?"

"Kevin Lyons."

Renee gasped as the shock of hearing that name gripped her. "He's *here*?" Struggling to keep her irritation at bay, she said, "Give me five minutes to get settled, then bring him to my office."

"Is this the same guy from New York?"

"Yeah."

"Do you want me to have security come to your office?" Kayla asked. "If you'd like, my Taser and I can join this meeting."

Renee chuckled. "You and that Taser… I'll be fine. Kevin is a jerk, but he's not going to get physical. He's scared of my brother."

Kayla didn't seem convinced. "I'll be close by if you need me."

"I feel safer already." She smiled and walked into her office, then sat down at her desk. "I'm ready," she called.

A moment later, their receptionist escorted Kevin to the door.

"Wow, this place is incredible," he said, his gaze scanning her office. He'd strolled in as if he were the one in charge.

"What are you doing here?" she asked, arms folded across her chest. Renee had absolutely no idea why Kevin would come to Charleston. *Why can't he just stay away?*

"Renee Rothchild, you're becoming a household name."

"You haven't answered my question."

He made himself comfortable in the chair

facing her. "From the looks of things, you're doing quite well for yourself."

She didn't respond.

"It's okay. You don't have to say a word, but I can tell. You have that fancy high-end boutique and now this building. I'd say you hit the big time."

"Why are you here?" Renee asked a second time.

He grinned. "I would say that I'm your muse, don't you think?"

She burst into laughter. "You can't be serious."

"Oh, but I am," Kevin uttered.

"You told me I was wasting my time—that I should've listened to my parents and gone to law school…anywhere but a fashion college." She fought back the memories of all the horrible things he'd said to her when they were together. That was all in the past.

"I knew it would make you more determined to succeed."

Renee rolled her eyes. "You have an answer for everything, don't you?"

"I figure you owe me."

She could barely contain the annoyance that had been building up since his arrival. "Owe you for *what*? Making my life miserable?"

"You don't really mean that."

"Yes, I do," Renee shot back. "Kevin, you were nothing but toxic. I spent most of our relationship feeling like something was terribly wrong with me—like I was inadequate or something."

"And you're blaming me for that? Look, you're the one who was always freaking out over nothing. Then there was that time you started beating your arm with your fist. It was crazy."

"I was having a panic attack, and hurting myself was the only way I could get it under control. All you did was stand there, looking at me as if I disgusted you."

He shrugged. "I thought you were having a mental breakdown."

"Yet you didn't do a thing to help me," Renee muttered. "You didn't even try to get help."

"It was embarrassing."

She huffed. "I'm sure you didn't come all the way here for nothing, so what do you want?"

It was obvious her words angered him. "Renee, you're not the one in control."

"Okay, end of conversation. Kevin, it's time for you to leave. And don't ever come back here."

"I don't think you really want me to do that."

"Oh, I definitely want you to leave." She leaned forward in her chair. "If you don't do so willingly, I'll have security escort you out. So, you see, I *am* the person in control."

He met her gaze head-on, but she didn't shrink back, even as he said, "I wonder how the fashion world will feel if word gets out that you're crazy. That you can barely function without medication."

"Is that your pathetic attempt to blackmail me? Because you're going to have to do a lot better than that." She shrugged, way past caring about his empty threats. "You can shout it from the rooftops that I have panic disorder—I really don't care. If anything, it'll probably increase my sales."

"Renee," he said in a softer tone, "all I'm trying to get you to see is that you need a man like me by your side. The fashion industry is filled with sharks. They will eat you alive. Sure, you're on top right now—but one failed collection and see what happens. I know that world." She knew that—because she was living it. And she'd gotten here without him.

"You know what? You talk about me being worthless, but have you looked at your own life, Kevin? You failed at being a model, a photographer, a politician, at marriage, and now you're even failing at blackmail."

He glared at her, but Renee didn't care. She wasn't afraid of him.

Kevin slumped in his chair. "I never should've gotten married, especially since I still loved you. That's why the marriage didn't work, Renee. And for the record, your friend kept running after me. I didn't want her. My mom thought we'd be good together."

She didn't believe Kevin. And it didn't matter even if he were actually telling the truth. She didn't love him.

"Why don't you get to the point of your visit? What do you want?"

"I want to talk about us."

"There is no *us*."

"I can accept that," he said. "We can help each other professionally. Let me photograph your new collection. We'd make a great team."

"I don't think so," she said.

"Why not?"

"It's all about control for you, Kevin. This would quickly become a toxic environment."

"You should seriously consider my offer, Renee."

"The lady already said no," Greg's voice

came from the doorway. "I doubt she's going to change her mind."

Renee was both surprised and elated to see him. She hadn't heard the door open or noticed him standing outside in the hall.

Kevin turned around in his seat. "We're having a private conversation."

Stepping inside, Greg closed the door behind him. "Not anymore."

Kevin sneered. "You don't have nothing to do with any of this."

"She doesn't want to work with you. Renee's made it clear that she doesn't want you around her at all. As for your threats to blackmail her—it's also not going to work. *I'll make sure of it.*"

Kevin stood up. "I don't know who you are, but this is between me and Renee."

"We're the men in her life, Kevin." He opened the door to her office to reveal Leon and Trey standing outside. "Me and her cousins. You see, we care about Renee, and we're not going to let *anyone* hurt her."

Kevin glanced over at Renee. "I see you've got your own security team." He gave a nervous chuckle. "Yeah, you've made the big time. Let's just see how long you stay there."

"*Goodbye*, Kevin. You come back, I promise I'll file charges against you for harassment."

RENEE MOVED FROM her desk and rushed into Greg's arms. "I'm so glad to see you. You're always here when I need you the most."

She looked past him. "Where did Leon and Trey go?"

"They most likely made sure Kevin left the building," Greg replied.

"We went by the law office and decided to stop here on a whim. We ran into Kayla, and she told us that Kevin was in your office. I wanted to make sure you were okay."

"He's been trying to get into fashion photography for years. Which is ironic because he tried to steer me away from the industry. I just thought he was bitter. I don't know what happened when he was modeling, but he must have burned a few bridges. No one wants to work with him."

"Do you think he'll try to come back?"

Renee shook her head. "No, but I wouldn't put it past him to try and cause trouble some other way."

"Well, you won't have to deal with Kevin alone. We're in this together."

She nodded and smiled. "I'm almost glad he

came. I think I finally saw Kevin for who he truly is—a desperate man. He spent so much time accusing me of being crazy and insecure, but he was the one who was insecure."

"Sounds like it."

Leon and Trey walked into her office.

"He's gone," Trey told her. "Honestly, cousin, I don't know what you ever saw in that dude."

"I have no idea," Renee responded. "I can't believe I was going to marry him at one point. I'm so glad that wedding never happened."

"So am I," Greg stated. "Because we never would've met."

CHAPTER TWENTY-FOUR

THE FOLLOWING NIGHT, Renee and Greg sat on the sofa, watching as singing sensation Serre stepped out of a sleek black limo as a sea of hungry photographers and reporters cleared a path to the door of the Wilshire Grand Hotel. She wowed everyone at the music-awards show in the peacock-colored gown she wore.

"You did a great job on that dress," Greg said.

Renee tossed the pillow she'd been clutching tightly only minutes before across the room. "She's wearing a Renee Rothchild original. *Yassss.*"

When one of the reporters asked who she was wearing, Renee leaned forward in her seat.

"This dress was designed by Renee Rothchild." Serre beamed. "She's a favorite of mine."

"She's the best-dressed artist there," Greg said.

She touched his cheek. "You're a bit biased, I'm sure."

"I am. I admit it." Greg pointed to the television. "Serre's first two records sold a combined three million copies."

"Over here, Serre," a photographer shouted.

Seconds later, a supermodel named Lyra made heads turn on the red carpet, and Renee gasped in surprise. "She's wearing one of my ready-to-wear gowns. I made four of them for the boutique."

Her phone vibrated.

Renee picked it up. "It's a text from Kayla. She's asking if I knew Lyra was going to wear one of our gowns. I had no idea. She must have ordered it online—none of the staff mentioned that she ever came to the shop." Renee couldn't contain her excitement at how much her brand had taken off.

Grinning, Lyra continued to pose for photos as Greg and Renee watched the awards show.

"You should be there," Greg said. "On the red carpet, posing right along with those women."

"I'm fine sitting right here, watching celebrities wearing *my* designs. This is so cool to me. I enjoy being behind the scenes."

"Looks like things are going great for both of us," Greg stated.

Renee nodded in agreement.

He wrapped an arm around her. "I think we're good, too."

She kissed him, enjoying the feel of his lips on hers once again. "We are," she confirmed. "Greg, I feel like we're better than good. We're not in the in-between place anymore." She felt safe. In his arms, Renee felt like she'd finally come home.

They sat there, holding each other close, neither one wanting to let go.

"How long do you plan on working tonight?" he asked when Renee answered her phone the following day.

She stole a peek at the huge clock on the wall in her office. "I'll probably leave here around six. What's up?"

"When you arrive on the island, I want you to meet me at 872 South Greene Circle."

"Okay. I'll see you there around six thirty-ish."

As soon as Renee pulled up to a gray house with white trim in the Ocean Forest subdivision, she broke into a smile. This was *the* house.

Greg arrived, parking his vehicle behind hers on the street.

She stood there, admiring the neatly land-scaped yard while waiting for him to join her.

He kissed her, took her hand and led her onto the porch. "Wait until you see the inside of this place."

"I love the outside already," Renee said.

Walking into the home, they were greeted by gorgeous hardwood floors and smooth ceilings that flowed into the open living area.

"It's beautiful," Renee nearly whispered. "I love the openness. This house is perfect for family dinners."

"It has four bedrooms and three and a half bathrooms," Greg said. "The ranch style features a split floor plan, with a screened-in porch off the living room and an open deck off the master bedroom."

"The kitchen is nice and large." Her eyes went wide as she took in their surroundings. "I love it."

"So do I," Greg said. They toured the upstairs and came back down to the main area. "The formal living room is large enough for two people to share an office, and there's a bonus room. Did you notice that the shower in the master is big enough for two or three people?"

She laughed. "Yeah, I saw that."

The selling point for Renee was the bonus room. She also liked that the yard was fenced in, with enough trees in the back to offer a measure of privacy.

"This house was meant for a family." Greg's eyes traveled around the space. "It has enough room for a growing family, and I love the huge backyard, too. It's minutes from the beach. This is *the* house."

"I'D BET MONEY that you dressed most of the women here in this room," Greg whispered as he escorted Renee to their table for the annual DuGrandpre Foundation Ball.

"Actually, Kayla designed Eleanor Du-Grandpre's dress," Renee said. "I designed the gowns Jadin and Jordin are wearing. And my gown, of course."

Renee leaned over and planted a kiss on his cheek. It still amazed her that he had so much faith in her design house. She was amused over his belief that practically every woman in the world was wearing her clothing. It was sweet and very touching.

Greg dipped down a little and whispered, "The truth is that you're the belle of the ball."

"You're looking pretty handsome, yourself.

Some of the women are already checking you out."

"Well, I'm already taken."

She grinned. "Oh, really?"

"Yep."

He pulled out a chair for Renee, then sat down beside her. They were placed at the same table as Leon, Trey, Rusty and their wives.

"Aunt Eleanor, you look stunning in that dress. That shade of blue looks great on you," Trey said.

"Thank you, suga. I love me some sapphire blue."

They made small talk as they waited for the food to arrive.

It wasn't a long wait.

They enjoyed a three-course meal of baby-leaf lettuce with marinated cucumbers and wedged Roma tomatoes; their choice of seared Ahi tuna, beef tenderloin or chicken breasts cooked in a white wine sauce and served with artichokes; goat cheese–mashed potatoes; and sautéed herbed Italian vegetables. Banana-rum bread pudding was served for dessert.

Halfway through the meal, Eleanor Louise DuGrandpre gave a short speech before introducing the entertainment for the evening. She acknowledged her son-in-law's generous donation. Amid thundering applause, Ethan stood up and smiled politely.

"That's Jordin's husband and Gia's business partner," Renee told Greg. "He doesn't like this kind of attention."

"Donating that much money, he should be walking around here with his head up high," he responded. "He's the CEO of a huge conglomerate," Greg added. "He might as well get used to this because it's not going away."

"I keep telling him that," Gia interjected.

Renee and Greg spent half the night on the dance floor.

At the end of the evening, the valet brought their car to the entrance, promptly stepped out and walked around to open the passenger-side door for her.

"I'm not ready for the evening to end. I know it's late, but maybe we can talk or watch a movie if you're not too exhausted," she said.

He smiled softly. "I'm not tired at all."

Several times during the evening at her condo, Renee had to sheath her feelings as a sense of inadequacy swept over her. It made her wonder if she had anything to offer Greg. She'd been working hard to refocus her thoughts and finding new coping strategies whenever she felt that way. She stole a peek at Greg, who appeared focused on the movie. The one ever-present thought that Renee couldn't always dismiss was the feeling that he deserved someone much better than her. Although it was a fleeting thought, she was determined not to let it take root.

SATURDAY AFTERNOON, GREG and Renee pulled up to a park in Charleston. Large oaks and maples provided shade around the playground area. Kids shouted and ran around the colorful swings and the massive slide.

Talei was playing in a fall soccer league and had invited them to her game.

Renee sniffed the air. "Must be a party in the picnic area. I can smell the meat someone's grilling."

"So can I," Greg said.

They walked past a family sprawled on a blanket. She smiled and waved at the baby watching them. "So cute," she murmured.

"Are you getting baby fever?" Greg said, his tone teasing.

She gave him a sidelong glance. "Not without a husband."

He chuckled. "I was just checking."

She held up her left hand. "I'm just saying…"

When he didn't respond, Renee said, "Too soon?"

"Just a little bit," he replied. He offered up a self-conscious smile.

She'd meant it in jest, but she knew now how deeply she'd hurt Greg on her birthday—how much they had the power to hurt each other. "Sorry," she said softly. And she *was* sorry—for all of it.

Greg wrapped an arm around her. "No apologies are necessary."

Renee glanced over her shoulder at the baby. Her heart caught. A longing to marry Greg and have his children shot through her with sudden ferocity. They'd decided to slow down the pace of their relationship, and it was working for them. If he proposed again, she wouldn't run away.

As they neared the soccer field, Renee saw the team and immediately searched for Talei. She spotted the curly ponytail first before she glimpsed her cute little face. They sat down on the bleachers by the soccer field.

Greg took her hand and gently squeezed it, sending a flood of warmth, love and hope through her.

She knew he hadn't fully recovered from the pain she'd caused him the first time.

What if he doesn't propose again? Renee shut out the errant negative thought that tried to come to the surface.

Soon, other families began arriving for the soccer game.

Looking around, she saw other kids wearing uniforms in various team colors.

"Looks like there's going to be more than one game today," she said. "Do you know if Talei's playing more than one game?"

"I think if they win," Greg responded. "You okay with that?"

"Yeah. Just might need a snack or two."

"They have a concession stand."

Smiling, Renee said, "Then we're good."

"You GOT IN late last night," Trey said. "Or should I say, early this morning?"

"Your cousin and I were watching a movie, and we fell asleep on the sofa."

Trey shrugged. "I'm happy the two of you are working things out. Y'all belong together. Speaking of which…when are you going to ask Renee to marry you?"

Greg knew that question would come up sooner or later. "Things are really good between us right now, so we're just enjoying each other. When the time is right, I'll propose. Renee's been so happy lately, and she hasn't had any panic episodes. I don't want to trigger her."

"How long do you plan on waiting for the right time?"

"As long as it takes, Trey. I love your cousin, and when she's ready, I'm going to make her my wife."

"Well, you already have the house."

"Yep. It's perfect for us," Greg said. "Soon, I'll be out of here so you and Gia can have your home back."

"We're fine. But before you leave, I need you to help me put the crib together. The instructions might as well be in another language."

Greg laughed. "We can get started on it this afternoon. You might want to see if Leon's available, in case neither one of us can figure it out."

CHAPTER TWENTY-FIVE

THE THIRD WEEK in November, Renee pulled the folds of her sweater together to ward off the chill as she walked briskly through the hospital doors with Greg. He'd called to let her know that Trey had taken Gia to the hospital. She was in labor.

A few weeks ago, they'd thrown a baby shower, and Greg had started moving out of his old home in North Carolina.

Time was flying.

"Come pick me up, and I'll go with you," she'd told him. "Or I can meet you there."

"Do you think we should go?" Greg had asked. "Trey's going to be with Gia. We'd just be hanging around."

"Yeah, we can wait in one of the waiting rooms. We should be there for moral support. It's what we do."

"Okay. I'll be there in ten minutes."

Leon was in the waiting room when they arrived.

"Have you heard anything?" she asked her cousin.

"She's definitely in labor," Leon responded. "Trey is back there with her. No idea how long this is going to take, so I called Rusty to let him know what's going on, but I told him not to bring Aunt Eleanor until after the baby is born."

Renee nodded. "How's Trey holding up?"

"He was a nervous wreck," Greg said. "I've never seen him like that."

"He loves Gia more than his own life," Leon added. "I think our family can handle almost anything until something affects the people we love."

"This is true," Renee murmured. She knew how much Leon and Trey both disliked hospitals. And after losing his first wife and daughter—this situation most likely triggered bad memories for Leon. She placed a hand on his arm. "How're you holding up?"

"I'm fine," Leon said. "Just can't wait for the baby to be born so I can get out of here."

Renee nodded in understanding. "Everything is going to be okay."

"Yeah, you're right." Leon nodded. "Misty delivered Leo with no problems. Everything was fine."

"Gia's gonna do great." Picking up her purse, she said, "I'm going to make a run to the cafeteria. I'll be right back."

Renee ordered coffees for Leon and Greg. She ordered an herbal tea for herself and returned with the drinks to the waiting room.

"Thanks," they said in unison.

A worried-looking Trey walked into the waiting area with the aid of his cane. "They're taking her to surgery. They have to do an emergency cesarean section."

"What happened?" Renee asked. She felt like she'd been doused with cold water. Gia and Trey had prepared for natural childbirth.

"The baby's umbilical cord has dropped through her cervix," Trey responded. "The doctor called it an umbilical cord prolapse. They have to take the baby out before the pressure on the cord cuts off the oxygen." He shook his head, leaning heavily on the cane. "Look, I gotta get back there."

"We're praying for her," Renee said.

"I know. We appreciate it." Trey left the room.

"Please let everything be okay," Leon whispered.

Renee took his hand in her own. "She and the baby will be fine. Everything will be okay."

She hoped if she said it enough, she would begin to believe it herself.

Still, later on when she'd stepped aside with Greg, she admitted, "This is one of those times that I really wish there was something I could do to help."

"Sweetheart, all we can do is just pray for the best outcome," he said gently. "No one has control over what happens."

She looked up at him. "That's what my therapist has been trying to get me to understand. I've spent so much of my adult life worrying and trying to keep bad things from happening. I've always tried to play it safe." She really got it now—she had to let go. "I haven't fully enjoyed my life. Trey and Gia are so happy and in love. I don't want anything to go wrong." She had been denying herself that with Greg, thinking she could keep bad things at bay—but she couldn't.

Her eyes filled with tears as she eyed her cousin, who'd been approaching them. "I remember how sad you were, Leon."

"I was heartbroken by the loss of Vee and my daughter," he responded. "I still miss them terribly. But I was blessed to find love a second time with Misty and have more children.

Greg's right. All we can do is pray and hope for the best."

Greg escorted Renee to a nearby chair. "Why don't you just lay your head on my shoulder and try to get some sleep?"

She wiped away her tears with the back of her hand. "I'll be fine. I didn't mean to get so emotional."

"Honey, it's understandable."

Renee placed her hand to her chest, and her breathing changed.

Greg kissed her cheek, then whispered, "Take your hand off your chest. You don't want that to be your focus. Slow down your breathing. Look at me. Keep your eyes on my face."

She did as he instructed, taking deep, slow breaths to calm herself.

"The doctors have everything under control."

When her breathing returned to normal, Renee closed her eyes and drank in the comfort of his embrace. She felt safe, secure and calm in his arms.

Patricia arrived. "I just got home from Savannah. What's going on?"

Leon pulled her to the side and shared what they'd been told about Gia.

"She and that baby are gonna be fine," she

declared as she took a seat. "I can feel it in my spirit."

Two hours passed.

The three of them all rushed to their feet at the sight of Trey.

Renee held her breath until she heard him say, "It's a boy. Gia and the baby are both doing fine."

She sent up a silent prayer of thanksgiving for sparing them the heartache that came with loss.

"I have a grandson," Patricia said, grinning from ear to ear. "I'm a grandmother."

"Congratulations," Renee said. She didn't bother to stop her tears from flowing. They were tears of joy.

"THIS WAS SOME NIGHT…" Renee murmured.

It was almost one o'clock, and they were on their way home from the hospital. They didn't get a chance to see Gia because she was in recovery, but they did get a peek at the newborn in the nursery.

"Trey was crying more than his son," Greg said. "I took a video."

"Ooooh, he's going to get you for that," she said with a chuckle. "I'm so very happy for him. You know, there was a time he thought he wouldn't be able to father a child. Even though the doctors told him there wasn't an issue, he wasn't sure he'd get the chance."

"I'm glad Gia and the baby are fine," Greg said. He didn't want to say anything, but he'd been afraid for Trey. He didn't want his best friend to suffer any losses tonight.

"He's a cutie," Renee said. "I think he looks like both Trey and Gia."

"You think so?" he asked. "I don't think he looks like anybody right now."

She elbowed him gently.

When they pulled up in front of her condo, Renee asked, "I know it's late, but can you come in for a bit? I need to talk to you."

"Sure."

They went inside and sat down in the living room.

"What's up?" Greg asked. He had no idea what Renee wanted to discuss, but he figured it might have something to do with her minor episode earlier. It pained him to see her suffering from panic disorder, but he vowed to never let her suffer alone. Greg continued to learn more about it.

"Tonight, I was scared for Gia and the baby. I felt helpless because I couldn't do anything for them. That's when it really became clear.

I realized that I have no control over certain outcomes in life. That's what has frightened me the most, Greg." She sighed. "Having no control and being vulnerable. Having to just sit and let the bad stuff happen. But I really get it now—what you and everybody has been trying to tell me, including my therapist. I've been hyperfocused on what I can't control. I've been trying to protect myself instead of enjoying life."

Leaning forward, Greg said, "I'm listening."

She took a deep breath and exhaled slowly. "Greg, I love you more than you will ever know. When we first got together, I felt like I was broken. First, I refused to date you because I was afraid that I'd lose you on one of your missions. Then I was scared that one day, you'd wake up and realize I wasn't good enough for you. Then, when I heard about your friend saving your life, it validated my fears."

Greg placed a gentle hand on her cheek. "I could never feel that way about you. I love you so much, Renee. My life hasn't been the same since we met. As for the other stuff—death is a part of life, babe. We can't control it. We just can't waste the time we've been given. We all have to make our peace with this."

"I'm not afraid anymore. I want to love and live each day intentionally."

He stilled. "What are you telling me?"

"I choose *us*. For better or worse. I don't want to waste another moment. We have a house. I'm ready to make it our home."

He could feel tears come to his eyes. "You have to know that you're the only woman for me." Greg pulled out the small velvet box he'd offered her not so long ago and got down on bended knee.

She gasped. "How long have you been carrying that around?" she asked.

"Every day. I've been waiting for the right time. I wanted to be ready when it came around," he responded. "Will you marry me, Renee?"

Greg opened it, revealing the stunning princess-cut diamond engagement ring he'd chosen just for her. "I sincerely hope that you'll say yes this time around," he whispered. "Because I've never felt this way about another woman. You own my heart."

"Yes, I'll marry you."

Greg slipped the ring on her finger before rising to his full height. He wrapped his arms around Renee, holding her close. "You've made me an incredibly happy man."

"I love you," she whispered. She peered at the ring on her finger. "I feel like I'm dreaming."

"It's no dream, sweetheart. I proposed, and you accepted. We going to become husband and wife."

She turned to face him. "I can't wait to start my life with you."

"So does this mean we're having a short engagement?" Greg asked, grinning. He was hoping she'd want to marry him tomorrow, but deep down, he knew better. She would want to have a wedding with all her family and friends present. In truth, Greg wanted his family and friends to witness this defining moment in his life, too.

"Not exactly," Renee replied. "I want enough time to plan a wedding—a small intimate one. Besides, I've always wanted a summer wedding."

AFTER MONTHS OF PLANNING, the day of Renee and Greg's June wedding arrived. They'd decided on a glam wedding theme using dramatic details, bold colors and silver sparkle. Renee added her own spin to give it more of an art deco vibe.

The Magnolia Ballroom at the Polk Island

Hotel was filled to capacity for their nuptials. The chic architectural lines of the building provided the perfect framework for their ceremony. Each row of chairs was garnished with lavish displays of white roses arranged with navy-and-teal-colored ribbons and baby's breath.

Upstairs, Renee stood in front of a huge full-length mirror in the dressing room designated for brides and their attendants. Her white satin wedding gown featured embroidered silver, with navy blue and teal beading around the front. The chapel train was in alternating colors of teal and navy. Her cathedral wedding veil, which had embroidered hearts filled with Renee's and Greg's initials in silver around the trim, had been designed by Kayla.

"You look so beautiful," Misty said from behind her. "You did an outstanding job on your gown. I can't wait to see Greg's face when you walk down the aisle."

"You look beautiful, too." Renee turned around to face her friend. "That color looks great on you." Misty wore a dark teal gown, with a high waist to accommodate her advanced pregnancy. Renee had chosen to have her bridesmaids wear different shades of teal, from dark to pastel. The men were all wearing custom dark navy tuxedos, their vests in varying shades to match the bridesmaid dresses.

Gia joined them. "It's finally happening. I'm so glad you and Greg are going to be husband and wife."

"No one's happier than me." Renee chuckled. "I feel like I've been waiting for this day all my life." It had taken her a long time to get here, but once she'd accepted Greg's proposal, this day couldn't come soon enough. She turned around to check her reflection in the mirror. "I don't know why, but I'm nervous."

"It's normal," Misty and Gia said in unison.

"You look great," Renee told Gia.

"You're the one with the skills." Gia smiled. "You had to alter my dress at least three times because of my weight."

Renee waved that off. "You just had a baby six months ago. It wasn't a problem."

Gia eyed her reflection in the mirror. "Well, I love it. This is one bridesmaid dress that's a keeper."

Pressing her hand to her swollen stomach, Misty said, "After I have this little girl, I want mine altered to fit my pre-pregnancy size because I love my dress, too."

"I can do that," Renee said. "I'm just glad

you both really love your dresses. I tried to make sure they reflected your natural beauty."

Snatching up a tissue, Misty said, "Please don't make me cry. I don't want to mess up my makeup."

Talei knocked, then entered the room. "You look so pretty!" she exclaimed when she saw Renee. "You look like a princess."

"Thank you, sweetie. You look like a princess, too." Talei's dress was navy blue, with a teal sash trimmed in silver.

"Mommy and I practiced last night. I know what to do with the flowers. I'm not gonna mess up."

"I'm not worried one bit about that, Talei." Renee smiled at the little girl. "I know you're going to be great."

Misty called for Talei. "C'mon, honey. We need to get ready for our entrance."

Renee's father appeared in the doorway just as her bridal party was about to exit. "It's almost time," he said with a smile.

Misty hugged her. "I'll see you at the altar."

Gia embraced her as well. "I'm so happy for you."

When they left the room, her father looked at her. "I can hardly believe how you've grown up on me. My baby's getting married..." he murmured after a moment. "I'm happy you got yourself a good man."

"Thank you, Daddy, for setting a perfect example of a good man," Renee told him. "You were my first date, and you set the standard by which I tried to choose the men in my life. Turns out, I wasn't very good at it, until now." She laughed. It never bothered her to think of that anymore. Her life had led her to Greg. "But I love you for showing me that I was worthy of love."

"I love you, too, sweetie, and I'm so very proud of you. I'm sorry for not telling you much sooner. I didn't know how to help you when you started having the attacks, so I just did nothing."

She shook her head. "I didn't come to you—I tried to deal with it alone until I couldn't anymore. I don't want you blaming yourself for anything, Daddy. I had to figure things out for myself. Everything is fine."

He swiped at his eyes, then gestured toward the door. "Now, let's not keep your husband-to-be waiting."

Taking his hand, Renee grinned. "*Husband.* That has such a nice ring to it. *I'm getting married.*"

Her father planted a kiss on her cheek. "Yes, you are."

Moments later, Renee floated down the aisle on her father's arm, toward the man she would love forever.

THE MOMENT THE doors opened to signal Renee's entrance, the room was engulfed in a sea of oooh's and ahh's. She was a vision to behold as she drifted up the aisle toward him. Greg's eyes filled with tears as he watched the woman who would soon become his wife.

He barely noticed the guests dressed in tuxedos and colorful dresses seated in the elegant space. Or the vivid paintings and photographs dotting the cream-colored walls.

Greg faced Renee when the time came for them to say their vows.

She spoke first. "Greg, you are my one true love, and I take you to be my husband. I will trust and respect you, laugh with and cry with you… I promise to love you faithfully, through good times and bad, regardless of the difficulties we may face together. I give you my heart, from this day forward, for as long as we both shall live." A tear slipped down her cheek.

"Renee, you are my best friend, and I want you to know that I'm eagerly anticipating growing old with you and falling in love with you a little more every day. I promise to support you and comfort you in times of sorrow and struggle. I promise to love and cherish you through whatever life may bring to our door. I give you my heart today and all the days of our life."

He could hardly contain his excitement as he waited to hear the words that would finalize their union.

"I now pronounce you husband and wife..."

These were the words he'd waited a long time to hear. They were music to his ears.

Greg pulled Renee into his arms, drawing her close. He pressed his lips to hers for a chaste yet meaningful kiss. The room erupted in applause and laughter throughout.

Grinning, Greg escorted his bride down the aisle and through the double doors at the back of the church. They escaped into a nearby room, waiting until it was time to go back into the chapel for the wedding photographs.

His eyes traveled down the length of her, nodding in approval. The dress she'd designed was stunning. "You look so beautiful, sweetheart."

Renee broke into a big smile. "We're married." She held up her left hand to show off the wedding set. "I can truly say that this is the happiest day of my life."

After taking hundreds of photographs, they were led to the ballroom next door for the reception.

Waitstaff navigated around the room with trays of miniature crab cakes, shrimp cocktail and frozen watermelon slices while the bride and groom and their family took personal photographs. Greg and Renee had selected signature drinks for their guests to try—watermelon-mojito cocktail paletas and basil gimlets in addition to the lemonade, sweet tea and sodas.

After their grand entrance as husband and wife, Greg guided Renee over to their table and pulled out a chair for her.

He dined on grilled rack of lamb with asparagus, while she chose the orange-soy-glazed scallops as her entrée.

He could hardly take his eyes off her. She looked so beautiful…almost ethereal. Greg felt like the luckiest man alive.

After they finished eating, he and Renee stood up and headed to the middle of the room to dance for the first time as Mr. and Mrs. Gregory Bowman.

Renee danced with her father next while Greg and his mother shared a dance.

"Son, I'm so very happy for you. Renee is a beautiful young lady, and I am honored to have her as my daughter-in-love." She placed a hand on his cheek.

"I want to thank you, Mom…for everything," Greg said. "I hope I didn't give you too hard of a time when I was growing up."

"Just know that whatever you did, you will get back in spades when you have children of your own," she said with a chuckle. Greg laughed with her.

When the song stopped, she said, "Go dance with your bride. I love you. I know your father's looking down on you right now, and he's so very proud of you."

Greg patted the white handkerchief in his pocket. It was the same one his father had worn when he married his mother. "I can feel him with me."

He made his way to Renee, who was dancing with Talei. Moving to the music, he joined them.

One song ended and another began while they were still on the dance floor. They participated in the line dance. Guests were dancing all around them, but Greg only had eyes for Renee. "I love you, sweetheart. With every fiber of my being, I love you."

"I love you back," she told him.

As the dance came to an end, Renee fanned herself. "Okay, no more dancing for me right now." They walked over to the table where the Rothchild family was sitting.

"Welcome to the family, Greg," Trey said. "You're never getting rid of us now. We're in your life forever."

Laughing, Greg placed his arms around Renee. "That's not a problem, because I love this woman more than my own life. I never really understood what that meant until now. I'm all in."

Leon kissed Misty's cheek, then said, "I feel the same way about Misty. She's definitely the better part of me."

A little while later, Greg and Renee eased out of the ballroom to get some fresh air.

As soon as they were outside, he pulled her into his arms, his mouth covering hers.

When he broke the kiss, Renee gazed up at him. "I'll never get tired of kissing you." She grinned.

And he would never get tired of looking at

her. His wife's eyes held the promise of love, life and a future that looked brighter than he could've ever imagined.

* * * * *

Get 4 FREE REWARDS!

We'll send you 2 FREE Books plus 2 FREE Mystery Gifts.

FREE
Value Over
$20

Both the **Love Inspired®** and **Love Inspired® Suspense** series feature compelling novels filled with inspirational romance, faith, forgiveness, and hope.

COUNTRY LEGACY COLLECTION

19 FREE BOOKS IN ALL!

Cowboys, adventure and romance await you in this new collection! Enjoy superb reading all year long with books by bestselling authors like Diana Palmer, Sasha Summers and Marie Ferrarella!

YES! Please send me the **Country Legacy Collection**! This collection begins with 3 FREE books and 2 FREE gifts in the first shipment. Along with my 3 free books, I'll also get 3 more books from the **Country Legacy Collection**, which I may either return and owe nothing or keep for the low price of $24.60 U.S./$28.12 CDN each plus $2.99 U.S./$7.49 CDN for shipping and handling per shipment*. If I decide to continue, about once a month for 8 months, I will get 6 or 7 more books but will only pay for 4. That means 2 or 3 books in every shipment will be FREE! If I decide to keep the entire collection, I'll have paid for only 32 books because 19 are FREE! I understand that accepting the 3 free books and gifts places me under no obligation to buy anything. I can always return a shipment and cancel at any time. My free books and gifts are mine to keep no matter what I decide.

☐ 275 HCK 1939   ☐ 475 HCK 1939

Name (please print)

Address   Apt. #

City   State/Province   Zip/Postal Code

Mail to the Harlequin Reader Service:
IN U.S.A.: P.O. Box 1341, Buffalo, NY 14240-8571
IN CANADA: P.O. Box 603, Fort Erie, Ontario L2A 5X3

#439 WYOMING RODEO RESCUE

The Blackwells of Eagle Springs • by Carol Ross

Equestrian Summer Davies's life is on the verge of scandal, so an invitation to host a rodeo comes at the perfect time. But with event organizer Levi Blackwell, opposites do *not* attract! Has she traded one problem for another?

#440 THE FIREFIGHTER'S CHRISTMAS PROMISE

Smoky Mountain First Responders • by Tanya Agler

Coach Becks Porter is devastated when a fire destroys her soccer complex, and firefighter Carlos Ramirez, her ex, is injured. Their past is complicated, but an unexpected misfortune might lead to a most fortunate reunion this holiday season.

#441 SNOWBOUND WITH THE RANCHER

Truly Texas • by Kit Hawthorne

Rancher Dirk Hager doesn't have time for Christmas...or his new neighbor, city girl Macy Reinalda. But when they're trapped in a snowstorm, Dirk warms up to Macy and decides he might just have time for his neighbor after all...

#442 HIS DAUGHTER'S MISTLETOE MOM

Little Lake Roseley • by Elizabeth Mowers

Dylan Metzger moved home with his young daughter to renovate a historic dance hall in time for Christmas. When Caroline Waterson reconnects with a business proposal he can't refuse, Dylan finds himself making allowances—in his business and his heart.

HARLEQUIN
PLUS

Announcing a **BRAND-NEW**
multimedia subscription service
for romance fans like you!

Read, Watch and Play.

Experience the easiest way to get
the romance content you crave.

Start your **FREE 7 DAY TRIAL** at
<u>www.harlequinplus.com/freetrial</u>.